I'M YOURS

SWEETBRIAR COVE: BOOK FOUR

MELODY GRACE

MELODY GRACE BOOKS

Thank you for reading!
Sweetbriar Cove is the start of a new series for me, set in a
charming small town on Cape Cod.
I have tons of happy memories of New England, and it was so
much fun inventing the town - and all its inhabitants. Mackenzie,
the heroine of I'm Yours, loves Christmas in her small-town, but
planning the annual Starbright Festival takes an unexpected turn
when a face from her past returns.

I hope you enjoy reading I'm Yours as much as I've enjoyed
writing it. So pour some cocoa, snuggle up, and enjoy this taste of
autumn wherever you are.
xo Melody

~

ALSO BY MELODY GRACE:

The Sweetbriar Cove Series:
1. Meant to Be
2. All for You
3. The Only One
4. I'm Yours
5. Holiday Kisses (A Christmas Story)
6. No Ordinary Love (2018)

The Beachwood Bay Series:
1. Untouched
2. Unbroken
3. Untamed Hearts
4. Unafraid
5. Unwrapped
6. Unconditional
7. Unrequited
8. Uninhibited
9. Unstoppable
10. Unexpectedly Yours
11. Unwritten
12. Unmasked
13. Unforgettable

The Oak Harbor Series:
1. Heartbeats
2. Heartbreaker
3. Reckless Hearts

The Dirty Dancing Series

The Promise

Welcome to Sweetbriar Cove: the small town where happily-ever-after is guaranteed.

Book Four

I'm Yours

Artist Mackenzie Lane is almost thirty and still single, which, according to her neighbors, pretty much makes her the Spinster of Sweetbriar Cove. She's sworn off terrible fix-ups, and is looking forward to her solo future of woolly mumus and cats. (Lots of cats). But a chance Halloween rendezvous awakens her reckless spirit, and makes her wonder if love might be in the cards, after all...

Jake Sullivan is back in town for the first time in years, recovering from a career-ending sports injury. He's dazzled by the mysterious woman he meets by chance - and even more intrigued when he discovers it's his high-school friend Mackenzie.

Ten years ago, Jake was the first (and only) guy to put a dent in Mackenzie's invincible heart. She's determined not to make the same mistake again, but when the pair are forced to team up to plan the annual Starbright Festival, old sparks fly - and new passion runs riot.

Soon, Mackenzie and Jake are risking it all. But will their connection last longer than the first snowfall? And can these old friends start a new chapter for love? Find out in the sizzling, romantic new novel from New York Times bestselling author Melody Grace!

---

*M*ackenzie was going undercover for the night. Her wild red curls were hidden under a sleek black wig, and she'd traded her usual funky dresses and knit sweaters for a tight black catsuit, complete with a pair of knee-high platform boots. She paused by the mirror, carefully touching up her smudgy black eyeliner, and felt a thrill at the stranger staring back at her. Usually, she went zany and creative for Halloween, but she'd spied the catsuit in the corner of the thrift store and impulsively grabbed it from the rack. Now, she felt unrecognizable in her disguise: sexy and mysterious, like some foreign agent on a secret mission, out to seduce and destroy.

She grabbed her keys, locked up, then slipped them under a flowerpot by the door. There was no room for a purse with this figure-hugging get-up, and besides, secret agents didn't carry a battered old tote bag. No, they got by on their wits, charm—and a switchblade hidden in their cleavage.

Mackenzie wouldn't need any deadly weapons at the town Halloween party, but her cleavage wasn't too shabby, she decided, thanks to the extra five pounds of ice-cream weight she'd put on over the summer. She set off down the street, an extra swing in her step as she imagined conquering exotic nations and seducing rogue spies, but the illusion lasted all of the five blocks it took her to reach the town square.

"Aww, Mac! You look so cute!" someone called the moment she approached the crowd.

"Great costume, Mac."

"Mackenzie! Where did you get that belt?"

So much for sexy and mysterious. Mackenzie sighed. This was what she got for living in the same small town most of her life. There was no going incognito here, not when everyone knew everyone else's business, and half the town had seen her dressed as an Oompa Loompa in the school play.

"Watch out!" A group of pint-sized ghosts charged past, clutching baskets of candy, and Mackenzie was sent spinning.

"Easy there!"

Mackenzie turned to find her friends Poppy and Cooper arriving, in matching 1920s bootlegger costumes. "Hey guys."

"You look amazing!" Poppy exclaimed, greeting her with a hug. "I almost didn't recognize you in that wig."

"Thinking about a new style?" Cooper teased, flicking the sleek, bobbed hair.

Mackenzie laughed. "Not anytime soon. The last time I tried short hair, it all puffed up into a frizzy ginger halo."

"I remember," Cooper grinned from under the brim of his trilby hat. "We called you Orphan Annie for months."

"Yeah, thanks for that." Mackenzie gave him a friendly glare. Between the bad hair, hand-knitted sweaters, and smelly home-packed hummus from her hippy parents, high school hadn't exactly been kind to her.

"Don't worry, nobody remembers that stuff now." Poppy linked her arm through Mackenzie's as they strolled through the busy streets.

"Spoken like a newcomer," Mackenzie shot back, laughing. "Sweetbriar never forgets."

"I can't believe everyone's costumes," Poppy continued, deftly changing the subject. They passed another crowd of trick-or-treaters, dressed up in a dazzling array of robot, witch, and Disney outfits. "Back in the city, I just had a couple of neighbor kids come to my door dressed in regular clothes, demanding candy."

"Haven't you learned by now?" Mackenzie asked. "We don't ever miss the chance for a party in this town."

Halloween in Sweetbriar Cove was a big deal. Well, pretty much any festival was a big deal there. Nestled in the crook of Cape Cod, Sweetbriar had built a reputation for its small-town charm—and for going all out with the decorations at the smallest excuse. There were harvest hay-bale mazes, and spring jamborees, and the winter Starbright Festival was the pride of the Cape, drawing thousands of visitors from all over the world.

Tonight, it was the Halloween Hoe-Down, cleverly recycling all those hay bales until they put the Tennessee backwoods to shame. The Town Hall was already lit up, with music and laughter spilling out into the brisk autumn night, and inside, crowds of people were already enjoying the food and dancing: a robot spinning around his zombie bride, while a trio of ghouls harmonized with a harmonica up on stage.

"Ooh, candy apples!" Poppy's eyes lit up when she saw the buffet along the back wall. "Be right back!" She grabbed Cooper and cut a path towards the baked goods, leaving Mackenzie to adjust her wig. It turned out, sleek and sexy was also itchy as hell.

"There she is." Debra, the unofficial town events planner, made her way through the crowd. Tonight, the older woman was dressed in flowing robes, with a magician's wand in hand. "Thanks again for helping out," Debra said. "The murals look great."

3

"Creepy enough for you?" Mackenzie asked. As the resident artist in town, she was always getting recruited to help out with decorations. This time, she'd painted some ghoulish backdrops, complete with cobwebs and tombstones, but Debra had kept insisting on more blood. Now, it looked like a murderous frenzy was splashed over the back wall.

"Just perfect!" Debra declared. She took a step back and looked Mackenzie over, getting a familiar glint in her eye. "You look very nice. I think I saw the Janowitz boy back from Colorado somewhere, dressed as Batman. You know he's a partner now in that law firm—"

"I know," Mackenzie cut her off. "You already told me. Twice. And so did Larry at the hardware store, and Franny when I saw her at the market. I'm surprised you didn't send a newsletter out: alert, eligible bachelor returns!"

Debra gave her a knowing look. "We're just looking out for you, sweetheart. It's about time you found someone. What are you now, thirty?"

"Twenty-nine," Mackenzie corrected, feeling a sting.

"Exactly. You're not getting any younger."

She blinked. "Gee, thanks—" But Debra had already steamed away—probably to find that Janowitz boy and corral him into asking Mackenzie on a date. Debra was out of luck. Mackenzie had already had an infamous coffee with Craig Janowitz, back after college, and she *definitely* wasn't his type, catsuit or otherwise.

In fact, Mackenzie would bet there wasn't a single guy between the ages of twenty-five and forty on the Cape that she hadn't been fixed up with at some point. It was par for the course, for the Spinster of Sweetbriar Cove, as she jokingly called herself, and she knew they only meant well, but all the good intentions in the world wore a little thin when everyone in town was worried you were going to die alone.

Alone, but with cats. Mackenzie had already decided the moment she hit thirty, she was adopting a litter of adorable kittens. If she was going to be a spinster, she may as well go all out: stop shaving her legs and give up on underwired bras, like that poem about getting old and wearing purple.

She was almost looking forward to it.

MACKENZIE DANCED FOR HOURS, with everyone from the mayor to her seven-year-old neighbor. The murals were a hit—judging by all the gruesome selfies people were snapping—and something about the costumes let even the most straight-laced residents let their hair (or wigs) down. She was breathless and laughing by the time she wound up doing a clumsy "Thriller" with Cooper, trying to remember the routine from years ago. Then music suddenly switched to a slow song, and there was a tap on her shoulder.

"Mind if I cut in?" Poppy asked with a smile.

"Be my guest."

Mackenzie stepped away, watching as the dance floor paired off. Poppy and Cooper, Riley and Brooke, Grayson and Summer . . . Looking around, she realized that all her friends had someone with them that night. Even the sworn bachelors among them were cradling their partners closer, gazing at them with pure affection in their eyes.

Mackenzie felt an empty pang.

Suddenly, her wig itched in the heat, and her catsuit was uncomfortably hot. The noise of the crowd felt like it was closing in on her, so she skirted the slow-dancing couples to the exit and slipped outside, letting the door clatter shut behind her as the cold night air hit her lungs.

She took a deep breath, and then another. It was late now, and the town square was dark, lamplights casting a warm glow over the still of the empty streets. Mackenzie could hear the music still echoing from the party, but instead of rejoining the crowds, she strolled slowly across the square, past the closed up storefront of her little gallery, and towards the green.

The wind whisked around her, sharp, and Mackenzie smiled. She loved winter on the Cape. They were famous for their summers—a parade of beach days, lobster rolls, and ticker tape fluttering in red, white, and blue—but Mackenzie preferred the blaze of fall colors and that first taste of snow. Already, she'd pulled the heavy blankets down from her wardrobe, and traded her denim cut-offs for thick wooly tights, and she had her snow boots waiting by the door, ready to crunch through the pristine snowfall the first morning it arrived.

Maybe this year, she'd do another set of snowflake ceramics. The tourists for the Starbright Festival had loved them last time around, and she could play around with different glazes to get that perfect wintery luster on the bowls and delicate tea cups . . .

Mackenzie climbed the stairs to the gazebo, still lost in thoughts of winter ahead; she didn't even notice somebody else was already sitting on the narrow bench until she knocked into a pair of outstretched boots. "Sorry," she exclaimed, stumbling hard on her stacked heels.

A pair of hands caught her waist, and then Mackenzie found herself pressed up against the solid planes of a muscular body.

"I've got you," the stranger said, moving out of the shadows. And suddenly, Mackenzie was gazing up into a pair of stormy blue eyes she would have sworn she'd never see again.

Her heart froze, right there in her chest.

It couldn't be . . .

But it was.

She blinked, disbelieving, but the mirage didn't shift. Sure, he had ten years on the gangly teenage boy she used to know: dark stubble on his jaw, and a weary look on that gorgeous face, but she couldn't have forgotten him, even if she tried.

Jake Sullivan. Her best friend, once upon a time. The first boy she'd ever loved. The only man to ever put a dent in Mackenzie's invincible heart.

And he was looking at her like they'd never met.

~

JAKE CAREFULLY PLACED the mysterious vixen back on solid ground. He'd been ready to snap at whoever stumbled in, interrupting his moment of solitude. Then he felt the soft curves pressed against him, and caught a glimpse of a heart-stopping face framed with inky black hair. Suddenly, he didn't mind the company.

"Thanks." The woman sounded breathless. "It's these boots, they're a hazard."

"Not your usual style?" he asked, amused.

She laughed, a bright, warm burst of sound that filled the dark space and immediately put him at ease. "Umm, no. Can you imagine hiking through the woods in these things?"

He took in the wicked boots. "Good point."

He could imagine her doing plenty of other things in them though. Clothing-optional things . . .

He shook his head, wondering for a moment if he'd wandered into some fantasy life. Then he remembered: it was Halloween. He'd been driving all day to make it back to the Cape, but it figured Sweetbriar would go all out when it came to the holiday.

"Let me guess, you're on a secret mission?" he asked.

"Well, if I told you that, it wouldn't be a secret now, would it?" The woman gave him an impish grin, and Jake chuckled.

"Unless you need a partner in crime. I could be useful."

"Oh, really?"

"Sure. I'm great at ordering takeout food and picking a good movie on Netflix."

7

She laughed. "Those are pretty important skills."

"They wouldn't see us coming," Jake agreed, smiling now.

The woman was looking at him carefully, almost like she wanted to say something, and Jake braced himself for the usual blink of recognition, and then the excited questions. He was used to it by now, after a career in the NFL—and the accident, which was splashed across ESPN for weeks.

But this woman wasn't a sports fan, or maybe she just didn't expect to see Jake Sullivan, star linebacker, moping in the dark of a small-town gazebo, because her expression smoothed out, and that playful smile returned.

"You're not in costume," she noted. "You better watch out, or someone will fine you for not having enough town spirit."

"Some things never change. I grew up here," he explained. "I'm just back for a visit. And who says I don't have a costume? The best spies blend into a crowd."

"Whoops. I'm not exactly blending in in this, am I?" She looked down, and Jake couldn't help but follow her eyeline back to the skin-tight black bodysuit.

Damn. Incognito she wasn't. Hell, she could stop traffic at twenty paces.

He snapped his eyes up. "That's OK. You can stun the enemy into submission, while I sneak in unseen."

"Sounds like a plan." She smiled, and Jake wondered what her story was. Definitely another out-of-towner like him, maybe visiting friends for the party. She couldn't have been a local. If they had women like this in Sweetbriar Cove, he would have found a reason to come back years ago, instead of flying his parents out to meet him wherever he'd been under contract around the country.

"So what about you?" the woman continued. "What would you be, if you could pretend to be anyone for a night?"

Jake felt the question ricochet straight to his heart.

God, if he could have anything, be anyone, he would pick himself—six months ago. Back when he had the world at his feet. Fame, money, women, a team he would have taken a bullet for, the chance to walk out on that field every Friday night and do what he loved best. He was living his dream, everything he'd spent his whole life training for, right up until the opposition linebacker smashed through the rest of his life.

But that wasn't a story for this mysterious siren. He swallowed back the pain and bitterness, and forced another easy smile. "I don't know. You've probably got the right idea. James Bond, I guess," he added. "Maybe then you'd meet your match."

"Is that right?" She arched an eyebrow, flirtatious. "You think you could handle me?"

He grinned. "You don't strike me as the kind of woman who could be handled," he quipped back. "But I'm sure I could give it a try."

"Promises, promises."

Their eyes met, electric, and Jake could have sworn there was something familiar about her playful stare. But he would have remembered if they'd met before.

A woman like this, you didn't forget.

The moment stretched, and he couldn't look away. For a moment, he could only hear his heartbeat, suddenly booming like thunder in his ears. They were alone in the dark shadows of the gazebo, and suddenly—inexplicably—he wondered how her lips would taste.

Would she kiss the way she laughed: warm and unbridled? Or were those gold-flecked eyes of hers hiding a wild, sensuous streak?

Then the woman glanced down, her cheeks flushing. "I should get back . . ." she said quickly, gesturing back to the Town Hall.

Jake knew he should let her get back to the party, and whatever lucky man she had waiting, but something stopped him from moving aside.

He didn't want to sit alone in the dark any longer, counting all the ways his life had blown apart.

He didn't want to face the fact that after ten years away, telling himself he was bigger and better than this small town, he was right back where he'd started, all over again.

He wanted to forget it all, just for a moment. Pretend that she really was some mysterious vixen, and that he was a man who had all the answers.

Before he could stop himself, he closed the distance between them and reached to push a strand of that sleek dark hair off her cheek. Her eyes flashed with surprise, but she didn't step away. She paused a moment, blinking up at him, and then her gaze dropped to his mouth.

Her lips parted. Her head tilted, moving in, and it was all the invitation he needed to slide his hands around her waist, pull her against his body, and kiss her, like it was the most natural thing in the world.

And it was. His mouth found hers, and just like that he knew: kissing her was as easy as breathing, and necessary as air.

Jake tugged her closer, feeling those curves pressed against him all over again. But now, he took his time—slipping his hands around her waist and feeling her melt against him, molded perfectly, like she was made to fit. Her lips parted, inviting, so he slid his tongue deeper to taste her: warm and sweet, with a whiskey kick that took him by surprise.

He should have known there was more to her than meets the eye.

The woman kissed him back, passionate and unleashed, and God, he could have lost himself in her arms. For the first time in months, everything just melted away, and he felt whole again: exactly where he was supposed to be. It was like walking out on the field, making that perfect spiral pass to the twenty-yard line with the wind behind him and the crowd cheering his name. A moment of sunshine, pure and bright cutting through the stormy shadows—

She suddenly pulled away. Jake was still caught up in the rush, and how *right* she felt against him, but the dark-haired woman was shaking her head in disbelief. "What are you doing?" she said, almost to herself.

"Wait—" Jake reached for her again, needing just another moment of sweet escape, but she was already backing away.

"This isn't me," she blurted, "it's the costume. And the boots. I told you, these are dangerous boots."

And then, before he could say another word, she turned and fled, racing down the gazebo steps and out into the night.

Jake sat down with a thump, his heart still pounding in his chest.

What just happened?

He took a breath, and slowly the world shifted back into focus: the streetlights calm on the fringe of the square, empty streets, and the distant call of music. Everything was exactly as it should be, just another night in Sweetbriar Cove. There was nothing to show his world had just been tipped upside down by a mysterious, intoxicating stranger.

And he didn't even know her name.

One week after Halloween, and Mackenzie hadn't heard a peep about Jake—which was a Sweetbriar miracle, considering how fast news traveled in their town. She already knew that Hank at the market had changed the brand of honey he stocked, so she would have thought that their conquering football hero returning home after all these years would have warranted an all-alerts broadcast. But even though she kept her ears open—and her eyes alert for that tall, muscular frame—as she strolled through town, there was still no hint of him.

She should have been relieved. Her cheeks still flushed when she remembered that night in the gazebo, and how she'd wound up melting in his arms. It was madness, making out like that with *Jake Sullivan* of all people, especially when he had no clue that she was the woman he'd been kissing.

Mackenzie flushed again, this time with guilt. OK, so she should have said something. They'd been friends, once upon a time. *Best friends.* She'd teased him, expecting him to figure it out at any moment, but the teasing led to flirting, the flirting made her heart race faster, and then suddenly, he was moving closer with that reckless look in his eyes, and the moment for confessing the truth melted away in a rush of pure desire.

She was a bad, bad girl.

But oh, it had felt so good.

Mackenzie reached her gallery and unlocked the front door. Inside, the bright, airy shopfront was filled with colorful pottery, stacked on pedestals and shelving, with their glazes gleaming in the fall sun. She loved to change her work with the seasons (and those tourist-friendly festivals), so her fall collection was out in full force: rich reds, orange, ochre, and gold colors, with tiny painted leaves edging the bowls and tableware, pretty as a walk through the autumn woods.

She stripped off her coat and scarf and looked around. She had a million things to do: orders to process and pack, fresh pottery to glaze, last month's accounts.

They could all wait.

She headed in back instead, to the studio she'd affectionately named her mudroom. It had clay-splattered floors, shelving crammed with tools and misshapen experiments, and, in the pride of position, her potter's wheel, waiting in the middle of the room.

She rolled up her sleeves, tied on an apron, and grabbed a handful of wet clay from the bucket waiting by the door. And just like that, her world made sense again.

Mackenzie smiled. She'd always been an artist. Even as a kid, her hippie parents had encouraged her to be creative, so she would spend hours in the yard making weird play figures out of twigs and material scraps, or mixing her own paints from a dubious collection of wild berries, eyeshadow, and cherry soda, but the first time she ever sank her fingers into a cool, squishy mass of clay, she'd known it was the beginning of a great love affair—one that had lasted twenty years and counting.

Now, she quickly kneaded the clay to remove any air pockets, then settled on her stool and threw it down hard in the middle of the wheel. It landed with a satisfying *splat*, so she nudged the pedal, and started it spinning.

What would she make today?

She had a list of orders a mile long, but Mackenzie could already see this piece taking shape in her mind: a beautiful serving bowl, with a gently-flared lip. Something simple; she would glaze in pure white and a cobweb of delicate snowflakes, her first nod to the winter season ahead.

She cupped the mound of clay firmly as it spun, exerting just the right amount of pressure with her palm and fingertips to guide the clay into shape. She formed the first dip in the center, gently bringing it wider, until the base of the bowl was formed, then pinched the clay up and out, shaping the slope of the body.

It was second nature to her by now, slipping into that focused dream state, totally absorbed by the project in front of her. She could have done it in her sleep, and sometimes, Mackenzie woke feeling like she had—hands molding around her blankets like she'd been shaping them into a new set of dinnerware. Today, she was glad for the distraction, putting all her attention on the smooth, steady spin, until she heard the bell jangle over the gallery door.

"Just a second!" she called, hitting the pedal and bringing the bowl to a stop. She rinsed her hands, then headed out to find a familiar face browsing the shelves. "Summer," she greeted her friend happily. "If you tell me that bag is full of sticky buns, I'll love you forever."

"You're easy." Summer laughed. She had a blue knit cap pulled over her hair, and a brown paper bag wafting sugar and butter across the room. "And yes. Cinnamon sugar buns, and some blackberry turnovers too."

"You're so good to me." Mackenzie wiped her hands off and skipped over. Summer's sticky buns were no joking matter: they'd turned her bakery into a massive success, and even fueled a cookbook and TV show. "It's kind of early for you to be out. Shouldn't you be chained to the stove, turning out pastries for your adoring masses?"

"My assistants are taking care of the adoring masses," Summer replied. Mackenzie took a bite of cinnamon dough and sighed with pleasure, as Summer glanced around the store. "I'm actually here on a mission. I need some new sets of plates for the bakery, I thought maybe I could commission you to do a special style." She turned over one of the bowls, etched with acorns. "Could you maybe do something like this, but in a simple white, with . . ."

"Blackberries!" Mackenzie finished for her. It was the bakery on Blackberry Lane, after all.

"Yes!" Summer lit up. "That's perfect. We could even sell them, so people can take a souvenir."

"Done and done." Mackenzie grabbed her order book and started checking dates. "When would you need them? I have to finish up an order for a gallery in Boston, but then I'm all yours."

"There's no rush," Summer reassured her. "Whenever you can spare the time."

"Then let me know what you need, exactly, and I'll get started." Mackenzie smiled. "I'll even give you the sticky bun discount."

Summer laughed. "Sounds good to me." She checked her phone. "I better get back, before they burn something. Have you heard how Debra is doing?" she added, heading for the door.

"No, did something happen?" Mackenzie frowned.

"She got tipsy on Hank's elderberry wine at the town meeting last night. She tripped and broke her ankle."

"Oh no," Mackenzie exclaimed. "Is she OK?"

"Aside from being laid up with a massive cast," Summer said. "I was going to take her these muffins, but I really should get back. Would you mind dropping by today?"

"Of course, I'll put together a care package," Mackenzie said.

"Great. Tell her I said hi!"

MACKENZIE CLOSED up early for lunch and headed over to Debra's farmhouse on the outskirts of town, stopping by the market first, for a stack of the trashy gossip magazines she knew Debra loved. She'd known the older woman for years; she'd been Mackenzie's art teacher in high school, and now as well as running all the big town festivals, Debra was also a regular participant (slash wine-drinker) at their monthly book club. When she rang the bell at the farmhouse door, Mackenzie was greeted with a riot of barking.

"It's open!" a call came from inside, so Mackenzie pushed it wider, and was promptly attacked by two fluffy German Shepard dogs.

"Brad Pitt! George Clooney! Down boys!" She managed to keep her balance under the cascade of wagging tails and enthusiastic licking.

"I'm in here," Debra's voice led her back to the cozy living room, where the woman herself was resting on the couch, her ankle in a massive cast that was propped up on a cushion. "What do you think?" she asked, nodding to the white shell. "I asked for something a little more colorful, but they only had white. Perhaps you can bring by your paints and jazz it up?"

"What happened?" Mackenzie asked, setting down her bag.

Debra sighed. "Contrary to what Franny says, I wasn't drunk. Well, not very. But one of those rascals left a chew toy out, and before I knew it, I was ass backwards down the stairs."

"Ouch." Mackenzie winced. "Does it hurt?"

"Not since the nice doctor gave me something for the pain," Debra grinned. "Speaking of, would you be a dear and grab my purse?"

"Here." Mackenzie passed it over. "And I brought some supplies, too." She unpacked the shopping. "Summer sends her best, and these muffins."

"Ooh, I guess there is a silver lining, after all." Debra swallowed a couple of pills and settled back, shifting position. "Cooper already came to fix my gutters, and Grayson stopped by with a box of rather naughty romance books from his store. I've half a mind to take to my bed every year."

"Don't get too comfortable," Mackenzie laughed. "I don't think Brad and George would cope too well."

The dogs were still racing around, full of energy. One bounded over to nudge at Debra. "That's my hint," she said, rueful. "I don't suppose you could take them out for a walk, could you? I let them out back to run around, but, well, you can see they're used to a real hike."

"I'd love to," Mackenzie agreed. "Things are slow at the gallery, so I was planning to get some fresh air anyway." She paused, scratching one of the dogs behind the ears as she fought her curiosity.

The curiosity won.

"I heard Jake Sullivan was back in town the other week," she said, trying her best to sound casual.

"Mmmhmm." Debra was busy picking through the bag of muffins. "Oh, yes, he's back. Staying at his folks' house while they're off on that trip of theirs."

Mackenzie's heart stopped. *Staying.* As in, present tense?

"I thought he'd already left," she said, her pulse suddenly racing. "He's still here?"

Debra looked up. "For the winter, at least. You should stop by," she said, getting a familiar gleam in her eye. "Welcome him to the neighborhood. Didn't I read in *Men's Health* he's still single? He was one of their top bachelors. I've got the article here somewhere—"

"No, thanks! I'm fine. Just . . . heard the gossip, that's all." Mackenzie leapt up, certain her cheeks were flushing bright red by now. "I should go take these guys out before they cause any more damage." She gathered her bag and the leashes, and was heading for the door when she added, "If you need anything else, just call."

"Well, there is one small thing." Debra said, stopping her. "The Starbright Festival."

"What about it?" Mackenzie paused. It was the pride of Sweetbriar Cove, a huge set of festive events leading up to the big candle-lighting ceremony on Christmas Eve, and Mackenzie loved every minute of it.

"I need you to run it."

Mackenzie snorted with laughter, but Debra looked deadly serious. "Wait, what?"

"I usually steer the whole thing, but as you can see . . ." Debra wriggled the toes peeping out of her cast.

"But . . ." Mackenzie blinked at the enormity of the project. "It's a huge festival. Thousands of people, and dozens of events!"

"Oh, don't worry, it practically runs itself." Debra waved away her concerns. "But, I suppose, if you don't have the time to help . . ." she sniffed, giving Mackenzie a frail look. "I could try and soldier on, and hope I don't do any permanent damage . . ."

"Don't play 'weak old lady' with me." Mackenzie stopped her with a grin. "You're in better health than the rest of us."

"But I can't get around." Debra pointed out. "Besides, I've been running the damn thing for over a decade. This time, I deserve to sip my eggnog in peace. Look, it's all here."

She heaved a massive binder up, stuffed with loose pages and handwritten notes peeking out. "The local businesses all know the drill," Debra continued, "you just need to crack the whip and keep them on schedule."

Mackenzie slowly lifted the binder. It weighed as much as a block of clay. "Why me?" she asked, feeling like she'd just been given a curse, not a blessing. "Ellie Lucas would be great at something like this, she's used to doing all the accounts. Or Riley's new girlfriend Brooke! She runs that hotel, spends all her time staging events. She'd be perfect!"

"They're in the honeymoon phase," Debra said, dismissing her. "Poppy and Cooper will be planning a wedding soon enough. You're the only one without any distractions, no man keeping you up at night—you'll have plenty of time for this!"

MACKENZIE LEFT the binder at her gallery, and then headed for the coastal trail with the rambunctious dogs in tow. Single-shamed for not having a boyfriend! She couldn't believe it, and from Debra of all people. But the older woman probably just knew Mackenzie was a soft touch, and she did love the holidays . . .

Christmas was her favorite time of year, and the Starbright Festival always made it special. The town was transformed into a twinkling wonderland, with Christmas trees on every corner, and the local businesses going all-out to decorate in new festive themes. Mackenzie did her best to top herself every year at the gallery, even hosting the annual Nog-Off eggnog competition, but she'd never been responsible for much more—let alone the whole thing!

It couldn't be too complicated, could it? Debra wouldn't risk the biggest tourist draw of the year just to have a nap.

Would she?

The barking of the dogs pulled her back to reality. They were out of town now, away from the main highway, so Mackenzie undid their leashes and let them run free into the undergrowth and along the winding trail that meandered up the coast, with the woods on one side, and the rocky shoreline on the other. It was a gorgeous fall afternoon, with a cool blue sky and leaves crunching underfoot, and Mackenzie took a deep breath of crisp air and felt her tension slowly slip away.

She could handle this, no problem. A project was good. Things had been getting a little predictable at the gallery, and helping with the Starbright Festival was her chance to shake things up. It would occupy her mind, and keep her from being distracted . . . like by a certain football star's unexpected return.

Jake.

Mackenzie felt her cheeks flush again, picturing his broad shoulders and blue eyes. She hoped Debra hadn't seen her feelings written all over her face before, but hopefully she'd played it off as just a casual question. They'd been friends, after all, long before he'd become the sports superstar everyone knew today.

Best friends.

Mackenzie smiled, remembering it. Back then, he gave her rides to school in his dad's beat-up truck, blasting mixtapes from the cassette deck. They did their homework together in the back corner of the library, and watched crappy movies in her basement on a Friday night—before he went off to whatever party was raging that weekend. They were an unlikely pair: the football star and the weird art girl, but thanks to the Sweetbriar School District's alphabetical seating policy, they didn't really have a choice. Mackenzie had arrived the first day in school, a transfer student with her chunky knit sweaters and that frizzy red hair that made her wince to think of it, and been assigned the seat beside him. It was her third move in five years, so she knew the deal: high-school gods like him didn't look twice at dorky mere mortals like her. But one afternoon during Calculus, she'd been deep in her sketchbook, when a tiny paper plane landed on her desk.

Can I see? the message read.

Jake had been watching her sketch and scribble all afternoon long. She'd been embarrassed at first, showing him her half-finished drawings and random notes, but he'd been so enthusiastic that she kept sharing. Art club let out the same time as football practice, so he'd offered her a ride home, and just like that, they'd become friends.

It would have been great, if she hadn't gone and fallen head over teenage heels in love with him.

Mackenzie winced. Her unrequited crush on Jake had consumed most of her junior and senior years, and the only silver lining to it all was that he'd remained completely oblivious. She'd come close to telling him how she felt, just once, the night of prom, but . . . well, that hadn't exactly gone as planned. (Unless the plan had been running half-dressed and humiliated through the Sweetbriar Town Square). But perhaps that was a blessing in disguise, because Jake stayed in the dark about her feelings—right up until the day he left for college on a football scholarship, and started what would become his glittering career. He hadn't stepped foot back in Sweetbriar since, and although she some-times thought of him—when a game was on TV at her parents' place, or when some old Jimmy Eat World song came on the radio —Mackenzie figured he was gone for good, just another wistful memory of the girl she used to be.

Until that Halloween kiss made him anything but ancient history.

The kiss . . .

She inhaled, memories rushing back to her. The broad, stacked planes of his body pressed hotly against her . . . The way she'd surrendered willingly to his tempting mouth, losing her mind, and her breath, as he kissed her like nobody had ever kissed her before . . .

She shook her head sternly. It was stupid to keep replaying that night. It had been a moment of madness, and now she had to face the consequences—or rather, try her best to avoid them. With any luck, Jake was just in town for a quick visit, and she wouldn't have to explain herself. She couldn't imagine him staying longer, anyway. He was rich and famous, and used to the city lights by now. He was—

Jogging up the trail in workout gear, heading straight for her.

Mackenzie froze.

Maybe she was imagining things, but nope: there he was, in loose gray track pants and a sweat-drenched blue T-shirt. She wondered if she had time to dive back into the trees and hide, but it was too late. He looked up and saw her.

"Mac?" he called, a grin spreading across his face. He slowed his pace, and came to a stop in front her, breathing hard. "Holy crap, I can't believe it. I haven't seen you in, what, ten years? C'mon over here and give me a hug!"

He held his arms wide, still beaming, and that's when Mackenzie realized:

He still had absolutely no idea that the woman from the gazebo was her.

*J*ake couldn't believe the woman standing in front of him, after all these years. He crushed Mackenzie in an enthusiastic bear hug and then stood back. "Look at you," he said, taking in her curly red hair, and the thick wool jacket all bundled up. She looked older than the gangly teenager he'd seen last, but still somehow exactly the same. "You got tall!"

"I've always been tall," she said, then cleared her throat, glancing away. "Umm, welcome back. I heard you were in town."

Jake came down to earth with a bump. It had been too long since he'd visited Sweetbriar—or sent so much as a vague email to Mackenzie. They'd drifted apart after he left for college, and even though he often wondered how she was doing, whenever he thought about reaching out, he always felt too guilty for leaving it so long.

"I'm sorry we lost touch," he said, "I mean it. I should have been better about calling, or emailing. But everything got crazy, and then, boom, it's ten years later."

"It's OK." Mackenzie gave an easy shrug. "I mean, it's not like you were busy or anything. They let anyone in the NFL, right?"

A teasing smile played on the edge of her lips, and Jake laughed with relief. She wasn't the type to hold a grudge. "Still, that's no excuse," he said, sincere. "I was actually going to look you up. Word is you have a gallery here in town?"

Mackenzie nodded.

"That's great! I always hoped you would keep pursuing your art."

She looked bashful. "It's just a small place. Mainly I do stuff for tourists, you know, plates decorated with sailboats, and ceramic lobsters."

"You still do that," Jake said, hit with a wave of familiarity.

"What?"

"Act like you're not crazy talented."

Mackenzie rolled her eyes. "And you still charm everything with a pulse, I see."

"I do my best." Jake grinned. God, it was good to see her. The sunlight was burning up the edges of her flame-red hair, and she had a wild striped scarf wound around her neck he just knew was handmade. It took him back to high school, driving the long way home from school with her after practice, stopping for fries and thick ice cream shakes and just talking for hours. Back when the world was full of possibility, and his bright future lay waiting.

"I missed you," he said, feeling a pang—for those sunset drives, and everything the happened after. Being back to Sweetbriar felt like a failure for him, a last resort, but seeing Mackenzie reminded him that there was a silver lining to his return. "I mean it," he insisted. "We need to catch up properly, get burgers from Astro like old times."

"Astro closed a few years back," Mackenzie replied.

"No!"

"Albert had a stroke, his son tried to keep it going, but they couldn't make it last," Mackenzie said with a rueful look. "It's a fancy bistro now, all white linen tablecloths and freeze-dried caviar."

"I guess a lot's changed since I've been away."

Jake paused. He wanted to ask more, find out everything he'd missed—all the gossip and news from her life—but Mackenzie still seemed wary. She was twisting the tassels of her scarf around her fingertip, the way she always used to do when she got nervous. Jake tried to rein in his enthusiasm. He was happy to see her, but maybe the feeling wasn't entirely mutual. He'd been the one to leave, after all, with barely a look in the rearview mirror. Who knew what her life had been like since he'd been away— what he'd missed, and who she'd become?

"Well . . . I'm around, if you want to get together," Jake said, deflating. "I'm back at my parents' place for now, so just give me a call, or swing by anytime. Fries or freeze-dried caviar. Your choice, my treat."

Mackenzie smiled. "Promises, promises," she said, teasing.

It sounded so familiar, he was hit with a sudden sense of déjà vu. And just like that, it came rushing back to him

Promises, promises.

The mysterious woman in the gazebo. Her playful hazel stare, so foreign and familiar at the same time. A pixie face hidden under the sleek, dark hair.

Jake's blood pounded in his ears as the two faces merged into one, standing right in front of him.

It was her. Mackenzie. It had been her all along.

"I . . ." He opened his mouth, frozen in disbelief, but she must have seen something because Mackenzie's eyes widened in shock.

"I have to go!" she blurted. "George Clooney! Brad Pitt!"

"What?" Jake stared, totally confused.

"The dogs," she explained quickly, and sure enough, two massive beasts came hurtling out of the woods. "Down boys! Down!" She managed to wrangle them under control, and then backed away. "I, um, good to see you!" she said, before turning and bolting away at full speed, with the dogs chasing at her heels.

But Jake could only stand, frozen in place.

The woman was Mackenzie.

He'd *kissed* Mackenzie.

Kissed . . . and held . . . and lain awake in bed all week, imagining the other sinful, wicked things he wanted to do with her, too.

With *Mackenzie*.

He couldn't believe it. That woman had been seductive and intoxicating, flirting like it was second nature—nothing like the brash, funny girl he'd known. Had she really changed so much? And why the hell hadn't she said something to him from the start?

He slowly started walking, feeling like he'd just been hit by a truck. His head was spinning, and memories of that night started replaying in his mind—in all their lush, sensual glory. It felt wrong somehow, knowing it was Mackenzie who was the subject of his lustful fantasies, but he couldn't help it.

Why didn't she say it was her?

Unless . . . she thought he'd known. And then decided to act like nothing had happened. Jake groaned, totally confused. So much for Mackenzie being the silver lining of his trip—now he was more mixed up than ever!

One thing was clear, though: He didn't know Mackenzie Lane as well as he thought. In fact, she was more of a mystery now than he could have imagined.

And damn if he didn't want to solve that riddle.

By the time Jake arrived back at his parents' house, thoughts of Mackenzie had been blotted out by the dull ache ringing in his injured knee. He'd done three miles, extra-slow, barely walking at a snail's pace by the end, but the pain told him even that had gone too far. Dammit.

He winced, limping inside and heading straight for the kitchen, where he grabbed an ice-pack and collapsed on a chair. It was strange to be home after all this time, it made him feel like he was eighteen again, bursting in after practice to grab a glass of water. His mom still had the clutter of photos and notes on the refrigerator door, and the sun fell through the windows on the worn, honey wood floors. It was a long way from his penthouse on South Beach, all glass and marble, with touch-button controls and wraparound views all the way to the ocean, but for once, he was glad to be a few hundred miles from city life. Back there, he was surrounded by reminders of the life he should have been living—and would be again, one day, just as soon as this damn knee healed.

His cellphone rang, and he retrieved it from the counter.

"Hey man, what's up?" the voice of his agent, Trey, boomed out, as if he were hollering from the twenty-yard line.

"Nothing much." Jake tried to be patient. Trey asked that every time, like the answer would be any different.

Not training with the team.

Not out on the field.

Not living the football star life that he'd worked so hard to achieve.

"How's it shaping up in Sweetapple?" Trey chuckled.

"Sweetbriar," Jake corrected.

"Same difference. I'm picturing you on a lobster boat, like an L.L.Bean commercial." Trey laughed again.

"No time for fishing," Jake said lightly. "I'm supposed to be getting back in shape, remember? I ran this morning, got weights this afternoon. The only thing missing is Coach yelling at me from the sidelines."

"That's great, man, but are you sure you're up to it? You heard the physio," he added, sounding cautious. "Rushing recovery could do you more harm than good."

"I've been in recovery for six months now," Jake said, his jaw clenched. "I can't just sit around doing nothing, not if I want to get back on the field."

"Hey, you'll get there," Trey reassured him. "I'm just saying, take it easy on yourself. I know you like pushing it to the limit, but things are different now. That knee of yours needs time. Hell, you were barely walking a few months back, you'll be fighting fit again, but not if you blow it out running laps in Sweetglen, or wherever you are. You know I'm right."

Jake scowled. The pain in his knee told him everything he needed to know, but he still didn't have to like it. "I'll ease up," he said reluctantly.

"I don't know why you sound so miserable," Trey added. "You've been busting your ass for ten years, and now you get a vacation! Have a few drinks, sleep it off. That cartilage will be healed in no time."

"Sure. Look, I've got to go. Talk later." Jake hung up before he said something he would regret. He knew Trey was just trying to cheer him up, but damn if he didn't have a skill for saying exactly the wrong thing.

A vacation?

Jake looked around the empty house and gave a hollow laugh. His vacations involved a white sandy beach and a girl wearing nothing much at all, not sleeping back in his childhood bedroom, going through his excruciating daily rehab routine, praying to God that the specialists were right, and that his injury would heal well enough for him to get back into the game.

But it was a long shot. He knew it, despite Trey's pep talks and his parents' cheery messages. They'd been the first ones on the plane out to visit him in hospital after that game. They'd sat by his bedside, helped him through those first, agonizing months, when even taking a single step felt impossible. Now, finally, he was on the mend, so he'd sent them off on a dream vacation to get away from it all. It was the least he could do, and to be honest, he needed a break from their smothering concern.

But now that he was alone, there was nobody to drown out those whispers of doubt. What if he never healed the same? What if his career really had ended with that brutal tackle from the Falcon's linebacker?

Football had been his life as long as he could remember. It was everything to him—and he was nothing without it. Just look around.

Jake slowly eased to his feet, and wandered through the house. There were his team photographs, lined up by the stairs. There were his trophies, still in pride of place on the living room shelves. And there was the photo of him up on the mantle, celebrating the day he got drafted, twenty-two, right out of college. His bedroom was no better, a shrine that hadn't been touched in ten years. Same posters on the wall, same rookie cards on the desk, same trophies and certificates proudly telling the story of how he went from college standout to rookie long shot and finally, a starting position on the team.

His career was all around him, he couldn't escape if he tried. A lifetime of sweat and dedication and training, every milestone like a dream come true for him.

So what if it was over?

What if five seconds and one bad tackle was all it took to send those dreams shattering to nothing?

Who was he supposed to be now?

4

_fter her run-in with Jake, Mackenzie needed some perspective.

Perspective, and carbs.

Luckily, she already had a girls' night planned, so she busied herself at the gallery for the rest of the day, trying to ignore just how good Jake had looked in his workout gear—or the look on his face when he put two and two together and came up with that kiss.

Busted.

She should have played it cool, laughingly come clean like sure, she dressed up in catsuits and made out with guys she hadn't seen in years *all the time*. Maybe then she wouldn't feel that jittery lurch in her stomach at the thought of him, or be making plans to become a hermit and avoid all potential contact with him for the next year.

But there was no hiding, not in Sweetbriar Cove. Which meant sooner or later, she was going to come face to face with Jake again, and when that happened, she would need a better response than just blushing bright red, turning, and running away.

Maybe she could move to Guam?

By six, Mackenzie hadn't come up with any better solutions, so she headed over to Poppy's beach house, with a bottle of wine and a family-sized bag of Doritos twice as big as her head.

"Yes! Chips! I'm PMSing like crazy." Poppy greeted her at the door and practically snatched them from her hands. "I'm so late, I'm ready to kill anyone who stands between me and calories."

Mackenzie gasped. "Late, as in . . ."

"No. Shush," Poppy said firmly, but there was laughter from the next room.

"She's in denial," Summer grinned, emerging with a glass of wine. She was barefoot in jeans, with a pink stain on her sweatshirt that looked suspiciously like frosting. "You can set your clock by her cycle."

Mackenzie blinked. So much for her own drama. "This is . . . amazing! Wow, congratulations."

"I said shhhh!" Poppy protested again. "I don't want to get my hopes up. I'm only a week late, and I've been working around the clock on my new novel. I haven't even said anything to Cooper yet. It's stress. "

"It's not," Summer said in a sing-song voice. Poppy glared. Summer laughed. "I'm sorry. You're right. We'll wait another few weeks before celebrating, OK?"

"I didn't even know you guys were trying," Mackenzie said, following them into the kitchen.

"We're not!" Poppy said. "And I can tell he's waiting until Christmas to propose. But, well . . ." She couldn't stop the smile spreading across her face.

Mackenzie squealed and gave her a hug.

"I said no celebrating!"

"OK, OK." Mackenzie pulled back. "I'm just really, really happy to be eating junk food tonight."

"That's better." Poppy smiled. "And you're in luck. I just called in our pizza order, Summer brought that popcorn she sprinkles with crack—"

"Cinnamon and spices," Summer corrected, laughing.

"And now we have wine." Poppy paused, her smile slipping. "Dammit."

"One glass is fine," Mackenzie reassured her, reaching for a handful of that crack-corn. "And you better have extra cheese on the pizza, if you're eating for two."

"I like the way you think." Poppy grinned. "But I'm serious, you guys. It's way too early to even be talking about it. We wouldn't, if Summer here didn't know way too much about my body."

"OK, my lips are sealed." Mackenzie mimed locking her mouth and throwing away the key. "So, we'll talk about something else. What else is new?"

"Besides the hot guy in town?" Summer lit up, and Mackenzie knew there could only be one man she was talking about.

Sure enough, Summer continued, "I heard he's some big-shot football star. Single," she added, giving Mackenzie a meaningful look. "And you're lucky I'm taken, because I saw him at the pub, and I swear, you could bounce quarters off that ass."

"Summer!" Poppy tossed popcorn at her.

"What? It's true." Summer grinned. "Have you seen him yet, Mac? We should go hang out there until you get a glimpse."

Mackenzie cleared her throat. They'd all become fast friends over the past few months, and talked about everything under the sun, but when it came to romance? It had always been her offering matchmaking advice for everyone else, not the other way around. It felt weirdly exposing to mention anything about her own tangled heart, but she knew she needed their opinions.

"Well, actually . . ." she began, but she was interrupted by the sound of the door opening.

"We're in here!" Summer called, and then Brooke joined them, still dressed in her crisp work outfit with her blonde hair pulled back in a braid.

"Leftovers from a wedding today," she said, holding up a couple of bags. "Who wants two dozen crab puffs?"

"Me!" All three women put their hands up at once.

Brooke laughed. "Done." She started to unpack the goodies. "What are we talking about, anyway?"

"The hot new guy in town," Poppy answered.

"The football player?" Brooke's eyes widened. "I heard he screwed up his knee, and can't play again. But that ass . . ."

"See!" Summer laughed. "It's undeniable."

Mackenzie thought back to the way the gray track pants had hugged Jake's body . . . And the blue of his T-shirt, bringing out his eyes . . .

"What's going on with you?"

She snapped out of her reverie to find Summer looking at her closely. "What? Nothing." Mackenzie shoved a handful of popcorn in her mouth.

"No, she's right," Poppy added slowly. "You just got this dreamy look in your eyes. I've never seen you look like that before."

"Sure I do. Every time I see a crab puff." Mackenzie reached across the kitchen counter, but Brooke pulled the plate back, out of reach.

"And you're all flushed, too. You're not getting any of these until you spill."

Mackenzie looked around. Three expectant faces stared back at her. She gulped. Suddenly, the casual girl talk felt more like an interrogation.

"I . . . know him. Or, I used to. We were friends in high school," she explained, feeling her cheeks blush bright red. "And I, um, maybe made out with him on Halloween and he had no idea it was me."

Brooke blinked first, then handed her the plate of crab puffs. "Talk."

ONE HOUR, two glasses of wine, and three slices of pizza later, Mackenzie had explained the whole humiliating mess to them all —from her unrequited crush to the impulsive Halloween kiss, and right up to their awkward encounter that afternoon.

"I love it!" Poppy said, gleeful. "A dark night, two strangers, who turn out to be old lovers—"

"We were never lovers," Mackenzie said firmly, but Poppy waved her away.

"Details! It's a great plot, like fate brought you back together again."

"Spoken like a true romance author," Mackenzie laughed, rueful. "Unfortunately, life doesn't exactly follow the outline."

"Yet," Poppy said, looking determined. "Who knows what the next chapter holds?"

"What I do know is that I can't ever show my face in town again," Mackenzie groaned, sinking lower into the couch cushions.

She was met with a chorus of protest.

"What? So you kissed the guy," Summer argued. "That's nothing. Franny practically caught Grayson and me doing it in the middle of his bookstore."

"Aunt June walked in on Cooper and me on the stairs," Poppy added.

"Let's just say, the harbor master has gotten an eyeful of me and Riley on his boat by now," Brooke agreed. They all clinked their glasses together in celebration of their very public scandals.

"Yes, but this is different!" Mackenzie exclaimed. "Jake didn't even know it was me. You should have seen the look on his face when he figured it out," she added, wincing. "It was like he thought he'd been kissing Angelina Jolie, and got me instead."

"Don't say that," Poppy said firmly. "You're amazing. And gorgeous, and sexy—"

"And your ass is just as fine as his," Summer agreed, laughing.

Mackenzie managed a grin. "OK, we'll pretend that part is true. But you don't understand," she added. "Jake always treated me like his kid sister. He never saw me as anything more, no matter how hard I tried."

"But that was ten years ago," Brooke spoke up. "A lot could have changed since then."

"Right," Summer agreed. "He could be a different person now. For all we know, he's turned into some arrogant man-whore— fine ass, or no fine ass," she added, warning. "You know these sports guys, a taste of fame and then suddenly it's all VIP clubs and bottle service."

"VIP what now?" Poppy joked. "The closest I've ever come is when Riley gives me extra fries."

"Ketchup is the only bottle service you'll ever need!" Summer cracked.

"Jake's not like that," Mackenzie said, when the laughter had died down. "I mean yes, he's older now, and hotter, but the way we were talking . . . He's still the same guy as before." She couldn't stop herself from letting out a wistful sigh, and the other women exchanged a knowing look.

"So, just play it cool, and see what happens," Poppy suggested, reaching over to steal another slice of pizza from the box. "I mean, this is Sweetbriar. You're going to find plenty of reasons to run into him. As long as you don't turn and flee in the other direction, you should be able to figure this out."

"She's right," Summer agreed. "You don't need to overthink it. Like you said, it was one kiss, you're both adults," she added reassuringly. "It doesn't have to be a big deal—unless you want it to be one."

"I guess . . ." Mackenzie felt her stomach do another slow flip just at the idea of seeing Jake again. She groaned. "Why am I even feeling like this? You know me, I don't get like this about guys."

"Maybe the other guys haven't been worth getting like this," Brooke replied with a grin.

Mackenzie stuck her tongue out at her.

"Real mature." Brooke laughed.

"That's me," Mackenzie said ruefully. "Partying like it's 2002 all over again."

She absently took another handful of popcorn. Maybe it was just the past talking: all her pent-up, unrequited teenage hormones back to haunt her all over again. That didn't mean she had to regress into her younger self, feeling panicked and timid at the idea Jake could ever discover how she really felt.

She was older and wiser, after all. And with a killer ass.

Jake would be so lucky.

Now, maybe if she repeated that to herself another three dozen times, she could start believing it. Some things may never change—but she had. And she couldn't let herself forget it.

~

Nothing had changed.

Jake strolled the town square, marveling at how it looked exactly the same. Sure, there was a new coffee shop and some quaint gift boutiques, but the feel of the place was just the same: antique streetlights lit the streets with a warm glow, and the windows were all decorated with fall colors and pumpkins, cozy and comforting. It was a long way from the neon lights he called home these days—South Beach bars spilling noise and music into the street past two a.m., the hustle of the main drag, and delicious Cuban food trucks on every corner.

His stomach growled. He could use one of those about now. It had been late by the time he stopped torturing himself with old ESPN recordings, and realized there was nothing in the house to eat. He was used to having a housekeeping service keep his place stocked with food, but of course, Sweetbriar didn't exactly come with round-the-clock delivery. He wasn't in the mood to stop by the pub and have to talk to anyone just yet, but luckily, he spotted a new pizza place across the way, so he ducked in just before closing and ordered up a large pie with the works—and one extra, for leftovers the next day.

"I thought you athletes were supposed to eat healthy."

He turned and saw an older woman sitting at the corner table, swathed in a huge knit kaftan. "Debra!" Jake exclaimed, smiling. "You caught me. I won't tell Coach if you don't." He winked, and Debra snorted.

"Same charm as ever," she said with a smile. "I'd get up, but as you can see, I'm moving slower these days. But, I guess you know a little something about that."

"News travels," he agreed.

"Still, good to see you up and about," Debra said approvingly. "Back on track?"

"Just taking it easy," he replied. "I'll be fine."

"So, you've got some time on your hands then?" Debra seemed to brighten. "Interesting."

Jake knew that look. It usually came right before a favor. Back in high school, he'd found himself hauling sets for theatre productions and cleaning out her gutters.

"Well, you know, I can't do too much," he added quickly. "I've got my rehab program, it's pretty demanding."

"Oh, shame," Debra said. "Poor Mackenzie could use the help."

"Mac?" Jake's head snapped up at the mention, and suddenly, his brain was flooded with images of her all over again.

Teasing in that sleek wig. Laughing with him in the woods.

Kissing him . . .

"She's running the Starbright Festival. All on her own." Debra gave a dramatic sigh. "She'll be run off her feet. But you take care with your rehab, I'm sure you have plenty to be busy with."

Suddenly, a bell sounded. Jake turned, confused. His order was up. "I should, umm . . ." He tried to remember what he'd been saying before Debra had mentioned Mackenzie, and all coherent thought went out the window.

"Good to see you, kid. Don't let it get cold," Debra said merrily, and turned back to her own meal.

Jake took the boxes and headed back outside, still thinking about Mackenzie's lips, and the way she'd melted into him. He stepped out into the street—

And got an earful of angry horn blast. He jumped back, just as a car rolled past.

Jake shook his head. He needed to get a grip. Spacing out every time he even thought about Mackenzie could be hazardous to his health, plus, he was acting like an idiot. It was just a kiss. He'd kissed plenty of women, hell, he'd probably lost count. You didn't play professional football without attracting your share of fans. Hot, sexy fans looking for a good time. He and his teammates hit the clubs after every game, and you could bet they never went home alone.

But this was different.

He headed back towards his truck, but something caught his eye across the square. A small gallery with colorful pottery in the window. This must be Mackenzie's place.

He crossed the street—carefully this time—and went to take a look. It was closed up, the lights off inside, but he could still see the shelves of ceramics, the bright glazes catching the streetlight gleam. Jake was impressed. He should have guessed it, she always had a way with paint, or clay, or even a cheap ballpoint pen. But this wasn't just some amateur school project. The spotless floors, the white walls, the glass display cabinets . . . It looked like the kind of place you would find in Boston, or some other big city: reining all those wild ideas into something polished and professional.

He wondered what path had led her here. There were ten whole years of her history blank, and although he'd always asked his parents for updates—heard about her going to art school, then moving back to Sweetbriar—it wasn't the same. He used to know all about her life, from the TV shows she was obsessed with to the music she loved to her latest crush of the week. Now, he realized, he didn't know a thing.

Was there a man in her life?

Jake immediately shot down that thought. Mackenzie had always been fiercely loyal, she sure as hell wouldn't be running around kissing him if there was another guy waiting for her back home. But it seemed crazy for her to still be single, after all this time. She was beautiful, and smart, and talented—

Not that it was any business of his.

He turned away from the gallery and headed back to his car. The pizza was getting cold, and he had no reason to be loitering out here on street corners, wondering what Mackenzie was doing tonight.

Impulsively, he pulled out his phone. He didn't know if she'd kept the same cell number, but he remembered her old one like it was yesterday. It rang, and rang, and then clicked to voicemail.

"Hi, Mac, it's Jake," he said. "It was good running into you today. How about getting that drink sometime this week? My schedule is pretty much open, so you pick, any time. It would be great to catch up, so . . . call me. Take care."

He hung up, wondering if he was going to hear from her again.

39

She'd bolted so fast that afternoon, it seemed like she couldn't get away soon enough. But that was crazy, they weren't going to let one little kiss get in the way of all their history.

Even if it was one of the most mind-blowing kisses in his life.

But if Mackenzie didn't want to mention it, then he could play that game too, Jake decided. It wasn't worth losing a friendship over, that was for sure. As far as he was concerned, it didn't mean a thing.

Not one, hot, sensual thing.

He definitely wasn't going to dream about her tonight, either. No, he had plans: pizza and a cold shower.

Make that two cold showers.

5

*I*t took Mackenzie less than forty-eight hours to seriously regret agreeing to steer the Starbright Festival plans. If the binder of doom wasn't enough, Debra also sent over another box worth of notes and files, covering everything from the regulations on twinkly light displays (white, yellow, and blue were allowed, but apparently pink was forbidden), to the size of holiday trees that should be ordered, and even a file of potential Santa Claus actors ranked on beard length, friendliness, and their CPS background check. By Friday morning, she was meeting with the Mayor, trying to take notes fast enough to keep up with his enthusiastic plans.

"The Cape usually gets over sixty thousand visitors in December alone," Albert said excitedly. "But this year, I really want us to hit the big one hundred."

Mackenzie gulped. "That's . . . ambitious."

"There's nothing like it!" Albert declared. "The Starbright Festival celebrates every religion and race, all coming together to share the magic of the holidays. And you know, tourism is the engine that keeps the Cape alive," he said over the top of his half-moon glasses. "Every person through that square doesn't just come to marvel at the lights, they book a hotel room and buy dinner and gifts for everyone back home."

"You don't need to convince me," Mackenzie said, pausing to flex her hand. It had cramped from taking so many notes for her to-do list. "I get half my business during the holidays."

"And it's that kind of creative, entrepreneurial spirit I know will make this year's festival a huge success!" Albert stood, and Mackenzie took that as her cue, too. "If you need anything, let me know. Now, what do I have next?"

"Chamber of commerce," his secretary Franny said, appearing briskly in the doorway. "Over in Provincetown."

"Ah, that's it! What would I do without you?"

Not much, Mac was sure. Franny was the secret power behind Town Hall, and had outlasted every mayor since before Mac could remember, quietly ruling from behind her non-descript secretary's desk. Once, a newly-elected mayor had decided to try and shake things up and brought in some highly-trained administrative assistant for the job. She'd lasted three months before losing her position in a surprise recall vote—that was a surprise to nobody.

Now, Mackenzie knew, if there was a secret to successfully pulling off this gig, Franny had it.

"Is that a new scarf?" she asked, following Franny back to her desk. "I love the color."

"They're in the basement."

"Excuse me?" Mackenzie blinked.

"Supplies from last year," Franny said, giving her a knowing smile. "That's what you're after, isn't it? Not sure what state they'll be in, but you're welcome to go down there and figure it out."

"Thank you," Mackenzie breathed. She'd caught a glimpse of the budget line, and wasn't sure how she was supposed to equip the whole town with festive cheer for such a small amount. "I figured all that fake snow had to go somewhere."

That somewhere was the second-level basement, deep below the town hall. Mackenzie ventured down the staircase, her enthusiasm dimming as she made her way past clean, bright storerooms, down into the dusty, dark depths of the basement. A dim gloom greeted her, and she fumbled around until she found a light switch. The bulb flickered ominously overhead.

"I've seen this movie," she said to herself, shivering. "It does *not* end well."

But she was a grown woman. She wasn't afraid of the dark. She squared her shoulders and set about hauling down boxes marked with Debra's familiar scrawl. "*Tree decorations,*" she read aloud, coughing as a cloud of dust billowed up from the box. "*Menorahs. Sex toys.*"

Wait, what?

Mackenzie gingerly peeled open the tape on that one, not sure what she would find. To her relief, it was a collection of holiday ornaments, complete with battery packs. Clearly, Debra had decided to have some fun with her packing—and, most likely, some of that prize-winning eggnog.

"No thank you," Mackenzie said aloud, eyeing the spikes on the two-foot light-up holiday tree. "Ouch."

A noise came from somewhere behind her. Her heart leapt, and she spun around. "Hello?" she called, brandishing the ornament in front of her. She peered into the shadows. "Is anyone there?"

Another noise came, louder this time.

"I'm warning you!" Mackenzie yelled. "I'm armed!"

"Whoa!" A reply came, and then Jake was stepping out from behind a teetering shelf of boxes. He took in the sight of her, and then laughed. "What were you going to do, brain me with Santa?"

"Jake!" Mackenzie exhaled in relief, her heart pounding. "What are you doing here? Trying to give me a heart attack?"

"Sorry." He looked around at the dim, cluttered basement. "Wow, this place is a death trap." His gaze stopped on the box she'd just opened. "Sex toys?" he said, eyes widening.

"Just Debra and her unique sense of humor."

"Shame." Jake flashed her a grin, and Mackenzie's heart kept on racing. Even in the shadows, she could see the stubble on his jaw, and the way he filled out that navy cashmere sweater. She still couldn't get over how his body had changed, or how his blue eyes crinkled at the edges now: a man's smile, not a boy's.

Her stomach turned a slow pirouette.

"You didn't answer my question," she said, trying not to be flustered. "What are you doing down here?"

"Helping you." Jake casually reached for the nearest box like it was no big deal. "Now, who wants to untangle half a mile of Christmas lights?"

Mackenzie didn't move. She fixed him with a look, and he finally explained. "Debra roped me into it. She said you were drowning, and in desperate need of a strong man to do some heavy lifting. So here I am." He reached up, and hauled another box down, and Mackenzie was momentarily distracted by the way his sweater rode up, revealing a strip of tanned, taut stomach.

And as for those arms . . .

She flushed. "You don't have to," she said quickly. "I can handle it."

Jake raised an eyebrow, and looked around at the basement—boxes strewn all over the floor.

"It's OK," he said, giving an easy shrug. "I have plenty of time on my hands. And besides, it could be fun."

Fun? Working in a dim basement in close proximity to all those muscles . . . Mackenzie gulped. That was one word for it.

Tempting was another.

"Sure. Great," she said brightly. "You can take that row on the left. Anything in good condition, we'll be hauling upstairs. Franny says we can use the storage buildings out back until everything's ready to install."

She turned away, and started blindly going through the nearest carton, praying he wouldn't say anything about the kiss—or his voicemail, that still sat, unanswered on her cellphone. She must have played it a dozen times over, but she hadn't called him back. She didn't know what to say.

Well, that wasn't true. She just didn't know what to say aside from, *Kiss me again. Now.*

"Look, Mac . . ."

Mackenzie glanced up, and found him looking at her with an awkward expression on his face. It was so familiar, it took her breath away, like he was seventeen all over again, reluctantly explaining to Chrissy Jenkins that he'd already agreed to take Mac to senior prom—just as friends.

It had cut her then, and it still did now. In an instant, Mackenzie realized what was coming: that same sincere rejection she'd watched him dish out to a dozen unlucky girls.

She couldn't be one of them. She couldn't bear him thinking she was another adoring fan-girl, eager for a moment of his time.

"Look, about what happened on Halloween," she said suddenly, before she could lose her nerve. "I know I should have said something, but I was tipsy from Bert's punch, and the costume, and the wig . . . Well, you know I can't hold my liquor." Mackenzie flashed a smile, hoping she was a good enough actress to pull it off.

"That's the truth," Jake answered slowly, his expression unreadable. "But, about that night. Maybe we should talk about it?"

"What's there to talk about?" she asked brightly. "I could tell you didn't recognize me. I was just planning on teasing you a little, but, well, one thing led to another. It happens," she said, breezy. "No hard feelings, I hope?"

"Not from me." Jake still looked unsure, so Mackenzie dialed up the "casual detachment."

"Good! So, we can just pretend like it never happened then. And you can tell me how you wound up on the cover of *Men's Health* wearing nothing but a speedo," she added, with a teasing grin.

Jake groaned. "You saw that?"

"Oh boy, did I see it." Mackenzie grinned, a sincere smile this time. "Someone pinned a copy to the town noticeboard. Your mom must be so proud!"

Jake laughed, looking embarrassed. "My agent made me do it. It was all staged, I swear."

"Oh, so you don't hang out in the gym in your underwear, surrounded by bulldogs?" she asked. "There goes my vision of your glamorous life."

Jake snorted. "Yeah, think five a.m. workouts and running drills all day."

"Poor baby," Mackenzie teased. "It's so hard living the dream."

Jake smiled at her, a real smile that warmed her heart and made her feel like no time had passed between them at all.

"I missed this," he said, like he was reading her mind. "Us. You."

"Me too," Mackenzie said quietly.

He exhaled. "It's been . . . a tough year. I haven't laughed like this in, well, a long time."

The accident. She had almost forgotten the reason he was back in Sweetbriar at all. Mackenzie felt the strongest urge to go wrap her arms around him, hold him tightly, and kiss away the pain in his eyes.

But she could tell he didn't want to talk about it, so she gripped an ornament instead, and gave him another bright smile. "I'm here to help. And so are you, so best get lifting. Chop chop."

She grinned. "What's the use in being my errand boy if you're not going to earn your keep?"

MACKENZIE KEPT her head down and tried to focus on the task at hand—and not the gorgeous man just a few feet away, close enough to touch in the cluttered, dusty basement. But the universe seemed determined to taunt her, flooding her mind with flashbacks to their kiss, and making her wonder why she couldn't just tug him closer and do it all over again.

Because that had been a moment of madness, she told herself sternly, putting three life-size plastic reindeer between them. And besides, that wasn't her. That was the woman in the wig. She'd just managed to laugh the whole thing off and save what was left of her pride, and a repeat play wouldn't exactly help with the whole nonchalant story she was spinning now.

The only thing worse than not kissing him again would be his inevitable rejection when she did.

"I can't believe this stuff," Jake said, sorting through a stack of old papers. "I mean, who thought this would make you want to celebrate the holidays?" He held up a poster showing a terrifyingly blonde child gripping a candy cane. "He looks like he's about to curse you, not bring on good cheer."

Mackenzie stifled a sigh. Sure, there she was trying her hardest not to fall at his feet, crying, *Take me now!,* and he was musing about the historical significance of candy canes. "I think we can leave all that stuff down here," she said instead. "It's just the decorations we want."

Jake paused and looked around at the many, many boxes they'd already stacked by the stairs. "Just how many snowman ornaments do we actually need?"

"Well, every store is supposed to put up a display," Mackenzie started. "Then there's the town square, the park, all the public buildings . . . And I only made it halfway through Debra's instructions."

"In other words, the North Pole will move a little south this year." Jake shook his head. "You know, I don't remember it being this crazy when we were growing up. We had the tree-lighting and carols, but that was about it."

"That's because we were too cool to go in for all this tourist stuff," Mackenzie teased, with a nostalgic smile. "We would fill up on cookies and hot apple cider, and then go to the movies instead."

"Sounds like a plan," Jake said, grinning back at her. "You in?"

Mackenzie laughed. "I think a hundred thousand hopeful tourists would have something to say about that."

She put her hands on her hips and looked around, doing a mental inventory. "We've found everything except the snowflakes. Can you see any more boxes anywhere?"

Jake checked the shelves. "No, we've got everything, I think."

Mackenzie shook her head. "They have to be here somewhere. They're my favorite, they go up on the gazebo every year. The light catches them just right," she said, remembering. "like you're in some winter ice palace, surrounded by snow. It's actually how I first started working with clay—I wanted to make them myself, for a project in art school," she confided. "I tried paints and different types of glass, but nothing worked until I started firing the glazes; it was the only way to get that glistening effect."

She stopped, feeling self-conscious. What was she doing, rambling on about snowflake ornaments when Jake clearly couldn't wait to get out of there?

She was just turning back, when she spied another box lurking in back on top of a cabinet. The snowflakes? She reached up on her tiptoes.

"I can get that," Jake said, moving closer.

"No, it's fine." Mackenzie stretched, grasping to get it. It was lodged behind something, and she had to tug to get it free. "I'm the errand boy, remember?" Jake tried to move her aside and grab it, but Mackenzie stubbornly kept pulling. She'd been doing just fine before Jake Sullivan came back to town. She was independent and capable, and she could reach a damn box without needing a man to get it, and push her up against the wall, and make her moan—

Wait, that wasn't the point here.

Mackenzie blushed, and finally stepped aside to watch Jake reach up with all six-foot-two of taut, lean muscle and effortlessly pluck the carton down. He opened the lid. "No luck," he said. "Unless you want to decorate the gazebo with reels of old microfiche."

"Never mind," Mackenzie said quickly, still feeling flustered. "I'm sure they'll turn up. Like you said, we have more than enough."

She turned away from his broad shoulders before she did something really stupid.

Like kissing him again.

6

*J*ake spent the afternoon in the basement with Mackenzie, helping her haul boxes up to the ground floor and check everything was in working condition. By the end of the day, he was sweaty, covered in dust, and ready to smash the next holiday ornament to cross his path.

He hadn't had so much fun all year.

"That's the last of it!" Mackenzie cheered, appearing in the main hallway with a final carton of tangled twinkly lights. She set it down and wiped her forehead, pushing sweaty red curls out of her face. Somehow, she looked more beautiful than ever.

"Remind me again why I volunteered for this?" she asked, sounding rueful.

"Because you're a good person," Jake replied. "And Debra is the queen of emotional blackmail."

"She's not so bad," Mackenzie defended, loyal as ever. "It's not her fault she got injured."

"Did anyone even see her fall?" Jake countered, teasing. "For all we know, she takes the cast off and dances around the living room the minute we're gone."

Mackenzie laughed.

"God, I need a shower," she said, tugging at her tank top. Jake's mind went blank for a moment and he fought the vivid mental images fighting their way through. *Mackenzie . . . naked . . . soaped up . . .*

"And food. And a cold beer," she continued, bringing him back to earth. Mackenzie looked torn for a moment, then shrugged. "The pub it is."

"You always did have your priorities straight," Jake said, trying to keep it together. He wasn't some asshole, drooling over every girl in sight, and Mackenzie deserved a hell of a lot more respect than this. He hoisted the cartons and took them out to the storage locker, hoping the shock of cold air would get his hot blood under control.

It hadn't been easy, working all those hours down in the basement with her. Every time she brushed against him, reaching for another box, he had to fight the urge to kiss her again.

Kiss her, and more . . .

But Mackenzie had made it clear she wasn't giving Halloween a second thought. *It happens*, she'd said, like it was no big deal, and maybe to her it wasn't.

Jake's pride burned at that. The most epic kiss of his life, and the woman in question just laughed it off?

Clearly, his technique needed some work.

Not that he'd get a chance to hone it with Mackenzie, he reminded himself sternly, shoving the last few boxes into place. She was off limits, and damn, it was already driving him crazy.

"Thank you," Mackenzie said when everything was locked up. "Really. It would have taken me all week to do this on my own. And I'd probably have given myself a hernia, too."

Jake smiled. "No problem. What's next on the schedule, anyway?"

Mackenzie looked surprised. "You still want to help?"

"If you still want an errand boy."

She seemed flustered, checking the massive binder she'd been toting around all day. "I . . . um, well, I guess we should go through the list of local businesses and distribute the decorations and schedule. We build with different events all through December," she explained, "and then the Festival itself kicks off on the twentieth with the tree-lighting ceremony and runs until Christmas Eve. But all that can wait until tomorrow," she added. "I'm beat, and you probably have better things to be doing."

He didn't. Jake's evening held nothing but another take-out meal, and that empty house, and a phone that didn't ring anymore. Nothing like a career-ending injury to show you who your friends really were. It was shocking, how quickly his buzzing social circle had melted quietly away, sending flowers and "get well soon" texts, and then nothing much more.

Jake lingered by the door. It wasn't just that a night alone held no appeal; he wanted to make the laughter last a little longer. "Well, how about I buy you those fries I owe you?" he suggested. "Before you get so hangry you sit on the ground in the middle of the square and refuse to get up until I bring you a bag of chips."

Mackenzie laughed at the reminder. "That was one time!" she protested. "And you're not much better. Didn't you make me drive to Boston just for a hot dog?"

"The Mighty Monster," Jake corrected her, smiling at the memory. "Two-foot chili-cheese dogs with extra cheese. And they were worth every mile."

Mackenzie giggled and fell into step beside him as they headed across the square towards the pub. "Mitch still keeping this place running?" he asked, looking at the new lights out front, and a chalkboard promising the best fish and chips on the cape.

"No, he retired. Riley bought it a couple of years back. You'll like him," she said, ducking inside. "He's fun. A charmer, like you."

Jake didn't know what to make of that comment, and when

Mackenzie crossed the room to enthusiastically greet the bartender, he couldn't help but tense up. The guy was tall and blonde, and Mackenzie hugged him without hesitation, laughing at something he said.

Just how friendly were they?

Jake slowly strolled over.

"This is Jake." Mackenzie turned to introduce him. "He used to be a local, before he abandoned us all for fame and fortune."

"Hey man, welcome back." Riley shook his hand. "Wait a minute, you look familiar. Linebacker, Miami, right?"

Jake nodded, as Mackenzie hit Riley playfully on the arm. "Since when are you a football guy?"

"I keep up!" Riley protested. "I'm a man of hidden depths."

"Sure you are," Mackenzie snorted. Jake looked back and forth between them, still trying to figure their relationship—and why it mattered to him so much. "Is Brooke around?" she asked.

"Upstairs," Riley said. "Want your usual?"

Mackenzie nodded. "Double portion, please. And whatever Jake's having."

"Hey, this is on me." Jake reached for his wallet, but Mackenzie shook her head so fast her curls shivered.

"No way. You've more than paid in sweat today. And there's more where that came from. You realize the Starbright Festival isn't for another month?"

He hadn't, but strangely, Jake didn't mind at all. "So then I'll get the next round," he said, sliding onto a stool at the bar.

Mackenzie smiled. "I'm not going to argue with that. Be right back!"

She ducked behind the bar and headed upstairs. Riley gave him a weary look and slid a pint of beer across the bar. "Make that a good half hour. Once those two get talking . . ."

Jake quickly put it together. "Your other half?" he asked casually, taking a sip of beer.

53

Riley nodded, and Jake felt a swift rush of relief. So they were just friends.

"Are you in town long?" Riley asked, giving him a look that Jake couldn't quite read.

"I'm not sure yet," Jake said, thinking of his huge apartment back in Miami—with a mortgage to match. "I figure on hanging out here for the holidays, at least."

"It's a nice time of year," Riley nodded, still giving him that inscrutable stare. "We have a poker night running, if you'd like to come by."

"Thanks." It wasn't exactly the warmest invitation, but Jake didn't have his phone ringing off the hook. "That sounds great."

There was a pause, and Jake felt Riley's eyes on him, sizing him up. Thankfully, they were interrupted by a newcomer, a tall, bearded man in a rumpled plaid shirt. Jake paused, double-taking.

"Cooper?" he asked in disbelief.

"Jake Sullivan!" Cooper broke out in a smile and slapped him on the back. "What the hell, man? It's been, what, ten years?"

"Look at you," Jake laughed. "Last time I saw you, you were a skinny kid, now you could give my QB1 a run for their money."

"Don't remind me," Cooper groaned. He turned to Riley. "This guy was always keeping me out of trouble in high school."

"I didn't have much choice." Jake grinned. "He would go wading into fights he didn't have a chance in hell of winning."

"At least not until you showed up." Cooper grinned. "Man, it's good to see you." His smile slipped. "I was sorry to hear about the injury. Tough break."

"Thanks." Jake changed the subject quickly. "What about you? What have you been up to? Besides hitting the gym."

Cooper snorted. "Try hauling timber. I do contractor work these days," he explained.

"He's being modest," Riley interrupted. "He restores historical houses, he's famous around here."

Cooper shook his head. "Architectural Digest kind of famous. It's not exactly TMZ," he said, giving Jake an amused look.

Jake coughed. That incident—stumbling out of a club at five a.m. with a Hollywood starlet—wasn't exactly his finest hour. His coach had made him run drills the next day until he was just about ready to collapse. "I don't make a habit of it, believe me," he said ruefully. "But it sounds like you're doing great."

"I've no complaints." Cooper gave a satisfied smile. "Hey, if you're looking for something in the area, just let me know. I need to put my old place on the market, or get a renter in, at least."

Jake didn't think he'd be sticking around long enough for that, but he nodded politely. "Thanks. I'll keep it in mind."

"And what about you?" Cooper took a seat beside him. "I hear you're already roped into this Starbright Festival affair."

"How did you—" Jake stopped and shook his head. "I forgot that gossip in this town puts the tabloids to shame."

"Poppy heard it from Aunt June who got it from Hank at the hardware store." Cooper grinned. "Welcome back."

"Some things never change."

"Sure they do."

Mackenzie's voice made him look up. She appeared back down the stairs, and danced out to the main bar, pausing to ruffle Cooper's hair and steal a French fry from the bowl he hadn't even noticed Riley set down. "I mean, I'm guessing your karaoke song has changed." Mackenzie gave him a cheeky smile.

Jake tried to look serious. "We swore never to speak of that again," he said, mock-stern.

Mackenzie just grinned back, totally unapologetic. "Statute of limitations, baby. Leave town for too long, and all your dirty secrets come spilling out."

"Is that a threat?" he arched an eyebrow at her.

"Think of it as incentive not to go forgetting us all over again." Mackenzie was still teasing, but he saw a flash of something else in her eyes, and Jake was reminded again that he was the one who had done the leaving. She was right. He'd stayed away too long.

"I won't," he said quietly. "And besides, something tells me you won't let me."

She smiled like him, and for a moment, it felt like the old days. The two of them against the world. But that wasn't right—because back then, he hadn't felt the hot flare of desire burning at the edges of every conversation, clouding his mind—and his body— until it was difficult to think straight.

Jake looked away and found Cooper and Riley watching them with matching expressions of curiosity on their faces.

He cleared his throat.

"How about we change things up?" Mackenzie said, thankfully changing the subject. "Who wants to play some pool?"

She was met with groans from the other guys.

"She hustled you, too?" Jake asked, grinning. They nodded.

"Took me for a hundred bucks the first night we met," Riley said, looking rueful.

"I should know better," Cooper agreed. "But somehow, she always makes me forget my last crushing defeat."

"Aww, you're no fun!" Mackenzie exclaimed. "Don't believe them," she added to Jake. "I'm not that good. I've gone rusty in my old age." She fluttered her eyelashes at him, and Jake snorted.

"You're not fooling me. But sure, why not? Winner buys me a Mighty Monster."

"Good luck," Cooper said, as Jake followed Mackenzie over to the pool table. He'd be needing it—but not for the game. He already knew there was no beating her, not once she got on a streak. Back in high school, he'd played the straight man to her pool shark routine, hustling unsuspecting tourists all over town.

No, it wasn't losing he was worried about. Because when Mackenzie racked the balls and leaned over to take her first shot —hair spilling over her shoulders, the V-neck of her sweater falling dangerously low, and a familiar look of total focus on her face—the game was the last thing on his mind.

She broke fast and clean, sending the balls scattering and two stripes into the far pockets. "So, game over, then?" Jake asked, only half joking.

Mackenzie pouted.

"Fine," he sighed, still teasing. "I'll stand here and watch you win. You know, I'm surprised they still let you play," he added, leaning back against the wall to watch her sink another ball with a swift, perfect shot. "Your mug shot should be pinned in every bar between here and Boston. *Wanted: hustler.*"

"It's not hustling to be good," she countered, circling the table and leaning over to eye the angle of her next shot. Jake caught a glimpse of creamy skin swelling beneath her sweater, and a hint of purple lace. His pulse kicked, and he forced himself to look away.

"It's hustling to pretend to be terrible so you can raise the stakes before you take the sucker for everything he has," he said instead, and Mackenzie laughed.

"Want to put your money where your mouth is?"

"Ha!" He chuckled. "I'm not about to fall for that."

"Pity." Mackenzie glanced up and winked. "I bet we could wager more than quarters these days."

She made her shot, but the ball bounced out of the corner pocket. "Whoops," she said. "Your shot. Still want to make that bet?" she asked, all innocence.

Jake shook his head, still smiling. "You did that on purpose," he said, selecting his cue. He chalked it up and gave the table an assessing glance. Mackenzie had a head start, but there were plenty of open shots for the taking. He lined up his cue, and quickly sank a couple of solids in quick succession.

Mackenzie whistled. "Someone's been practicing."

He smiled and leaned over to take another shot, but just as he was drawing back his cue, Mackenzie started to gather her hair up into a messy bun. Her arms lifted, and her back arched with the motion, her sweater lifting to graze her ribcage, revealing a pale band of bare skin—

He mis-struck, sending the ball ricocheting across the table. "Damn."

Mackenzie looked over. "Your winning streak over already?"

"Guess I'm out of practice, after all." Jake cleared his throat. What was he playing at, panting all over her? She was wearing a wool sweater, for crying out loud. A sweater, and jeans that hugged her curves in all the right ways . . .

"Oh crap." Mackenzie suddenly ducked back, peeking around the corner to the main bar.

"What is it?" Jake was glad for the interruption.

"This guy I went on a terrible date with." Mackenzie peered out again, and Jake had to go see who she was talking about. There was a man at the bar with a ponytail and a brown leather jacket. Jake laughed in surprise.

"You went on a date with Moose Conway?"

Mackenzie looked surprised, then she sighed. "Oh, right, you guys were on the team together."

"While he wasn't cutting practice to go do wheelies on his dirt bike." Jake didn't know whether to be amused or jealous. "Since when is he your type?"

"Since I'm twenty-nine, single, and get fixed up with every available man between here and Connecticut." Jake thought he heard a note of tension in her voice. "Anyway, the date was a bust, obviously. But he keeps calling and— He's seen me! Crap, he's coming over!" Mackenzie ducked back and looked wildly around, but there were no nearby exits. She grabbed Jake's arm. "Pretend to be my boyfriend."

"What?" Jake blinked.

"For five minutes, otherwise he'll—Pete, hi!" Mackenzie's voice changed, and she was suddenly all smiles as the guy approached. "How's it going? Everything good at the track?"

Jake was confused, until he remembered that was Moose's real name.

"Mac, babe, look at you." Moose grinned at her. "Got some sugar for your neighbor?" He held out his arms for a hug, but Mackenzie nimbly stepped back and placed one hand firmly on Jake's chest.

"Sorry, I'm all out. You remember Jake, don't you?"

"Sullivan, my man!" Moose lit up, and slapped Jake on the back. "What's up? Should've known you'd grab the prettiest girl in town."

"Oh, stop," Mackenzie said, still trying to escape Moose's hands. "Really, stop."

Jake planted himself firmly between them. "Well, you know Mackenzie. Who can resist her charms?" he said, turning to her with a grin. "She's so sweet, and agreeable . . ."

Mackenzie fixed him with a look, but she played along. "What can I say?" she shrugged, slipping an arm around Jake's waist. "I'm just a doll when it comes to my Jakie-poo."

"Is that right?" Jake couldn't resist pulling her closer, feeling the warmth of her body. He caught a breath of her shampoo, something light and coconut-y, and just like that, he was back in the gazebo again, holding her tightly and claiming that tempting mouth for his own.

"You're a lucky man," Moose said, looking enviously at Jake.

"Yes, yes I am." Jake squeezed Mackenzie's waist. "My pumpkin doesn't give me any complaints."

"Well, see you around, I guess." Moose didn't look too crushed. "And Sullivan, anytime you want to pound a brewski, you holler. Peace." He gave Jake a fist-bump and strolled away.

"Pumpkin?" Mackenzie fixed him with a look. "My dad calls me that!"

"Jakie-poo?" he countered, grinning. He was still holding her, and he had no desire for that to change anytime soon.

"Would you prefer 'snookums'?" Mackenzie laughed. "You look like a snookums."

"I'll pretend I didn't hear that," Jake said. Mackenzie seemed to realize she had her arms around him, and took a step back, about to let him go.

"He's still watching," Jake quickly lied. And then he did what any pretend-boyfriend would do.

He kissed her.

It was just a brief brush of his lips against hers, swift and light, but it felt like finding gravity: drawn by some power beyond his control. Mackenzie tensed against him in surprise, but then she softened, pressing one palm to his cheek, which blazed with heat as he slowly tasted her, savoring every moment.

His blood surged. What he wouldn't give to yank her closer and claim her lips the way he'd been dreaming: hard and hot, until she was begging for more. But he hadn't lost his mind completely, and that would turn every damn head in town.

Reluctantly, he set her down and stepped back. "He's gone," he said, heart pounding.

And so was he.

Mackenzie blinked, looking flushed. "Uh, thanks," she said, tugging on her sleeve. "For, you know, playing along."

Jake would have happily kept the performance up all the way back to his bedroom, but that wasn't an option, not tonight.

Not with her.

"Sure. Anytime." He cleared his throat. "I should get going."

"Oh." Mackenzie's face fell. "What about the game?"

Jake had totally forgotten about the pool table, abandoned behind them. "Let's take a raincheck," he said hurriedly. "I'll need a good night's sleep to prepare for whatever festival heavy lifting you need tomorrow," he added, and she seemed to relax.

"Sure thing, errand boy."

Jake left her to it before he said or did anything else to make a fool of himself. What was it about her lips that turned him into a stammering idiot?

Her lips, and body, and smile—

Nope.

Jake stopped himself before his imagination could get him into trouble all over again. She'd needed a favor—a *platonic* favor—and he'd pushed his luck, as usual.

Some friend he was turning out to be.

He took in a breath of crisp night air, and looked around at the dark town square. This was all temporary, he reminded himself. He was just passing through. He'd help Mackenzie with this festival of hers, give his injury time to heal, and be back to his old life before the New Year. Getting tangled up in anything else was just a recipe for disaster—however good it might feel at the time.

His head knew all of that, he just had to make his body get with the program.

And as for his heart?

It needed to play by the rules.

7

For someone determined to keep a safe distance from Jake Sullivan, she sure was doing a terrible job of it. Mackenzie woke after another night of fitful, restless sleep and sighed. Two kisses and counting. It was either a spectacular failure . . . or just plain spectacular.

The problem was, she didn't know which anymore.

She swung her legs out of bed, wincing as her bare feet hit the cold floorboards. She tried to leave the heat off for as long as possible in winter, to keep her heating bills down and give her an excuse to bundle up in snug flannel bedclothes. She hurried quickly to the bathroom and turned on the shower, the pipes shuddering in protest before releasing a rush of hot water, quickly filling the blue-tiled room in steam. "That's right," Mackenzie cooed, patting the faucet. "Don't you go freezing on me yet."

She stripped off and stepped under the flow. For all its quirks, she loved her old cottage. It was nestled back from the main town, down a winding country road, surrounded by wildflowers and willow trees. It was just one bedroom, with a cozy living area, kitchen, and wrap-around porch, but Mackenzie had filled it with brightly-colored paintings, pottery, and other art pieces until it overflowed with color and life. The dirt-cheap rent helped, thanks to a forgetful landlord who had long since moved out of town, and Mackenzie was slowly putting savings aside, hoping to one day convince him to let her buy it from him outright.

For now though, she was content to bide her time, building up business at the gallery and securing placements for her pottery in high-end design stores up and down the coast. It had taken years, but she was developing a name for herself, with most of her trade coming via Sweetbriar's tourists, flocking to the many festivals they hosted in town. Which was why the Starbright Festival was so important. It wasn't just Mackenzie who depended on it for her winter trade; vendors all over town were counting on the visitors to see them through the icy winter months, before the summer beach-goers returned.

So, just the fortune of the entire town resting on her then. No problem at all.

Mackenzie tugged on a sweater and jeans, caught her hair back into a braid, and headed for the door. Then she stopped. She was meeting Jake at the gallery first thing, and this was what she was wearing?

She back-tracked to her closet and flipped through the rails. An array of chunky knit sweaters, brightly-patterned dresses, and quirky jackets stared back at her.

Mackenzie groaned. Didn't she have anything that said, 'I'm effortlessly sexy, but never give it a second thought?'

Apparently not.

She looked deeper in the closet, feeling like she was seventeen again, agonizing over her outfit before Jake came to pick her up from school. Maybe *this* sweater would make him finally notice her, or *that* lip gloss have him realize what was staring him in the face. But of course, nothing did. To Jake, she'd always just been plain old Mac—buddy, pal, and utterly invisible—as a girl, at least.

Her phone rang, and she scooped it up, trying to find something that didn't look like an explosion in a yarn factory.

"I dress like a spinster," she said in greeting to her friend Eliza. She was a journalist up in Boston who was fast becoming a part of the Sweetbriar gang.

"What? I love your style!" Eliza exclaimed. "You always look so comfortable."

"Comfortable!" Mackenzie echoed in despair. "That's saying I look like your favorite couch."

Eliza laughed. "I do love my couch. But where's all this coming from?"

"Nowhere," Mackenzie said. "I just didn't realize how complacent I've gotten. I mean, I'm not going to walk around in full makeup and a skin-tight dress, but still, I'm single. If I want to find a boyfriend, I should be making some effort, right?"

"Is this about Jake?" Eliza asked knowingly.

"Yes. No. I don't know." Mackenzie grabbed a plain black turtleneck down. She never wore it, which is why the fabric still had some shape, at least. "I guess having him around is making me realize my love life has been DOA for years."

"You date!" Eliza protested. "Which is more than I do these days, I'm working all the time."

"I go on first dates," Mackenzie corrected her. "And maybe if I didn't dress like I'm upholstery, I would go on seconds dates, too."

"Since when have you even wanted a second date with any of those guys?" Eliza countered. "And if a guy only wants you dolled up in three-inch heels, he's not a guy worth having."

"You're right," Mackenzie agreed. "Of course you're right. I wear overalls because I get clay all over them, and boots because it's muddy out, and hats because my ears get cold. I don't know why I'm overthinking this."

"Maybe because a certain football player is scrambling your brain. He's really that hot?" Eliza asked, sounding sympathetic.

"So hot. Dangerously, wildly, unacceptably hot," Mackenzie said. "So I'm probably better off dressing like Aunt June's furniture. At least that might keep him from kissing me again." She put the turtleneck down.

"Again?" Eliza's voice went up an octave.

"Oh. Yeah. That. He didn't mean it," Mackenzie explained quickly. "He was just covering for me."

Eliza laughed. "Kiss me once, shame on me. Kiss me twice, and . . . I don't know how that goes, but it definitely wasn't an accident."

"You think so?" Mackenzie picked the sweater up again.

"I know so," Eliza reassured her. "Anyway, I was just calling to ask if you would sit down and talk me through your festival planning. I mentioned to my editor you were hosting, and he suggested it would be a fun behind-the-scenes piece. You know, how you make the magic happen."

"I don't know how much magic there'll be, but sure, any time," Mackenzie agreed. "Any publicity is good publicity."

"Great. I'll put something on the calendar," Eliza said. "And don't worry," she added, "you're the sexiest couch I've ever seen."

That decided it.

Mackenzie hung up and pulled on the black sweater. Sure, it was a hell of a lot tighter than anything she usually wore, but what was a little suffocation between friends?

MACKENZIE WALKED the few short blocks to the gallery and found Jake waiting outside, looking handsome as ever in a thick navy peacoat with a coffee cup in each hand. "Still take it with ten sugars?" he joked as she unlocked the front door.

"Eleven, but I'll make do. Thanks." Mackenzie took the coffee and led him inside, feeling self-conscious as she watched him look around. "It's just a small space, I know," she found herself apologizing. "Most of this stuff is for the tourists. They love the kitschy designs. Anything with a ship on it they snap right up."

"I think it's great." Jake sounded sincere. "I mean it, I'm really impressed."

"Oh." Mackenzie blinked. "Thanks. My studio's back here," she said, showing him the way. "We can get started with the schedule."

Jake quirked an eyebrow at her. "All business, huh? You have changed."

Mackenzie flushed. "I figured you must be busy . . ."

Jake gave a hollow-sounding laugh. "Me? Sure. My phone's just ringing off the hook these days. Injured players are in high demand."

There was a beat, and she saw that shadow flit across his face again, that echo of something dark and almost hopeless.

"I'm sorry," Mackenzie said gently. "I keep forgetting. I mean, you seem to be getting around fine. I would never guess you were injured from looking at you."

"No, I'm sorry." Jake let out a sigh. "And you're right, my recovery has been great so far. I shouldn't complain, not when it was a question if I'd even be walking again. But . . . walking isn't playing."

"Do you know when you'll be back on the field?" she asked.

"Soon, I hope. I have an appointment with my physio later today, but she always just tells me to be patient."

He was clearly frustrated, and Mackenzie knew how hard this must be for him. "Well, if anyone's pig-headed and stubborn enough to make it happen, it's you."

"Gee, thanks," Jake said, but he smiled again. "Now, are you going to show me where the magic happens?"

Mackenzie paused, her mind racing somewhere not entirely PG-rated.

"Your studio," Jake added.

"Oh, right." Mackenzie showed him in back, to the chaotic, cluttered space. Jake chuckled.

"That's more like it," he said, looking around. "I was wondering where you kept the mess."

"You mean, the raw, creative genius," she corrected him. She shoved a stack of books off a chair and kicked it towards him.

"That too." Jake took a seat and looked with interest towards the corner. "What's over there?" he asked, nodding to the sheet she had draped over one of her works-in-progress.

"Nothing," Mackenzie said quickly. "Just something I'm playing around with."

The truth was, it was one of her personal projects, the sculptures she never let anyone see. These weren't the tourist-friendly pottery she churned out for the gallery, but intricate, personal, abstract works that Mackenzie toiled away on after hours—and then promptly locked in her storage room and never let see the light of day. She certainly wasn't going to show them to Jake, so she quickly heaved Debra's festival binder onto the desk with a thud.

Jake looked at it with trepidation.

"It's not too late, you know," Mackenzie said lightly. "Go, now, save yourself."

"And leave you to shoulder it on your own?" Jake shook his head. "I told you: we're in this together."

God, she was going to have to build up her resistance to that smile. Mackenzie averted her eyes before she started drooling, and started stripping off her coat, gloves, and scarf. "Well, we've got a full inventory of the decorations, that's the first thing," she said, going to hang her winter gear up. As usual, there was no space to put it, so she shoved her coat aside on a stack of books. "Now we just need to make a list of what each business in town is doing, plus there's the toy drive, and the main tree—" She turned back and found Jake staring at her. "What?" Mackenzie asked, self-conscious. "Do I have paint all over my ass again?"

Jake coughed. "No. You're . . . fine. OK, I mean," he corrected himself. "No paint."

"Good." Mackenzie sat down, relieved. "Also, maybe it's crazy to be planning extra stuff before we even get started, but I was thinking it could be fun to do a Winter Art-Walk. You know, have different local artists display their works around town and put together a map for tourists."

"Sounds great." Jake took a sip of his coffee.

"You're sure? Not too much?"

Jake laughed. "Last year, I spent the holidays with takeout and ESPN, so pretty much anything we're planning here counts as 'too much.' But it'll be good," he added, reassuring. "There's no such thing as too much holiday spirit in Sweetbriar."

"That much is true." Mackenzie relaxed. "OK, let's get started on this schedule!"

BY THE TIME they were done divvying up the Sweetbriar schedule, Jake knew more about the politics of holiday ornaments than he ever thought possible. With anyone else, it would have been a chore, but Mackenzie made everything fun—dropping scandalous gossip in with every new item, so he was fully up to date on everything he'd missed in town. It was strangely comforting to hear all the news again: no high-stakes drama or million-dollar contracts on the line, just the ongoing feud between the Cartwright sisters over the family orchard, and the time Grayson at the bookstore caused a local scandal by selling some middle-schoolers a box of steamy erotic romance novels.

"Well, on the plus side, everyone in town is going to hate me for making them do all this work," Mackenzie said brightly, sitting back. "Which means fewer invitations, and more time alone with my work."

Jake chuckled. "Liar. You could charm them into anything. I bet you'll have people lining up to volunteer."

"Sure." Mackenzie sounded dubious.

"I'm here, aren't I?" Jake said. Mackenzie caught his eye, and he suddenly had a hard time remembering why he'd stayed away from Sweetbriar for so long.

Get a grip.

Jake forced himself to take another swig of coffee, long since cold. At least he was looking above her neck this time. When she'd taken off her coat to reveal that skin-tight sweater . . . Jake felt like he'd just run laps at the stadium. Pulse racing, shortness of breath —an NFL workout had nothing on five minutes alone with Mackenzie Lane.

A rumbling noise broke through his thoughts. He looked up to find Mac blushing furiously. "I guess that's our cue to break for lunch," she said, rubbing her stomach.

He laughed. "Loud and clear."

Mackenzie got up. "Want to run by the bakery and grab something? Summer is trying out savory stuff for fall. She does these cheese and herb pies that are just . . ."

She pressed her hand to her chest in a swoon.

Jake felt torn. "Wish I could, but I have my physio appointment up in Boston, and I should hit the road."

"Right. Of course," Mackenzie agreed quickly. She looked away. "We can pick this up another time."

"Can't wait," Jake replied, and Mackenzie snorted with laughter.

"Sure," she said, grinning, and Jake didn't have the heart to tell her he'd meant every word.

8

He grabbed a sandwich in town and then hit the road, driving the slow-winding route down the Cape, through villages and trees. It was a familiar road, nothing but him and the radio, until he crossed the Sagamore Bridge to the mainland, and suddenly, the sandy highway became five, six lanes wide, and the flow of traffic thickened all the way up the coast, until the Boston skyline came into view on the horizon. It wasn't far, just a couple of hours if you timed it right, but the city felt like a world away from the sleepy Sweetbriar streets, thick with traffic and bustle and pedestrians. Jake navigated his way downtown, then parked on a side street a couple of blocks back from the big medical center.

He'd spent enough time in hospitals to last him a lifetime, but the smell still hit him, every time: a mix of disinfectant, and air freshener, and something that reminded him of despair.

"Can I help you?" the woman on the main desk called over as Jake was scanning the listing on the wall.

"I'm looking for Dr. Lashai's office."

"Third floor, to the left."

"Thanks."

Jake got into the elevator, trying not to look at the guy beside him in a wheelchair. That had been him, only six months ago—hating every moment and feeling trapped in his body. This time, at least, he wasn't on the surgical floor, or the in-patient wards; he followed the nurse's instructions until he found himself in a quiet, bright wing full of private offices, far away from the chaos downstairs.

"Jake, hi, come on in." His new physio was younger than he was expecting, a smiling woman in her thirties, with long, dark hair.

"Dr. Lashai?"

"Please, call me Padma." She waved him in, opposite a wall covered in certificates. He took in the framed achievements and relaxed a little. His coach back home said she was the best in the Northeast, and Jake wasn't about to pull any punches, not with his career on the line.

"So I've reviewed all your files and progress," Padma began. "And I've talked with your physicians back home, and the team doctor, too. Do you mind if we run through some basic movements, so I can get a look?"

"Sure thing."

Jake followed her sequence of movements, stretching and pivoting as she made notes and felt around his knee. The pressure from the exercises made him ache, but Jake grit his teeth and did his best to hide his discomfort. Finally, she gestured to the couch by the window, and Jake took a seat.

"What's the verdict, doc?" Jake asked, suddenly nervous.

"You're right on track." Padma smiled. "Exceeding it, even. ACL injuries can be tricky, recovery isn't a set path. But from your last scans, and the way you're moving now, I'd say the reconstructive surgery is looking good."

Relief flooded through him.

"So when can I start training with the team again?" Jake asked eagerly.

Padma's smile dimmed. "Let's not get ahead of ourselves," she said gently. "You've still got a long way to go."

He bit back his frustration. It was the same story he'd been hearing for months now. "But how am I supposed to get back in shape if I can't train?"

"The most important thing right now is not putting any stress on the tendons while they're still healing." Padma sounded firm. "The rigor of a pro football routine is the worst possible thing you could do."

Jake took a deep breath, controlling his temper. "So how long will it take?" he asked. "Another three months? Six? Longer?"

Padma looked apologetic. "I'm afraid there's just no way of knowing. The body heals in its own time. I don't want you to get your hopes up," she added with a warning look. "I know your progress has been encouraging, but there's still no way of saying how your mobility and endurance will develop."

Jake felt a shard of panic, ice-cold. "But I will get there, right?" he asked, not realizing how much was riding on that question until he let himself ask. "I can make it back onto the field?"

Padma paused. "I don't know," she said finally. "I'm sorry, I know you want answers, but you have to understand your recovery has already been miraculous. To be walking, pain-free, with the kind of mobility you have right now—it's incredible. And any other patient would be thrilled."

"But I'm not any other patient," Jake said grimly.

She smiled. "No. Professional athletes don't judge themselves by normal standards. I understand you want to resume your career, but Jake, maybe it's time to start thinking about alternatives."

"Alternatives to what?" He stared back at her.

"A professional football career always has a lifespan." Padma seemed to be picking her words carefully. "You've been playing now for ten years. You always knew there were limits to what your body could take."

Jake shook his head. "Guys on the team go for longer than this. Peyton Manning won a Super Bowl when he was thirty-nine."

"At what cost?" Padma asked. "Look, I'm not saying this to challenge you. We're going to keep working, rehabbing that knee, and who knows? Maybe you'll find your way back onto the field. But you've put your body through hell for the past decade, you've pushed yourself to the limit. Sooner or later, it has to stop. Why not now? The next time you take a hit—and believe me, there will be a next time—you might not be so lucky."

Jake heard his blood pounding in his ears. He knew her words made sense—he'd heard them many times over the years, from his parents, coaches, even former teammates—but after everything he'd been through that year, every painful moment of dogged determination, he didn't want to hear it.

He couldn't.

"That all, doc?" he asked, getting to his feet.

Padma looked like she wanted to argue, but she just pressed her lips together instead. "For now. I'll send over a new set of exercises, you can rotate them daily. And rest. I mean it," she warned him. "No running, no standing on it for long periods—"

"No line dancing?" Jake joked.

"Not this month." Padma smiled. "But hang in there. You've come so far already."

Jake knew he had. He could tell they all thought he was ungrateful. After all, his surgery had worked perfectly. Still, it had been a grueling road to recovery, long hours at the rehab center pushing through the pain, until he'd come so close to giving it up and saying "no more."

But he hadn't. He'd stuck with it, no matter how much it hurt. He wasn't about to quit on his dreams, he'd worked too hard for that. Because he knew, if he just kept trying, he'd be back on the field soon enough, with his teammates. Where he belonged.

But soon enough wasn't coming any time soon. And now, feeling that familiar needle of pain in his knee as he made his way back down to the street, he wondered if it was on the horizon at all.

Was he kidding himself believing he could make it back? Or was the doctor right: was it time to give up the ghost and stop pushing so hard just to put his body through hell all over again?

He wasn't as young as he used to be.

Jake found himself walking past the intersection, farther out, all the way to the river. There was a path that wound along the waterfront, and he sat himself down on a bench there, watching the crowds. A rowing crew was out on the water, pulling hard, even in the autumn chill, and farther up the path a group of runners kept pace, sweaty and determined.

That had been him, ten years ago. Workouts and training, drills, and routine. Ever since he'd picked up a football and thrown that first, spiraling pass, he hadn't paused for breath. His body had become his weapon, fine-tuned and fueled just right. Sure, he knew how to let off steam with the guys, but they never let it get in the way of their real work. Five miles on the clock every morning, the right foods for lean muscle and speed. His world revolved around training, and those precious moments out on the field come Friday night. Day after day, year after year, the same grueling workouts to get the same all-star results.

Now that he thought about it, this was the longest he'd been off the field since high school. Eight months and counting. Jake hated to admit it, but it felt . . .

Good.

Like he could finally breathe.

He slowly exhaled, watching the water. It was a betrayal, even thinking it. Coach would probably kick his ass if he knew. But the past few weeks back in Sweetbriar Cove had almost been a relief.

The worst of rehab was behind him, with nothing to take its place. No five a.m. alarm calls. No watching his glucose intake like a hawk. No falling into bed every night with an exhausted ache he felt all the way to his bones.

He'd had no choice but to take it easy, doctor's orders, and although his body was itching to get back out there again, he couldn't deny the part of him that recoiled from the idea, too.

Imagine, not putting himself through it again.

Imagine, he could just *be*.

But be what?

That was the other side of the blade, the thing that had kept him pushing for so long. If he wasn't Jake Sullivan, all-star player, who was he? This was his life—his team, his passion—and no matter what the doctors said, he'd fought way too hard to just walk away.

Jake impulsively pulled out his cellphone, scrolling through his contact list until he found DeJay Yate's number. DeJay had been a teammate, close to three years on the frontline together until a brutal tackle had sent him off the field on a stretcher. His ankle had been shot, and he quit that year and switched to sportscasting instead: running commentary from the box in a sharp suit every Sunday.

Now, Jake could hear the kids in the background when DeJay picked up. "Jake!" He sounded happy, that big voice booming. "What's up? How's that knee of yours?"

"It's getting there," Jake said. "You know the doctors, they'd have me on bed rest if they could."

DeJay laughed. "Yeah, I remember. You must be climbing the walls by now."

"Almost." Jake looked out at the water. "What about you? Things good with the family?"

"Can't complain. The youngest picked up a football the other day, I said, 'No thanks,' and steered her over to a science kit."

"Don't want her following in your footsteps?" Jake teased.

"Lord, no. Can you imagine me on the sidelines? I got banned from Little League last year, they said I was causing a ruckus. If anyone laid a hand on my baby girl . . ."

Jake laughed. DeJay always did have the loudest voice on the sidelines, and racked up a half-dozen reprimands for trash talk every season. "I saw you commentating the game last week. Very smart."

"Thanks man. We're renegotiating my contract, my agent's pressing for a wardrobe allowance this time around."

"You ever miss it?"

Jake didn't even realize the reason for his call until the question was out there, in the chill of the cloudy afternoon.

DeJay paused. "Sometimes," he said at last. "You love something that much, you can't just give it up overnight. But I don't miss the travel, or Coach screaming at me every time I missed a throw," he said, sounding rueful. "I get to spend time with Mindy and the kids instead of training, and that commentary box isn't the field, but it's close enough." He paused again, his voice turning sympathetic. "You thinking about calling it a day?"

"I don't know if I'll get the choice," Jake said quietly. "My whole life's been football."

"But you have your exit plan, right?"

"Yeah, I'm good," he sighed. He hadn't blown his money on fast cars and big mansions like some of the other players. He'd been careful with his paychecks, and made solid investments. He and his family were set for life, but that wasn't the point. "Not as good as some people," he added. DeJay had bought into an energy drink a few years back and watched the company skyrocket.

DeJay laughed. "You'll figure it out then. And any time you

want a game-day spot on air, just holler. The network will go crazy for your baby blues."

Jake laughed. "Yeah, yeah. Not all of us want the spotlight."

"That just leaves more room for me!"

They said their goodbyes and hung up. It was getting darker out now, but the crew were still on the river, rowing back and forth with hard, steady strokes. Maybe they were training for a big race, or maybe this was just a regular afternoon session. If Jake was back in Miami, they'd just be wrapping up right now. Hit the showers, head out onto the town. He'd be in the VIP section of a new, hot restaurant, basking in the glory he'd worked so hard for.

All year, he'd been wishing he was back there, and he could still feel that restless burn. But it had faded a little, with distance and time, and now that world seemed more than a few hundred miles away—it was a different lifetime. Now, he pictured Sweetbriar Cove instead. A warm fire burning, a cold beer, a quiet night.

A redhead curled up beside him, with that tempting smile.

Jake shook his head, pushing the image aside. Where the hell did that come from? Mackenzie wasn't his to go home to, and he wasn't about to risk their friendship on his mixed up emotions, not when she deserved much better than him.

This injury was temporary—and his time in Sweetbriar was, too. He would get it all back, no matter how long it took. This doctor didn't know him, didn't know how determined he could be. A few months more recovery and rehab, and he'd be back on that field where he belonged.

He finally got to his feet and left the river behind.

9

*I*t was Thanksgiving.

Somehow, between the Starbright Festival and Jake sending her emotions flipping upside down, Mackenzie hadn't even registered the holiday coming. It wasn't until people started leaving the bakery early on Wednesday, while she was still savoring her lunch, that Mackenzie realized something was different.

"Don't rush," Summer insisted, even as she began flipping chairs over around Mackenzie's table. "I just want to get a head start. We're meeting my mom in New York for the weekend," she added with a grimace, "and the traffic will be a nightmare."

Mackenzie blinked as it finally dawned on her. The paper turkeys lining the counter should have been her first hint. "Thanksgiving! Right."

"I'm just hoping my mom breaks her diet. She's much easier to handle with carbs," Summer grinned. "Do you have any plans?"

"I'm not sure yet," Mackenzie replied, her mind racing. "I'm sure I'll figure out something."

She left the bakery—with a goodie bag of pastries—and called around, seeing if anyone wanted to get together to celebrate. But Poppy and Cooper were visiting her folks back east, and even Riley was closing up the pub and heading out of town.

"We're taking the boat down the coast," he explained with a smile. "I never thought Brooke would take the time off work, so I'm getting her out of cellphone range before she changes her mind. What about you?"

"Just family, I guess," Mackenzie replied, but when she called her mom, she got a brief text message in reply.

We'll be at a silent retreat until Monday. Have fun!

It looked like she was spending Thanksgiving on her own.

Mackenzie tried to ignore the pang of loneliness. It was just another weekend, she told herself. And sure, everyone else was celebrating with loved ones, but she could do the same: all she needed to do was stick her favorite pot pie in the oven and cue up a classic movie marathon.

There was nothing wrong with being alone.

SHE WORKED LATE that night on some sketches, and woke early on Thursday to find the streets of Sweetbriar eerily silent. Strolling to the gallery, it almost felt like a ghost town, empty, save a few anxious-looking men loitering outside the market with lists crumpled in their hands. She was lucky to be saving herself the stress of a big dinner, Mackenzie told herself firmly, as she unlocked and made her way to her studio in the back. A whole day just to focus on her art without distraction. That was something worth being thankful for.

Right?

There was a list of orders waiting, but Mackenzie moved her potter's wheel aside and dragged her favorite work bench into the middle of the room. She tugged down the sheets she had covering her sculptures, and stood back, assessing her progress.

It was a new series, a trio, she imagined, although she was still working on the first piece, the figure of a woman, sleek and abstracted, a suggestion of the human form instead of something recognizable. Arched, reaching, in motion—Mackenzie was trying to capture a feeling more than anything, and although some days she looked at her progress and felt stupid for even trying, today, in the silvery morning light, she could see where she was going.

It was a start, anyway.

She put on some music, hauled a chunk of wet clay from the bin, and set to work, this time on the next figure. He would be reaching too, and the third piece would be the two of them, intertwined. Inevitable.

At least, that was the plan.

Mackenzie didn't share this side of her art with anyone. It felt too personal, too out there to just put on display for everyone to see—and judge. They knew her for her cute bowls and pretty ceramics, and Mackenzie didn't want to imagine what people would say if they were faced with this side of her art: weird and abstract, and hard for her to even put into words.

Still, she loved it. Here, in the privacy of her studio, with the clay sinking under her fingertips and the light falling through the windows just right. She lost track of time, smoothing and molding the clay just right, until a second figure was slowly shaped in front of her: not reaching and open like the first one, but holding back. Restrained. Closed, and careful.

Just like Jake.

Mackenzie paused, coming out of her reverie. You couldn't see it in the abstract form, but now that she stood back and assessed the sculpture, she could see it was him.

Or rather, the heart of him.

Leaning back while she was reaching forward. Always drifting out of reach. Without even realizing it, she'd been sculpting their relationship, committing her own foolish yearnings to solid clay.

It was like she was seventeen all over again.

Mackenzie flushed, remembering her big plan to finally come clean about her feelings. She and Jake had agreed to go together to prom, and despite everything, she couldn't help getting caught up in wishful fantasies about their romantic night together. Every smile, every glance . . . Mackenzie wondered if this was finally the moment he would realize she was more than just a friend.

After the dance, the party moved to his place, and—fueled by too many teen movies and a dose of peach schnapps—Mackenzie somehow decided a dramatic romantic gesture was in order. She snuck away up to Jake's bedroom, peeled off her dress and arranged herself in a seductive pose, and was just about to text him to come meet her there, when she'd heard voices outside the bedroom door. Jake, and some of his football buddies.

She froze.

"Mac's looking hot tonight, man," one of the voices jeered. "Didn't think she had it under those sweaters."

Jake's voice came, sounding annoyed. "Come on, quit it."

"So you're really not getting any?"

"No way, man." Jake laughed. "She's like a sister to me!"

"Sweet. So you won't mind if I hit that!"

The voices moved further away, and Mackenzie sat there, frozen in place, her blood rushing hot. She'd known that Jake was probably oblivious to her feelings, but hearing him laugh along to their crude jokes was too much. The rejection sliced through her, knowing without a doubt that the boy she'd spent so much hope, and energy, and sleepless nights on didn't even see her, not as a girl who mattered.

Then, just when she thought her humiliation couldn't get any worse, Jake's voice came again. "Hold up, let me grab that CD—"

Mackenzie panicked.

She bolted up, grabbing for her dress. They were on the second floor, and the only other way out was the window. She yanked it open as she struggled to pull her dress on again. It was a ten-foot drop, but she didn't hesitate for a moment.

A broken ankle was better than Jake finding her there, so, saying a quick prayer, Mackenzie clambered out the window, and dropped to the ground.

RIIIIP.

Her bodice caught on the ledge and tore clean away. Which is how she wound up sneaking home through the Sweetbriar town square in nothing but half her prom dress and a nude strapless bra. Somebody must have seen her, because soon the gossip spread, but Mackenzie never said a word. They all assumed she'd had some scandalous hook-up, and she let them go right on believing. Better some sexy story than the humiliating truth. Jake left for college a few months later, and as far as Mackenzie was concerned, she was taking her secret to the grave.

And here she was, spending precious time and energy on Jake all over again. Except this time she had more to go on than wishful thinking. Two whole kisses more, and the kind of chemistry than her teenage self could never even dream about.

But had anything really changed?

Mackenzie looked at the sculpture again. She was tempted to smush the whole thing down and start over, but something made her leave it. There was a beauty to the longing, at least, and even if her own romantic dreams were nothing but that—dreams—at least it was good material.

She rinsed off and cleaned her things away, and when she emerged from the gallery, she was surprised to find the streets dark in the late afternoon. The whole day had disappeared, but it always went that way when she got lost in a piece. Even when she was back in high school, she would get so deep into a painting or project, that her teachers would have to clap out loud to get her attention again.

She pulled her coat tighter and started walking for home.

Then she saw a familiar figure on the other side of the street, his head bent against the wind.

Mackenzie couldn't see his face, but she already knew. It had been thirteen years since she'd learned his steady gait by heart, and time may have changed a lot, but it didn't change that.

Jake looked up and saw her. Mackenzie raised her hand in a wave. He crossed the street, smiling as he reached her. "Another Thanksgiving orphan?" he asked. "I thought you'd be with your folks."

"Mom's dragged them to some retreat," Mackenzie explained. "You?"

Jake shrugged. "I pretty much forgot about it, until I went by the pizza place, and they were closed."

"You should come over." She made the invitation without thinking. "For dinner, I mean. Us orphans have to stick together."

Jake's face softened. "I'd like that," he said. "If you're sure I'm not interrupting anything."

"Cary will understand."

Jake raised an eyebrow.

"Cary Grant," she explained. "I had a hot date planned with him and Gene Kelly."

Jake chuckled. "Then sure, I'd love to come."

"Give me an hour?" Mackenzie looked down at her clay-stained hands. "I'm on Primrose Lane. The one with the blue door."

"Alright then. See you later." Jake saluted and strolled away. It wasn't until he was around the corner and her pulse had just about returned to normal that Mackenzie realized what she'd just signed herself up for.

Thanksgiving dinner from scratch in an hour?

She better get a move on.

~

JAKE STOOD on Mackenzie's doorstep with a Tupperware container in one hand and a bottle of wine in the other, feeling like he was fifteen years old and picking a girl up for a date for the first time. His shirt collar was tight around his neck; he'd figured he should make an effort for the occasion, but now he felt over-dressed and just plain awkward.

He used his elbow to knock, and a moment later, the door flung open.

"Hey! Come on in." Mackenzie was barefoot in jeans and a tank top, her red hair damp from the shower and falling out of a messy bun. Her smile lit up the night, and Jake tried to remember how to speak.

"Ignore the mess," Mackenzie continued, gesturing him in. She headed inside, calling back over her shoulder. "It was either a clean house or food, and I figured you would only care about one."

Jake stepped inside and carefully wiped his boots on the mat. Music was playing, some jazz song on the old-fashioned record player that was sandwiched on a cabinet between a stack of art books and a bowl of yarn, and everywhere he looked, there was bright, haphazard clutter: paintings on the wall, and colorful throws on the furniture, and even a carved wooden panther sitting waist-high beside the fireplace.

It was totally, perfectly Mackenzie.

He followed the sound of clattering pans into the small, blue-tiled kitchen, where Mackenzie was tasting something at the stove.

"I thought about going traditional, but it turns out, I don't have turkey, potatoes, or any veggies," Mackenzie said, looking over. "So I'm doing my classic, spaghetti and meatballs."

"Is it safe?" Jake teased, and Mackenzie hit him lightly with a tea towel.

"Hey! I'll have you know, I'm an excellent cook now. This recipe is the real deal," she added, returning to the simmering pans. "My roommate in art school was from a big Italian family. I used to beg to go home with her on the weekends just to get a taste of Nona's sauce. Here." She offered Jake the wooden spoon, and he took a taste.

"That's great," he said, hit with the tomato flavor, warm with spices.

"You don't have to sound so surprised." Mackenzie grinned. "I couldn't go around burning toast forever."

"I can," Jake said. "Ordering takeout is about the height of my skills in the kitchen."

"We'll see about that," Mackenzie said, then noticed the Tupperware he was holding. She lit up. "Is that . . . ?"

"My mom's famous pecan pie? Yup." Jake set it down on the counter and stripped off his jacket. "You're lucky, this was the last one left in the freezer."

Mackenzie gave an appreciative groan. "Your mom makes the best pie. Don't tell Summer I said that," she added quickly. "But it's true. You know she used to bring one over for my folks every year when they lived in town? It was so sweet."

"She's good like that," Jake agreed. "She even tried to mail them to me, out at college, but they kept going missing. Somewhere, there's a very fat postal worker."

Mackenzie laughed. "Well, what are you waiting for? Open that bottle, and let's get Thanksgiving started right. With dessert first!"

Jake poured them both a glass of wine and set the table, a safe distance away from Mackenzie's enthusiastic chopping and stirring. She cooked the way she painted: by instinct, adding a dash of this and a sprinkle of that, pausing to taste with her eyes half-closed, contemplating.

"This is a cute place," he said, looking around. Pans dangled from a rack over the range, and there was an antique china cabinet along one wall filled with mismatched plates and plant pots. "Did you come straight back to Sweetbriar after art school?"

She nodded. "I always knew this was home. I had this picture of a little gallery, right off the square. It took a few years, selling at farmers' markets and gift shops, but I finally made it happen."

Mackenzie looked proud, and she had every right to be. Jake knew she'd done all this on her own. Her parents had always been supportive—in an absent-minded way—but Mackenzie was the stubborn one. When she wanted something, she didn't quit.

"What about you?" she asked, leaning back against the counter. "How was your appointment in Boston? Or, do you not want to talk about it?" she added quickly, looking concerned. "Because we can do that, too."

Jake gave her a rueful smile. "It's fine. She said pretty much what everyone else has been telling me. Healing takes time." He said it casually and shrugged, like he hadn't been agonizing over those words all night.

But Mackenzie could always see through him. "I'm sorry," she said quietly, reaching over to touch his arm. "I know you must be frustrated with the recovery."

"I'll get there." Jake said it with determination. He had to believe it was true.

"I worried about you," she said quietly, turning back to the stove.

"You did?" Jake stared at her, surprised. "When?"

She shrugged, stirring a pot. "Always. All those reports about injuries . . . concussions . . . Even back in high school you'd take the worst hits."

"You never said." He frowned.

"Yeah, well you would never have listened." Mackenzie gave him a look. "You all thought you were invincible."

"We were." He chuckled, remembering the old team.

"Not anymore." Mackenzie seemed to realize what she'd said. She flushed. "I'm sorry, I didn't mean—"

"No, it's OK." He stopped her. "You're right. I'm not. If this year taught me anything . . ." He trailed off, forcing a smile. "But come on, if I'm not a player anymore, then who am I? It's not like I know how to do anything else."

"Sure you do!" Mackenzie protested.

"Like what?"

"Well, you're pretty great at bar trivia," she said. "Your pool game could use some work—"

"Hey!"

"—but you make a mean martini," she finished, and he smiled.

"So basically, I should go work for Riley at the pub then," Jake said.

"You could figure it out," she reassured him. "You know you can do anything you set your mind to and make it look easy. It's actually pretty irritating."

"Oh yeah?" Jake teased, smiling.

"Yup. If you weren't my best friend, I'd pretty much hate you." Mackenzie grinned back.

Jake's chest tightened. "Best friend?" he echoed.

She turned away to grab some dishes down. "Maybe. The spot's been open for a while, we'll see if you've got the goods."

He swallowed. Mackenzie had always been his closest friend, the one person he could share everything with, and even after all this time, that hadn't changed.

But the way he was looking at her had.

Friends didn't notice the way her tank top clung to her curves, or the purple bra straps peeping out beneath. Friends wouldn't imagine gently tugging the rest of her hair down, loose around her shoulders. Or licking the sauce off the edge of her lips. Lifting her up on that countertop, and tasting her mouth again, kissing her slow, and hard until—

"It's ready." Mackenzie's voice broke through his fevered thoughts. She tipped the spaghetti into a serving bowl, and ladled the rich meat sauce on top. "Grab the plates, will you?" she asked, flushed from the steam and totally oblivious to his cravings. "And since you're the guest, I'll even let you choose: *Casablanca* or *High Society.*"

"The last one," he said, reining himself in. The last thing he needed was slow-burn passion, on the screen or anywhere else.

He didn't need anything giving him ideas. Not when he already had so many of his own.

10

They gorged themselves on spaghetti and pecan pie, then collapsed in front of the TV, the fire flickering merrily in the corner. Mackenzie yawned, barely paying attention to the movie playing on screen. How could she, when Jake was sprawled just a few inches away?

She watched him, lit by the screen. She must have gazed at his face a thousand times, but still, somehow, it always seemed brand new. The strong line of his jaw, the smile that lingered on the edge of his lips—

Mackenzie stopped herself, reality crashing down on her.

She was doing it again.

Falling into the same old crush that had pulled her under a decade ago. Pining after someone who had never felt the same.

Doing exactly what she swore she wouldn't that very first night he'd arrived back in town.

"What's up?" Jake nudged her with his knee, and she realized with a jolt that the movie was over.

Mackenzie stifled a sigh. "Just thinking about those pie left-overs," she lied.

Jake groaned. "Seriously? I won't eat for days."

"Right." Mackenzie smirked. "I bet you a hundred bucks you'll be hunting in the fridge for a midnight snack."

"No bet." Jake gave her an irresistible grin. "Want to just pack me up a doggie bag instead?"

"Pack it yourself." She kicked him playfully, her feet bare, and Jake caught them, pulling her legs into his lap.

Her breath caught.

"Purple?" he asked, arching an eyebrow at her toenails.

Mackenzie wriggled them. "I couldn't decide between pink and blue," she said, fighting to sound casual, even though her heart was racing.

"I like them." His hands lingered on her feet, warm, and Mackenzie could have sworn that his thumb gently stroked the bare arch of her foot.

She bit back a sigh.

It wasn't fair, to be consumed with this desire, while the object of her affection was lounging there, totally oblivious.

"So, you and Moose, huh?" Jake's lips quirked in a teasing grin.

Mackenzie fixed him with a look. "Ancient history."

"Aww, I think you'd make a cute couple."

"Not funny," she warned him. "And you wouldn't be joking if you lived here. I bet you a hundred bucks that Debra, and Franny, and your mom would be fixing you up with anything that moved."

"Is it really that bad?"

"Worse," Mackenzie said lightly. "You're looking at the spinster of Sweetbriar Cove."

Jake frowned, and she realized she hadn't mentioned her nickname for herself before. "It's inevitable, don't you think?" she said. "Give me a few cats and a muumuu, and I'll be good to go."

"You'll find someone," he said, with such quiet certainty in his voice that it made her chest ache.

"I haven't yet." She looked away.

"There hasn't been anyone serious?" Jake asked, and Mackenzie bit back an empty laugh.

"Nope. I mean, I date. I've probably been on more first dates than anyone." She gave a rueful smile. "You know what it's like in town here, everyone's got a nephew, or a college friend, or a stepsister's aunt's kid out of college. But . . ."

She paused, not ready to say the words that came after.

But despite all the hopeful introductions, nobody clicked.

But being on her own seemed better than half-hearted hookups.

But none of them were you.

"Well, it never worked out," she said instead. Mackenzie gave a half-shrug. "Guess I'm not everyone's flavor."

"Their loss," Jake said with conviction, and she felt a pang. It was *his* loss, but he didn't see it that way. He never had.

Mackenzie shook her head. "What about you?" she asked, changing the subject. "Any football fans waiting for you back home?"

She realized too late that she didn't want to know the answer, so it was a relief when Jake chuckled and shook his head. "No, not for me. I mean, I've dated some, but . . ."

He trailed off with a shrug. Mackenzie suspected that "some" was plenty, but she didn't ask any more. She could already imagine the hordes of adoring women waiting in line for his charms—she'd caught the previews in high school, and that had been enough.

"You seem to have figured it out now." Jake looked around. "The gallery, your art, you've really built a life here."

He gave her an admiring look, and Mackenzie flushed. "I guess I realized I was never going to fit into someone else's schedule. You know, 9–5 job, following orders—"

"You think?" Jake laughed, and she lightly kicked him again.

"It was touch and go for a while, trying to make ends meet

when I first opened the gallery," she admitted. "And I had to take a crash course in running my own business. I made such a mess of my books, Ellie Lucas had to come straighten them out," she said, naming the girl whose family ran the inn, just outside of town. "But at least this way I make my own rules. If I want to close the store and spend all day up to my elbows in clay, I can. I just have to make sure I have enough orders to see me through," she added.

"But things are going good now, right?" Jake asked.

She nodded. "I have a steady list of vendors, and the website works too. Plus, there are always tourists around. I make out like a bandit over summer with my nautical collections, and the red, white, and blue pottery. Still . . ." She paused, and Jake arched an eyebrow, waiting for her to continue.

"Sometimes it feels like I'm playing it safe," she admitted out loud for the first time. "Don't get me wrong, I love making things that people enjoy, and the steady paycheck is great, but . . . I used to want to make great art. You know, something that makes you stop and really feel," she said ruefully, thinking of the sculptures hidden in the corner of her studio that would never see the light of day. "My polka-dot sugar bowls are cute, but they don't exactly shake you to your soul."

"Those would have to be some sugar bowls," Jake agreed.

Mackenzie looked away, suddenly feeling self-conscious. "Anyway, it's nothing. You're right. I've got a good thing going."

"Good can always be better," Jake said easily. "Maybe you can find a way to do both. Find some of that soul-shaking magic."

Their eyes caught again, and Mackenzie knew she didn't have to go looking for any magic. It was sitting right there in front of her.

Out of reach.

"Maybe," she agreed quickly. The fire had burned low, and she made to get up, but Jake beat her to it.

"Let me."

She watched him place another couple of logs in the hearth, and nudge the embers into a shimmer of sparks, blazing high again.

She knew how they felt. A touch or two from Jake, and feelings she'd almost forgotten were possible came roaring back to life.

Desire, snaking low in her belly. Building in her bloodstream, a taste of something sweet and dangerously intoxicating.

Jake detoured to the kitchen. "You win," he said, emerging with the pie plate leftovers. "You know me too well," he added, flashing her a grin as he scooped her legs into his lap and settled back on the couch beside her.

Not well enough.

Mackenzie sucked in a breath and tried to gather her heated thoughts. Was it just her, or was he sitting closer now, his thighs pressed against hers, and his broad frame sprawled near enough for her to feel the heat, radiating stronger than that fire?

Her pulse kicked up a level, the steady drumbeat skittering, but Jake didn't seem to notice the shift. He had a fork in his hand and was happily digging into the pie.

"Where's mine?" Mackenzie asked, fighting to stay cool.

"Right here." Jake's lips curled in a tempting smile. He loaded the fork with pie then held it out to her.

She leaned in, and took the bite, her eyes never leaving his.

Oh.

Even he couldn't have missed the heat that surged between them. Mackenzie forced herself to swallow, licking a crumb from her lips.

Jake's gaze dropped to her mouth, and she could have sworn she saw something hungry there, that same need that had drawn her to him that Halloween night in the gazebo.

The same need that was spiraling through her now, making her blood run hot and one tantalizing thought echo, louder with every heartbeat.

She could kiss him, right there.

Mackenzie froze. With a pounding heart, she dragged her stare away.

What was she thinking?

Suddenly, the room was stiflingly hot—or maybe that was just her body, prickling with awareness and painfully attuned to every shift of Jake's body, every breath. Their casual, friendly dinner had taken an intimate turn, and now—in the flickering firelight, with him so close—it was hard to remember why she was keeping her distance.

Because he doesn't feel the same way about you.

Except, was that really true? He was the one tracing semi-circles on her bare foot, his other hand resting gently on her knee. He was the one giving a sleepy smile, and snuggling deeper into the cushions.

He was the one looking at her like she was the only woman in the world

Mackenzie's blood thundered in her ears. She felt a giddy lurch in her stomach, that clench of exhilaration that always signaled a very, very bad idea.

"More?" Jake asked with a lazy smile. He held out a forkful of the pie again, and Mackenzie's heart flipped over.

"Please."

Before she could take it back, Mackenzie leaned in. This time, she bypassed the fork, and brushed her lips against his mouth instead.

Jake startled, drawing a breath that she felt all the way through her. He froze, suspended there on the edge of her kiss, and for one terrible moment, humiliation loomed. Then, with a groan, he pulled her closer.

It was hot and sweet, and somehow, more right than any kiss had been before; Jake's mouth pressed against her urgently, easing her lips apart before his tongue slid deep to taste her.

Mackenzie sighed in pleasure. She didn't know what happened to the pie plate, or their wine glasses, all that mattered was Jake tugging her into his lap, her arms fast around his neck, her body crushed against his.

God, it was heaven.

She bent her head, letting the curtain of her hair fall around them, blocking out the world. She kissed him, savoring every moment; the sweetness of the pecans, and that masculine taste that was pure Jake.

The heat grew, lazy at first, but smoldering, liquid fire trickling through her veins until her whole body was ablaze. His grip on her grew tighter, and the kiss deepened, passionate and raw. She could have lost herself in it, let the whole world burn down around them, as long as he didn't stop. Mouths, and hands, and low, ragged gasps; she was closer than she'd ever been, and she couldn't get enough—

Jake pulled back. "Wait," he said, his breath coming heavy. "We shouldn't . . ."

He lifted her aside and practically fell off the couch in his hurry to put distance between them.

No!

Mackenzie fought for breath. Her pulse was still racing, her body on fire. That was the hottest, most epic kiss in the history of the world, and Jake was . . . stopping?

"I should go," he said, pushing his hair back. He was avoiding even looking at her, already grabbing his jacket and backing towards the door. "I, uh, Happy Thanksgiving."

The door was slamming shut behind him before Mackenzie could even say a word.

She turned and buried her face in a cushion, and let out a frustrated scream.

Why was he pushing her away? One minute he was the one

kissing her like it was all he wanted in the world, the next, she couldn't see him for dust.

But who in their right mind would walk away from a kiss like that?

Mackenzie sank back and groaned. She couldn't deny it, no matter how hard she tried.

She wanted him.

It had always been Jake, but things were different now. Maybe she should take the slamming door as a hint, but she'd made herself a promise, and she was going to stand by it. She wasn't going to swallow back her feelings and let them turn to misery, pine after him like she had done when she was seventeen and too scared to take a leap. Whatever the risk of going after what she wanted, it couldn't be worse than keeping it all bottled up inside and bending over backwards to hide the truth, boxing her feelings into tiny spaces until they turned to dust.

She was going to do this. Make her move.

The question was . . . how?

11

*M*ackenzie deliberated for the rest of the weekend, which meant cleaning every square inch of the cottage and ticking half a dozen items from the Starbright schedule like a woman possessed with denial and productivity. Finally, when there was nothing else to distract her, she admitted defeat. She needed advice, the kind that wouldn't pull any punches in figuring out Jake's hot and cold routine.

"I need a man." Mackenzie threw herself onto a stool at the pub and fixed Riley with a plaintive stare across the bar.

"Want your gutters cleaned out again?" he teased. "No pun intended."

"Very funny." Mackenzie smiled. "And no. I can clean my gutters just fine alone. I need advice this time, from someone on the other side of . . . *things*."

Riley arched an eyebrow, looking interested now. Mackenzie knew she never talked about her love life—not that there was one to talk about—and clearly, he wasn't about to let this go lightly. "So, you finally accept my superior knowledge when it comes to matters of the heart?" Riley puffed out his chest. "I knew this day would dawn, and you'd come begging—"

"I'm not begging."

"—for me to solve all your problems." Riley grinned. "Go on then, child, tell me your woes."

Mackenzie shook her head, but it was hard not to smile when Riley was hamming it up like this. And the bowl of fries he nudged across the bar didn't hurt either.

"It's Jake," she finally admitted, feeling her cheeks flush.

"Well, of course it's Jake." Riley gave her an exasperated smile. "Everyone for fifty miles knows it's Jake. The question only was if you knew."

Mackenzie decided not to take offense. "Oh, I know," she told him. "I wish I didn't, believe me. But know that I do know, there's no way to un-know it! And he doesn't seem to know at all."

Riley shook his head. "OK, you lost me there. Plain English?"

Mackenzie swallowed. "I can't figure him out," she said at last. "He kisses me, and then pretends like it never happened. *I* kiss *him*, and he pretends like it never happened. He acts like we're just friends, but something tells me that friends don't make out like this!"

"Sadly, no," Riley said. She mournfully ate another fry, and her inner turmoil must have shown, because he finally put down his drink and looked serious. "So what do you want from him?"

"Lead with the easy questions, why don't you?" Mackenzie sighed.

Riley chuckled. "I'm sorry. I just mean it'll be easier to figure out how to get what you want from him if you actually know what it is you want."

"That's annoyingly sensible." She frowned. "Since when are you Mr. Rational?"

"Don't you know I've turned over a new leaf?" Riley grinned. "All it took was the love of a good woman. And old age."

Mackenzie laughed. "Somehow, I don't think so. Didn't I hear something about you skinny-dipping in the Chesapeake Bay?"

"Don't change the subject on me." Riley grinned. "It's your life we're trying to fix here."

"Mac needs fixing?"

She turned to find Cooper leaning against the bar, looking interested.

"She's dealing with affairs of the heart," Riley explained. "Obviously, she came straight to me."

"Something I already regret," Mackenzie grumbled, trying to hide her embarrassment. At this rate, half of Sweetbriar would know her emotional state before dinner.

"Ah." Cooper nodded. "So Jake hasn't got his act together yet?"

Mackenzie whimpered and slumped over, burying her face in her arms like she was in school all over again. "Does everybody know?"

She heard Cooper chuckle. "Just the people with eyes," he said, and gave her a comforting pat. "So what's the story?"

"He's pulling that whole 'just friends' routine," she heard Riley explain over her head. "Giving Mac mixed messages."

"Ouch," Cooper replied. "So what does she want to do?"

"So far, sit around and eat fries," Riley said, sounding amused.

Mackenzie lifted her head. "This isn't funny!" she protested, even as a smile tugged at her lips. "I don't know what to do! I told myself I wouldn't fall for him again, but here I am, ten years older and not one bit wiser."

"Again?" Cooper studied her, and then his face changed. "High school, huh? I always figured you guys were just friends."

"So did everyone. Including him." Mackenzie stole a swallow of his beer.

"Wait, was he the one from prom night?" Cooper asked suddenly. Riley perked up.

"The infamous town square incident?"

Mackenzie cleared her throat. "Nope, and you know I'm taking that one to my grave. So, come on, what should I do?"

"Have you tried seducing him?" Riley asked.

Mackenzie snorted. That plan had worked so well last time around.

"I'm serious," he insisted. "Take all your clothes off, see what he does. Boom, you'll have your answer."

"And if the answer is 'Sorry, Mac, I just don't feel that way about you,' then I'll be standing naked waiting for the ground to swallow me up," she pointed out, cringing at the thought. It had been bad enough watching him bolt from her cottage the other night; imagine if she'd been semi-dressed at the time.

Mackenzie shook her head. Talk about high school all over again. Throw in a cheap corsage and some slow jams, and she was right back at prom.

"Sorry." Cooper looked apologetic. "But sometimes the only way to get a straight answer is to ask a straight question."

"You guys are no use at all," Mackenzie informed them, frustrated.

Riley laughed. "Come on, men are simple creatures, at least where women are concerned. Sometimes you just need to make it blindingly obvious before we get the hint. Have you even told him how you feel?"

She paused. "Not in so many words. But it's obvious by now," she added quickly. "I've practically thrown myself at him, more than once. He has to know!"

Riley and Cooper looked dubious.

"Doesn't he?" Mackenzie paused, thinking back over the past few weeks. And all the effort she'd put into casually acting like she couldn't care less. "Oh God," she breathed, the truth dawning. "Maybe he really doesn't know."

"So, give the guy a break," Riley suggested. "Ask him out, flirt, be obvious."

"Obvious," Mackenzie repeated, taking another gulp of Cooper's beer. "I can do that."

Before she could chicken out, she pulled out her phone.

Want to grab lunch tomorrow? she texted, and hit send.

Riley reached over and took her phone. "Grab?" he quoted. "That's still friend-talk."

"What do you want me to say?" Mackenzie countered. "Come over right now and rock me all night long?"

"Works for me," Riley grinned. "Coop?"

"Yeah, that'd get the message across."

Mackenzie shook her head. Her phone buzzed.

Sure, call me whenever.

It wasn't exactly a heartfelt declaration of love, but it was a start. "Obvious," she repeated, feeling her stomach start to tangle with nerves. "Flirting. I can do that."

" 'Atta girl," Riley said. "And remember, when in doubt, undo another button. He'll get the hint eventually."

"Here's hoping it's before I get arrested for public indecency," Mackenzie cracked, but inside, she was getting more nervous by the second.

After spending ten years trying her hardest to hide her feelings, could she really throw herself at Jake just to see if he felt the same?

What the hell. She was about to find out.

JAKE NEARLY CANCELED lunch a half-dozen times. What was he playing at? He'd barely escaped the other night without giving in to temptation, and now he was heading straight back into the flames again.

But somehow, he couldn't say no to her.

He had a serious problem.

It didn't feel like a problem when Mackenzie was panting in his arms, and that was the dangerous part. For those few, brief moments, he forgot who he was: a washed up former player with his future hanging by a thread. He forgot he had no plans to stay, or reasons to leave, forgot that she deserved far better than him. All he wanted was her. And if she was anyone else, then maybe he'd give in to the desire burning through him, to hell with the consequences.

But this was Mackenzie. His Mac. He knew her better than anyone, and he knew without a doubt she deserved the best. A man who could be there for her, and treasure every second. Build the life she wanted, and spend forever by her side. She wasn't the kind of woman to hook up like it didn't mean a thing. And if they really went there . . . Jake already knew there could be no going back.

It would mean everything.

He couldn't do that, not to her. Which was why he was determined to turn the clock back to when they were just friends. Simple, uncomplicated friendship. No mind-blowing make-outs or fevered, hot desire. Today, he would tell her the kissing had to stop. No more sultry evenings alone in front of a roaring fire. He had to save their friendship while he still had the chance.

Jake pulled into the parking lot of the address she texted, surprised to find a quiet, rustic-looking carriage house set back from the street. He'd been expecting something basic—fried seafood by the waterfront—but when he stepped through the doors, he found a classy restaurant, already humming with the lunch rush.

So much for keeping things casual.

He looked around, already out of place in his jeans and flannel shirt. Mackenzie was at the bar, talking to some guy, and he could hear her laughter clear across the room.

Jake cleared his throat. "Hey."

Mackenzie turned at his voice. "Hey you." She smiled and walked over to greet him.

Damn.

She looked incredible. She was wearing a figure-hugging blue sweater dress that hit three inches above her knee, and was made out of some soft, fluffy material that just begged to be touched. Her hair was down, spilling over her shoulders in a cascade of wild, red curls, and there was a playful smile on her lips as she leaned in to brush a kiss against his cheek.

Jake breathed in her perfume, something subtle and spicy, and felt light-headed. What had happened to baggy overalls and sneakers Mac? The girl who wore jeans and no makeup, just one of the guys? In her place was a total bombshell, with curves it took him everything to resist holding onto.

"Uh, hey." He finally recovered. "You look . . . dressy."

"This old thing?" Mackenzie shrugged. "I wear it all the time."

He swallowed hard. "I . . . I didn't realize we were eating someplace fancy," he said, dragging his attention away from her. The restaurant was warm and rustic, but he could see thick linens on the tables and gleaming silverware. "I would have put on a decent shirt."

"No need." Mackenzie placed one hand on his chest and smiled softly. "I think you look great."

Jake felt her touch burn through him. He lurched back. "Good. OK. We should . . . get started."

"The hostess is right there." Mackenzie smiled, and Jake tried to pull himself together.

"Sure. Right."

As they were shown to a table by the windows, he chided himself for acting like a fool. They were both adults, and sure, it seemed like they couldn't spend more than a few hours together without someone getting kissed, but Jake had some damn self-control.

He cared about Mackenzie too much to let desire ruin a good thing. She deserved better than that.

Better than him.

He just had to remember that.

They settled at the table, and Jake took a gulp of ice water. "This place is new," he said, looking around again.

"Declan opened it a couple of years ago," Mackenzie replied, glancing at the menu. "He's the best chef on the Cape."

"Make that the tristate area," a voice interrupted them.

It was the guy she'd been talking to, a tall, dark-haired man with a cocky smile on his face. Mackenzie laughed and rolled her eyes. "Add 'modest' to that list," she grinned up at him.

Jealousy hit Jake hard. Was this the reason she was all dressed up?

"You're the chef?" he asked, forcing himself to play nice.

"For my sins," the man replied. "Declan Nash," he said, shaking Jake's hand. "I saw you play against the Packers a couple of years ago. Pure poetry."

"Thanks." Jake felt weird accepting compliments these days, like taking credit for something in a former life.

"Declan was running high-end restaurants in Vegas before he quit it all and opened here," Mackenzie explained.

"The slow pace of life agrees with me."

"You mean, the staff don't all quit at your tantrums," Mackenzie said, still teasing.

"Don't believe her." Declan winked at Jake. "I'm reformed. I only smashed three plates this week."

"Progress," Mackenzie laughed, and Jake felt that burn of envy again. He didn't want her looking at some other man, laughing with him like that.

He wanted to be the one to make her smile.

"So what's good today?" Mackenzie asked, and Declan took the menus from their hands.

"Trust me, I'll blow your minds." He sauntered back to the kitchen, and Mackenzie shook her head.

"He's an arrogant bastard, but the man can cook."

"You come here often then?" Jake asked, still trying to figure if this Declan was more than just a friend.

"Only for special occasions." Mackenzie fixed him with a smile, and just like that, he felt like the only man in the world.

Their server arrived with a basket of fresh-baked bread and a crock of butter. Mackenzie tore into it with a sigh of satisfaction. "God, I love carbs," she swooned, her eyes falling shut as she tasted the food. She looked the way she did when he kissed her, that same blissful expression that sent all his blood rushing south.

Jake took another gulp of water.

"So. The festival," he said, trying to get things back on track. "What's left to plan?"

Mackenzie looked amused. "Not much," she said. "The local businesses are all putting up their displays, I'm having the main tree delivered this week, and I even confirmed the local choir for the tree-lighting ceremony. It was a busy weekend, don't you think?" she added innocently, and Jake couldn't help remembering just how busy.

He coughed and looked around for the server. "Can we get some more ice water over here?" he asked.

"Or we could get some wine," Mackenzie suggested.

"No!" Jake blurted. "I mean, it's the middle of the day."

"Suit yourself." She shrugged, and her sweater dressed slipped off one shoulder, leaving it bare.

Dear Lord. Alcohol was probably the last thing he needed, but he was going to need something to get through this lunch without sweeping the table clean and pulling her across it. "You know, on second thought, I could use a drink," Jake said hurriedly. "I'll take a scotch on the rocks."

Mackenzie arched an eyebrow. "Cutting loose, huh? I'd like to see that."

She held his gaze, something like a challenge in her stare. He looked away, relieved when the server set down a platter of food. "Looks great," he said, grabbing something blindly. He barely tasted whatever he put in his mouth, he was focused so hard on not watching Mackenzie savor another morsel, her tongue darting out to lick sauce from her lips.

This woman was going to be the death of him.

His drink arrived, and he took a gulp as Mackenzie ran through the other festival plans. She had been busy, and it seemed like everything was all set—from her art walk and carriage rides to the town Secret Santa gift exchange. "All this, just for a few days of celebrations?" Jake asked, still in disbelief that a simple holiday required a month of military planning.

"Tourists will start arriving this weekend. December is one long party," she added with a smile. "We've got Hanukkah, Kwanzaa . . . there are even some Wiccans who throw a pagan Yule party."

"Only in Sweetbriar." He shook his head.

"Admit it." Mackenzie leaned forward, her eyes shining in the sunlight. "You wouldn't want to be anywhere else."

She was right. At that moment, Jake felt like he was exactly where he was supposed to be.

With her.

Home.

He dragged his thoughts back to reality. Whatever happened to having that platonic conversation?

Ground rules, he told himself.

"We also need to make a trip to Santa's grotto."

Jake looked up. "Santa's what now?"

"It's this big holiday warehouse up in Boston," Mackenzie explained. "Debra says that's where we get the rest of our supplies

—decorations and gifts for the toy drive. I've already placed our order, so we just have to go pick it up. Or I could get someone else to drive . . ." She looked around, as if searching for her chef friend.

Jake thought about Mackenzie sharing the long drive with Declan, cozy in the cab of his truck. "I can go," he said quickly.

"Great." Mackenzie ticked it off her list. "We'll go this week. There. Business is all done." She tucked her notebook away. "Now we can get back to the pleasure part of lunch."

Pleasure.

The word made Jake's body tighten, and he flashed back to the other night in front of the fire: Mackenzie straddling him, with her hair falling softly around them.

He gulped. "You know what?" he said, shoving his chair back and getting to his feet. "I forgot, I have to . . . meet Cooper."

Mackenzie looked confused. "Now? Why?"

"I'm going to rent his place. Maybe." Jake scrambled for a reason to get away. "He said he'd give me the tour, and I totally blanked. I'm sorry."

"But—" Mackenzie started to protest, but Jake couldn't stick around to listen. If he spent one more moment with her, he didn't know what he might do.

Chances were it wouldn't be platonic.

"Sorry," he said again, and bolted for the door before he could change his mind. It wasn't until he was outside, breathing in a lungful of crisp winter air, that he realized he'd stuck her with the check.

Damn, he'd have to make it up to her. But not today, when she was looking like that.

He knew his limits, and he'd just reached them.

*J*ake drove the long way back to Sweetbriar to clear his head. When he arrived back in town, he found a familiar figure leaving his parents' front porch.

"Coach Wilson?" he asked, getting out of the car.

"I just dropped by to say hello," the old man said. It had been ten years since Jake had seen him yelling from the twenty-yard line, but that weathered face was unmistakable—and the faded old baseball cap he wore in blue and white. School colors. "Heard the rumors you were back in town."

"I'm sorry I didn't come see you yet," Jake said, chastened. He knew Wilson would want all the NFL news, and to tell the truth, he hadn't been ready to put on a smile and pretend everything was going to be OK.

"That's OK, kid." Wilson smiled. "I know you've been busy, with the festival and all."

For once, the gossip mill was on his side.

"Come on in," Jake said, holding the door wide. "Can I get you something to drink? Coffee, beer?"

Wilson snorted, following him to the kitchen. "My day-drinking days are long behind me. Cindy would raise hell. You know she's got a chart up on our fridge, tracking my cholesterol?"

"Water it is then."

"Well, if you're opening a bottle . . ."

Jake chuckled, and grabbed a couple of beers from the fridge. Wilson settled at the kitchen table and looked around. "How are your parents enjoying their trip?"

"They're loving it." Jake smiled. "Mom texts me a picture of a new beach every other day. She's already talking about their next cruise."

"Ha. Good thing you've got that NFL contract to keep them on the water. Don't you?"

That was Wilson, straight to the point.

"For now," Jake said.

Wilson gave him a sympathetic look. "ACL. Helluva injury, that one. When I saw you go down like that . . ." He winced.

"You were watching?"

"Never missed a game," Wilson said simply, and Jake felt that shot of guilt all over again.

Wilson had been his biggest supporter back in the day—and his hardest critic. He'd seen Jake's natural talent on the field and pushed him to take it to the next level. "Anyone can be a high-school hero," he would say, sending Jake out to run another set of laps. "But it takes commitment to make it as a pro."

Jake took those words to heart, and it sent him all the way to his college team and beyond. He owed a lot to Wilson, and the donations he'd made anonymously to the high-school athletic department didn't even begin to cover it.

"I'll be back out there soon enough," Jake said. "It'll heal."

Wilson looked skeptical. "And if it doesn't?"

Jake paused. He didn't want to think about that part. "A lot of guys go into sportscasting," he said with a shrug. "Or switch to the business side. Managing, training."

"Makes sense," Wilson said, and quietly took another sip of beer.

It did. It also would feel like a failure to Jake, to stand on the sidelines, talking about someone else's game. Sure, DeJay loved the spotlight, and would happily gab a mile a minute to whoever wanted to hear, but it didn't hold the same appeal to Jake.

And as for becoming an assistant coach, or consultant—just one more guy in the massive NFL roster . . . Maybe it was his ego talking, but he was used to being a part of the action, not just a cog in the machine.

"You know, I could use some help with the team, when school starts up again," Wilson added casually. "It's not the pros, but there's a couple of good kids this season, they've got potential. We're hoping to make it to state, maybe even pick up a couple of scholarships for them. Could use your experience."

Jake was flattered. "Thanks, but I'm not sure I'll be here by then."

"Bright lights calling you back to the city?" Wilson asked with a smile.

Jake just shrugged. It had been a few weeks, but Miami felt even farther away: loud and brash in his memories after the peace of the coast. "We'll see. Like I said, it all depends how I heal. I'm working hard on the rehab," he added, not liking the doubt on Wilson's face. "Making real progress."

"That's good, son. Real good to hear. But you know, there are worse places to call home than right here," Wilson said, giving him one of those clear-eyed looks of his. "Settle down, start a family . . ."

"You sound like my mom," Jake replied lightly.

Wilson chuckled. "Maybe she's got the right idea."

He set his beer down and got to his feet. "I won't keep you any longer. Think about swinging by, we could use some pro pointers on the field."

"You're the only pro they need." Jake showed him out and watched Wilson stroll back down the street. It seemed like only yesterday he was at practice, back in high school, when everything was still ahead of him. Full of possibilities.

He looked around. The trophies on the mantel, the pictures on the wall. Suddenly, it all felt suffocating, like some kind of shrine to the man he'd spent his life trying to be.

Was he still that man anymore?

Jake grabbed his keys. He was already out the door before he called Cooper about that rental. He might as well look at the place now, especially since he needed an alibi. He hated lying to Mackenzie, and at least this way, there was a kernel of truth in his cover.

COOPER MET him at the barn, a soaring, rustic space in the woods just outside of town. It was hidden down a dirt road, surrounded by peaceful trees and the sound of running water from a nearby stream. "I'll take it," Jake said, getting out of the car.

Cooper arched an eyebrow. "I haven't even opened the door yet."

"You're the master architect, right? I trust you." Jake stopped a moment, listening to the quiet and the sound of birds in the trees. It really was a beautiful spot, and—most importantly—it didn't have trophies of his former winnings set on every surface. He already knew he couldn't spend another night in that place. He'd take a room at the motel if he had to, but something told him Cooper's place would be a step up from that. "I can sign a lease right now if you want."

Cooper waved away the offer. "It's fine. I'll know where to find you." He pulled out the keys. "Let me show you around. The furnace is temperamental, but there's a trick to it."

He led Jake inside. Just as Jake predicted, the place was great:

the original barn converted into a big, open-plan living space with a sleeping loft in the back. Sun filtered through the iron-paned windows, spilling onto the wooden floors and giving the whole room a warm, relaxed feel. "I can take the furniture, or leave it," Cooper said. "Whatever suits."

"It would be great if you could leave it," Jake said, looking around. Cooper's style was simple and hand-crafted, and he smiled. "My teammates are paying interior designers a small fortune to get this look," he said, chuckling. "I'm guessing you didn't pay ten thousand bucks to have this table imported from Italy."

"Hell, it sounds like I'm in the wrong trade," Cooper laughed.

"I'll hook you up," Jake said, as Cooper finished giving him the tour.

"There's enough wood on the porch to see you through winter, and a back-up generator, too, in case of storms," Cooper explained. He paused, giving Jake an assessing look. "Just how long are you planning on staying?"

The million-dollar question—and it seemed like everyone wanted an answer.

Jake gave a vague shrug. "I don't know. But I can cover a couple months' rent up front, just in case."

It didn't seem like the reply Cooper was looking for, but he nodded. "How are the festival plans going?" he asked, as they headed back inside.

"Fine," Jake replied. "Mac's pretty much got everything figured. I'm just there for the heavy lifting."

"Welcome to the club," Cooper grinned. "Debra's had me hauling trees the past five years running."

"Gee, thanks. I guess I'm the new errand boy in town," Jake cracked, but Cooper was still looking at him with that careful expression.

"It's a big deal, you know," Cooper continued. "It matters to a lot of people."

"Sure," Jake agreed, checking out the kitchen area. Not that he'd be using it. "It's the big tourist draw."

"And locals," Cooper said with a steady look. "If things got messed around, if someone didn't take it seriously, then there would be a lot of unhappy folks around here."

Something told Jake they weren't talking about the Starbright Festival anymore.

"It matters to me too," he said carefully. "But I'm just lending a hand. I'm not sticking around here, so I won't get involved."

"No?" Cooper looked surprised. "Why the hell not?"

Jake opened his mouth, but nothing came out. All his silent arguments about friendship and commitment and what Mackenzie deserved suddenly didn't even seem worth saying out loud.

"Yeah, I figured." Cooper smirked. "But a word of advice, landlord to tenant. Don't take too long figuring it out, because she's not going to wait around for you again."

He left the keys on the counter and sauntered out the door, leaving Jake alone with the lingering threat—and the one word that lodged uncomfortably in the back of his mind.

Again?

He checked the time. He needed to go pick his stuff up and apologize to Mac, so he headed back into town again, stopping by the bakery for some "sorry" muffins. With any luck, she would be too engrossed by the carbs to remember what a fool he'd made of himself at lunch. He pulled up across from the gallery, just as another car slowed by the curb outside.

It was Mackenzie in the passenger seat, smiling and talking to the driver.

Declan.

Jake tensed. What was she doing with him?

He watched as she climbed out of the car, still smiling. Declan followed, circling around to walk her to the gallery door. They lingered there, talking for a moment, Declan gesturing widely and Mackenzie laughing along. Then she leaned up and kissed him on the cheek and headed inside.

It wasn't until Declan had driven away that Jake exhaled. He realized that he was gripping the steering wheel so tightly, his knuckles were white.

What was he playing at?

It shouldn't matter who Mackenzie was friends with. He wasn't staying around, remember? He had no claim to her, and had been going crazy trying to keep it that way.

He should be glad there might be another man in her life.

Glad, and not filled with a pure, hot jealousy that made him want to burn the world down.

He gulped down a ragged breath, and turned the keys in the ignition again. Mackenzie's love life was none of his business.

Maybe if he repeated that often enough, he'd start to believe it was true.

13

---

*F*lirting hadn't worked.

Mackenzie pored over their lunch, trying to figure out exactly where she'd gone wrong. From the way Jake had been looking at her, it wasn't the dress—or the conversation. They'd been chatting, having a good time, tension crackling between them so sharp her heart was beating faster even before their appetizers arrived.

OK, maybe she'd laid it on a little thick, sighing and moaning like that. But in her defense, it was worth the praise. Declan was the best chef around.

And then Jake had bolted, leaving her with a table of delicious food and no company.

Mackenzie didn't know what to do next. Should she admit defeat already? Just when she thought Jake was off limits for good, he did something to make her head spin all over again. Like kissing her. Or showing up on her doorstep bright and early on Friday morning with a rental truck, a bag of muffins, and an unreadable expression on his face that could still take her breath away.

"Ready to hit the road?" he asked, as if there was nothing weird about embarking on a road trip with the woman he'd been seducing there just a few nights before.

Hell, if he could play it cool, then Mackenzie would just have to call his bluff.

"Sure thing," she beamed. "Just let me get my coat."

It was a cool, crisp day, with snow clouds lurking on the horizon, so she grabbed some gloves and a scarf too, bundling up before she left the house. "I hope it snows soon," she said as she followed him out to the van. "It usually comes these first weeks in December. But I guess it's been a while since you had a white Christmas," she added with a smile.

Jake gave her a blank look. "I spend the holidays in Aspen most years. We get plenty of snow out there."

Mackenzie blinked. Jake's tone was as cool as the wind slipping under her collar, but she didn't have time to think; he was already back in the driver's seat, starting the engine.

"Don't leave without me!" Mackenzie climbed inside. "For a start, I'm the one with directions."

"Great." Jake's voice stayed even. "Just program them into the GPS."

Mackenzie did as instructed, shooting him a sideways look as they drove out of town and hit the highway down the coast. He was looking at the road straight ahead, but she could have sworn there was a tense expression on his face.

Had something happened? Bad news from the physio, maybe, or his teammates back home? Mackenzie knew he hated to talk about that stuff, so she changed the subject. "Mmm, chocolate chip," she said, digging into the muffin bag. "My favorite. Thanks for picking them up."

"Don't get so excited, they're a day old," Jake replied shortly.

Mackenzie paused. *Okaaay.*

"I'm surprised they're still around, then," she said, trying to be upbeat. "Since when do you leave a pastry unattended?"

"I was going to drop them off yesterday," he said, still staring straight ahead. "But you weren't at the gallery. Did you have big plans after our lunch?"

She frowned. After Jake had made his quick exit, she'd hung out at the restaurant for a while, then Declan had given her a ride home—

She stopped. Declan. Was that the reason Jake was in such a mood? But it made no sense at all. Declan was just a friend, and even if he wasn't, did Jake just expect her to sit around waiting for him to swing by with apology muffins after running out on their lunch?

She felt a flash of annoyance. She was the one trying to lay her cards on the table, and he was just running hot and cold.

"Let me see," she replied at last, matching his cool tone. "I'm always so busy, it's hard to keep track. Hmm, I spent some time with Declan, I think—tasting his new recipes. He's very talented," she couldn't help but add.

Jake scowled. "Yeah, he seems like a real charmer."

"It's the accent," Mackenzie continued, musing. "There's just something about British guys."

"The women, too," Jake replied, and her good mood slipped. "They can't get enough of a real American man. Trust me on that." He gave her a smug wink, and Mackenzie's muffin turned dry in her mouth.

She didn't want to trust him. Hell, she didn't want to think about what he'd been doing with all his many women these past ten years, so she turned on the radio instead. It was programmed to a classic rock station, and Foo Fighters were playing, and just like that, she was seventeen again, feet up on the dashboard of Jake's car, driving back from practice down those dark country roads.

Mackenzie smiled and started singing along.

"Remember?" she asked, looking over at him. "You kept getting the lyrics wrong."

Jake started to smile. "And you made me look it up on my parents' computer, just to prove you were right."

"Which I was."

"Not that you'd let me forget it."

Mackenzie laughed. "I'll take my wins wherever I can get them. And speaking of which, don't you owe me a Mighty Monster hot dog for that pool game?"

"You don't forget a thing, do you?"

"Mind like a steel trap, baby," Mackenzie laughed. "And a stomach to match. Although I ate so much yesterday, I might give that foot-long dog a miss. Pro-tip, never become friends with chefs if you want to keep to a healthy diet. Especially when they think butter is a basic food group."

"Right. Your friend Declan." Jake's smile disappeared. He stared out at the road, stony-faced again.

Mackenzie stifled a sigh. Two hours to Boston? It was going to be a long ride.

BY THE TIME they arrived at the destination on the GPS, Mackenzie had given up trying to decipher Jake's mood. He could feel free to spend the day scowling, but she didn't have to let him spoil her fun too. They were spending the day in the happiest place on earth—or damn near close to it, anyway—and she was going to enjoy herself, down to the very last reindeer ornament.

"Are you sure we're in the right place?" Jake got out of the car and looked dubiously around. They were in front of a warehouse on the outskirts of the city, with the freeway overpass thundering nearby, and nothing but gray, run-down buildings all around.

"Freeman's Costume and Supplies," Mackenzie read the name off her order receipt. "Look, it says it on the door, right there."

She knocked, but there was no answer, so she pushed the door open on her own. Immediately, she stepped inside a grotto that could have put Santa's workshop to shame.

It was a massive warehouse, with aisles stretching all the way out of sight. Fake Christmas trees loomed thickly in the lobby, with displays of every decoration under the sun: from plastic cartoon characters and superheroes all the way through to delicate glass ornaments, glittered and spinning on their strings. Upbeat holiday music pumped through the speakers, boxes of toys were stacked sky-high on every shelf, and there was even fake snow falling in one corner, a constant stream from a line of machines all whirring away—on special discount, this week only.

"Elf costumes!" Mackenzie exclaimed in glee, spinning around. "We should get them for the Santa photo booth. Ooh, and look at those holiday lights! You can program them to spell out words!"

"Easy there," Jake said, finally cracking a smile. "Debra's already placed our order. We're just here to pick it up."

Mackenzie fixed him with a look. "Are you seriously telling me you want to grab our boxes and leave, without even looking around?"

"Well—"

She didn't wait for an answer. Mackenzie grabbed a cart and took off down the first aisle. To hell with the budget. She wanted to see everything they had in stock. Like those inflatable snowmen. And red-and-white feather boas. Mackenzie pulled one down and wrapped it around her neck, adding a floppy Santa hat as she happily browsed. There was a whole aisle of stocking stuffers—small gifts like toy cars and marbles that would be perfect donations to the toy drive—and soon, her cart was full to the brim.

Jake caught up to her while she was picking out train sets.

Mackenzie braced herself for more stony displeasure, until she caught sight of his fluffy Santa beard and red jacket. She burst out laughing.

"What do you think?" Jake grinned from behind the massive beard. "Do I get the gig?"

"You need to put on a few pounds," Mackenzie teased, poking his stomach with a candy cane. "Santa doesn't have a six-pack!"

"Sure he does!" Jake protested. "Hauling that sack of toys around the world? That's a prime core workout, right there."

"Sexy Santa . . ." Mackenzie mused. "You know, I'm sure there's a club in Vegas that would kill for your routines. Do you have a dance?"

"Do I have a dance?" Jake scoffed. "Baby, I was born dancing."

He began to thrust and gyrate with cheesy disco moves as Mariah Carey sang overhead.

"Stop!" Mackenzie cried. "My eyes!"

Jake kept dancing down the line, and she couldn't help but laugh. They turned a corner, almost bumping into a pair of bored-looking clerks, but Jake didn't skip a beat, he just slid to the side and kept on jiving.

Mackenzie shook her head, smiling. Jake turned to face her, moonwalking in time with her stride. "We're going to need a bigger van," he said, eying her cart. "What have you even got here, glitter pens?" he asked, picking the box out. "Since when does hot pink say holidays?"

"When you have a grade-school mural going up at the library," Mackenzie told him. "You can never have too much glitter."

"I agree." Jake nodded solemnly. "That was our unofficial team motto, in case you didn't know."

She laughed, silently giving thanks that even Jake couldn't resist the feel-good spirit of the holidays. "It looks like we've got everything," she said, looking around.

"Did you find those snowflake ornaments you were looking for?" Jake asked.

Mackenzie sighed. "Nope. I emailed them some photos, but they didn't recognize them. The town must have got them someplace else."

"Then we better get you out of here before that cart gets any fuller."

Mackenzie paused, looking around. "Unless you think the mayor will bump our budget so we can get a twenty-foot inflatable reindeer to sit in the town square?"

"It says a lot about Sweetbriar that my first answer isn't no," Jake laughed. "Come on. Let's leave some sparkle for the rest of them."

They headed for the check-out to get everything boxed up, and collect the order Debra had phoned in, too. Mackenzie was bracing herself for the final total, but when she emerged from the stock room after signing their delivery papers, she found that Jake had already taken care of the bill.

"Think of it as my donation to the good cause," he insisted. "All this stuff is making sure everyone gets to enjoy the holidays, even kids who don't have much at home."

Mackenzie was touched. "Then I'm treating you to dinner," she said as they stepped outside. "Your choice."

"Does that include my Mighty Monster dog?" Jake asked with a grin.

"Absolutely!"

But by the time they'd loaded up the van, it wasn't exactly food-truck weather. The gray snow clouds had turned a threatening shade of purple, hovering low on the horizon, with a few stray flakes already spiraling to earth. "We should probably head back to Sweetbriar if we want to beat the blizzard," Jake said, warily checking the skies.

Mackenzie's heart sank. She was in no hurry to get back home

—not when it meant Jake might flip the switch again and turn as moody as the winter weather. "Come on," she said lightly. "Since when has a little snow ever stopped you from getting fed?"

"True enough." Jake flashed her a grin. "I'm game if you are."

Mackenzie checked online for that old food truck, and found they'd upgraded to a permanent location. She directed Jake across the river and into the heart of Boston, navigating the narrow city streets until they found it crammed down a non-descript alley-way, sandwiched between a liquor store and an all-night launderette.

"Not exactly the five-star dining you're used to," she joked as they ducked into the neon-lit joint. Clearly, the legend of the foot-longs lived on, because it was packed and bustling with people escaping the cold, jostling for space at the narrow counter.

"Five stars are overrated," Jake said, shrugging off his damp coat. "Give me a classic with all the toppings and a beer any day."

"Amen." Mackenzie spied a couple of people leaving, and zipped through the crowd to steal their places. She victoriously hopped up on a stool as Jake arrived behind her, laughing.

"I haven't seen you move so fast since the market almost sold out of donuts." He nudged her good-naturedly.

"Hey!" Mackenzie laughed, nudging right back. "Not all of us are crazy enough to run five miles for fun every morning."

Jake made a face. "Don't remind me. I've been slacking off these past weeks."

"Only running three?" she teased, and he smiled again.

"Walking. Fast."

"That's more than me," she said, reaching over to grab them a pair of laminated menus. "Dad got me one of those step-counters for Christmas a couple of years ago. He thought we could do it together, you know. Bonding." Mackenzie grinned. "My count was so low, he called me up after the first week to check I turned the thing on."

Jake laughed. "You don't need to worry. You're in great shape."

His eyes drifted lower, skimming over her body, and even in a sweater and jeans, Mackenzie felt every inch of his stare.

She checked the menu, her blood humming again. It didn't matter that she had a couple of frat bros shoved up behind her, and the smell of French fries clinging in her hair. Jake was close enough to touch, right there beside her, stubble on his gorgeous jaw and his blue eyes crinkled happily at the edges. It made her pulse skip, too good to be true, all her old feelings roaring back to life in an instant.

Her heart caught. Why had she thought this was a good idea?

Because she still held out hope of breaking down that wall he'd put up and finding out once and for all if those blazing kisses could ignite something real. Maybe she was being a fool, but Mackenzie couldn't forget how it felt in his arms—and how Jake had looked at her, like she was the only one he wanted.

She cleared her throat. "Looks good," she said vaguely, even though the menu type was a blur to her.

"What looks good?" Jake asked.

Mackenzie bit her lip to keep from answering, *You.*

"Everything," she said instead. "Shopping is hungry work."

Jake chuckled. "I thought you hated it. You always whined whenever we had to get back-to-school supplies."

"I didn't whine!"

"Right," Jake grinned. "You just complained in an annoying voice until it was done."

Mackenzie stuck her tongue out at him, and he laughed. "Oh, how you've grown."

"You're one to talk," Mackenzie replied. "It was like pulling teeth trying to get you a tux for prom."

She stopped, remembering that night so vividly—and how it ended in humiliation. She flushed and took a gulp of water, but thankfully Jake didn't seem to notice. He flagged down the guy behind the counter to place their orders, and Mackenzie picked something at random, while Jake declared, "Foot-long with chili-cheese and all the trimmings," with such a satisfied look on his face that she had to laugh.

"I guess that's one thing I don't have to worry about now," he said, his smile dimming with the reminder of his injury. "Eating healthy, all those supplements and vitamins."

"For now," Mackenzie reminded him gently, and he nodded.

"For now."

THE FOOD CAME FAST—AND kept coming. Jake insisted on making up for lost time by sampling all the newest flavor combinations, and the evening passed in a deep-fried blur as they sat elbow-to-elbow, filling in the blanks of the past ten years. By the time the restaurant staff started wiping down the counters and kicked them out, Mackenzie's stomach—and heart —were full.

She hadn't had so much fun in years.

Just a couple of hours in a cheap fast-food dive put every date she'd ever been on to shame. And watching Jake bundle back up in his coat and scarf, a smudge of mustard still on his chin, she hadn't wanted a man more in her life.

Mackenzie swallowed hard. She turned away and pushed out of the door, trying to pull herself together again. It was snowing now, a steady fall of cold, icy flakes on the dark street. She looked up at the skies and stuck her tongue out, tasting the cool flakes in her time-honored tradition.

"Some things never change."

She looked back to find Jake watching her, his hands shoved in his coat pockets and a curious smile on his face. "You always loved the snow."

"And you always said you'd move someplace tropical," she

replied, putting her hands out to feel the flakes. "I guess we both got what we wanted in the end."

"Not everything," Jake said, his eyes never leaving hers. Mackenzie's heart stuttered in her chest. He took a few steps closer, and it took everything she had not to move closer too, not to go to him, no matter what.

But she'd tried that already. Tried and failed, and all the romantic, softly falling snow in the world wouldn't make a difference if Jake didn't want her.

He took another step closer.

"Don't look at me like that."

The voice came from somewhere inside her, braver than she'd expected.

Jake stopped. "How am I looking at you?"

Mackenzie swallowed, fighting to keep her voice light. "Like you want to kiss me again."

Jake glanced away, and then back at her with a boyish, charming smile. "Would that really be so bad?"

She tried to remember to breathe. "No," Mackenzie replied, as if this kind of heart-stopping flirtation happened all the time. "It's what comes after I don't want to repeat. The part where you suddenly regret everything and bolt."

"I don't regret anything."

Jake's voice was rough, suddenly deep with emotion. Mackenzie inhaled in a rush.

"So why do you do it?" she whispered. He was too close now, close enough she could see the snowflakes resting on his eyelashes, and the look in his gaze, so intent and possessive it took her breath away. "Why do you keep pushing me away?"

"Because I never knew what was good for me."

Jake's expression changed, a glimpse of something raw slipping through his smile, and then he was kissing her, and Mackenzie stopped thinking at all.

14

*J*ake knew there was no turning back.

He'd been fighting to resist her all day, ever since that damn feather boa in the warehouse. She'd twirled down the aisles, so full of excitement, it had taken everything he had not to pull her closer and kiss here right there in amongst the fake plastic trees and confetti snow. But there on the dark street, with real flakes tumbling from the sky and catching in her curls, all his control melted clean away.

Why was he still fighting this? She was inevitable. Necessary. The realest thing he'd felt in so long. And she was standing right there in the snowfall, almost challenging him to make a choice.

She should have known he'd made that choice a month ago when he kissed her for the first time. Because now that he knew how it felt to hold her, he wasn't going to stop until he had it all.

His lips found hers again, and he pulled her closer, losing himself in the exquisite rush. Her cheeks were chilled from the night air, but her mouth blazed hotly, pressing closer as the inferno sparked to life, and Jake fell headlong into the fire, and taste, and feel of her—*his Mackenzie*.

He wrapped his arms around her, drawing her as close as he could, hands sliding under her coat to feel the soft shape of her body as their mouths burned together, a slow dance of lips and tongues that only made him want more. God, what she did to him . . . This was more than just lust, thundering in his veins. This was something primal, a need that blotted out everything in the world but her. He kissed her harder, desperately, and who knew what he would have done if there hadn't been a distant blare of horn cutting through the night.

He pulled back, feeling drugged on her sweetness. The horn blared again, and he realized they were blocking the narrow street. He tugged Mackenzie back out of the way, and she stumbled after him, her cheeks flushed and her eyes bright and she was so damn beautiful, he had to kiss her all over again, up against the wall like a couple of kids, not caring who was around to see.

Mackenzie hooked her arms around his neck and dragged him eagerly down to her, pressing kisses along his jaw and nipping lightly against his earlobe until Jake groaned and captured her mouth again. He slid his tongue deep, needing to taste every inch of her, make her feel this burning desire that was consuming him. She sighed against him, her body arched and pressing, and damn the layers of clothing that kept them apart. He wanted her naked and moaning. He needed her to come apart in his arms, for him.

It should only ever be him.

Mackenzie finally dragged her lips from his, panting for air. There was something bright in her eyes, and for a moment, the face that was so familiar looked like a stranger to him: full of depths he'd never realized, the parts of her he'd never even dreamed.

"What now?" she whispered, the desire on her face giving way to uncertainty.

The question loomed, bigger than he wanted to deal with, but maybe Mackenzie felt the same, because she added, "We should hit the road, if we want to beat the snow."

She paused and drew a breath. "Or . . ."

The word hung between them, full of possibilities that roared hard through his body.

"It's late," Jake managed to say. "We should stay. Here. In the city tonight."

Mackenzie's lips curled in a smile. "That seems like a good idea." She nodded, still breathless. "The sensible thing to do."

To hell with sensible. Jake was on a one-way road to reckless, and he was going to savor every damn moment. With another searing kiss, he pulled Mackenzie after him down the street, back to wherever the hell he'd parked the van. He wasn't sure how they made it across the city, to a hotel by the park, he only knew that the moment the elevator doors closed behind them, they were up against the wall again: hard and hot, and too good to ever forget. Mackenzie let out a moan against his mouth, and Jake felt his whole body scream to life, demanding more until—

Ding!

The elevator doors opened, too early, to reveal an older couple standing in the hallway. They blinked, looking shocked to see Jake and Mackenzie still holding tight, their breath coming hard.

"Well I never . . ." the woman said, her lips pursing in disapproval. "Sorry," Jake managed, reaching over to hit the button again. "This one's occupied."

The doors closed, and Mackenzie dissolved into laughter. "Oh God, did you see their faces?" She giggled. "Anyone would think we were naked!"

"Soon," Jake growled, landing a kiss on the bare curve of her neck. Mackenzie shivered against him, and if the elevator hadn't arrived at their floor, he would have given those strangers something to complain about for sure.

Mackenzie grabbed his hand and pulled him down the hall.

She somehow managed to find their room, swiping the keycard even as she kissed him again. They tumbled backwards into the room, the door slamming shut behind them.

"Multi-tasking." Jake yanked her jacket off. "I'm impressed."

"I'm good with my hands, remember?" she teased, sliding her cold palms under his coat and sweater, making him flinch with the touch. He caught her wrists and pulled her hands away, catching them behind her back as he kissed her again.

This time, he took it slow.

Easing her mouth wider, sliding his tongue deep inside—Jake tried his best to go slow, even as his body demanded it all. He wanted to remember every moment, every breath. Mackenzie seemed to melt in his arms, swaying closer as he teased kisses along her jaw and down the curve of her neck. He peeled her sweater over her head, leaving her in just a thin camisole and bra. Her skin was flushed, not just her cheeks but the freckled surface of her chest too, and he bent his head, impatient to lavish every last freckle with the attention she deserved.

"Wait." Mackenzie broke away. "Shouldn't we . . . you know, talk about this?" She gulped, and Jake could see the nervousness slip into her eyes.

"Sure." He took her hand and began to kiss his way up her arm. "You talk. I'm all ears." He nuzzled in the crook of her elbow, and Mackenzie let out a breathy sigh.

"Jake, I'm serious," she said. "What are we doing?"

Her body was so close, so tempting, but he dragged himself back. She was worried, and he didn't have to ask why. This was unchartered territory for them, the brave dawn of something unknown, but he knew in his bones that there was nothing to be afraid of.

"It's OK," he promised, looking into the eyes he'd seen a thousand times, but never like this. "Whatever happens, it'll be alright. It's *us*."

He didn't know any other way to explain it, the feeling of total rightness that wrapped around them, making the real world seem like a million miles away. But maybe Mackenzie knew exactly what he meant, or maybe the tension between them was too much to resist, because either way, he saw her face change—from questioning to something certain.

She kissed him, and this time, she didn't stop.

∼

MACKENZIE TUMBLED backwards onto the bed.

What had happened to learning from her past mistakes, being older and wiser this time around? She knew all the reasons why this was a very bad idea, but somehow, pesky things like "sense" and "logic" didn't seem to matter at all, not with Jake's mouth hot on hers, and his hands sliding under her clothing, skimming over her skin and making her moan at the touch.

She wanted him. And for the first time in her life, he was right there for the taking.

She wasn't going to waste another moment.

Jake wrapped her legs around his waist, burying his face against her neck as she pulled his sweater over his head. God, that body . . . It was an athlete's physique, all taut, tanned flesh and curved muscle, and she wasted no time exploring every inch, from the swell of his biceps to the chiseled line of his abs. She dropped a dozen kisses, teasing him with her tongue as she made her way over the expanse of his broad shoulders, loving the way his body shivered under her mouth. He was tugging her camisole away from her, and she gladly obliged, stripping it off and tossing it to the floor.

"God, you're so beautiful," Jake breathed, staring up at her. But before Mackenzie could feel self-conscious, he rolled her beneath him, pinning her to the sheets. His mouth grazed over the lace of her bra, and her breath hitched in anticipation.

Almost . . . almost . . . *there.*

He closed his mouth around her, teasing as Mackenzie swooned back into the covers. The sensations were overwhelming: his steady weight, and sliding hands, and *God,* that miraculous mouth, sending her soaring as he stripped the last of her clothing away and lay her out, naked beneath him.

Her breath caught.

He was looking at her, really looking, the reverence in his gaze like nothing she'd ever seen before. Slowly, his eyes skimmed over her body, and she felt their path like a burning touch, bringing every part of her to life until she was panting, tension sweet between her thighs. She could have stayed like that forever: suspended on the edge of something, with anticipation burning in the air, but Mackenzie's patience was already long gone.

She'd been waiting ten years for this, and she wasn't going to waste another moment.

She reached for him, hungry, and then his clothes were joining hers in a mess on the floor, and there was nothing separating them anymore. Just the delicious, hot tangle of hands, and limbs, and bare skin, and searching mouths. The kisses she'd dreamed about all those innocent nights—and so much more. She didn't want to stop, not for a moment, and a small part of her felt almost desperate with desire—as if any pause, even for a moment, would pierce this reckless haze and it would all slip away, before she could possess him the way she craved.

But Jake didn't stop. His touch was ravenous, electric, as he spread her open and explored every inch, driving Mackenzie higher with a hungry touch until the storm was dancing, cresting, just out of reach. When he peeled away from her, she moaned in frustration, but he was only gone a moment, long enough to grab a condom from his wallet on the floor, and then he was back, yanking her against him, and it was her turn to explore: feeling the shifts and shudder of his breath beneath the rake of her fingernails, devouring him, teasing him in all the ways she could have imagined. She could have spent hours discovering the planes of his body, but Jake let out a ragged groan, and then he was rolling them again, pinning her beneath his delicious weight and easing her thighs apart.

When he moved inside her, Mackenzie lost her mind.

Something took her over, a raw, animal need she'd never known before. Hot and pulsing, demanding more. Harder. *Now.*

Jake rocked higher, and she heard herself cry out, as if from far away. She was clinging to him, meeting him stroke for stroke, wild with desire as he surged inside her, thick and deep and *God*, right there. She bit down on his shoulder to keep from screaming with pleasure, and Jake let out a raw, ragged cry. His pace became frenzied, their bodies a slick blur of sweat and gasps and wild abandon. She couldn't think, she couldn't breathe, all she could do was hold on for dear life, feeling the fire take her over, burning the world down in the blaze of his touch until she was poised on the edge of the precipice, a live wire sparking in the night.

"Jake," she gasped, drowning in him, in the wild, sweet fever of it all. "Oh God, don't stop. *Jake!*"

He shifted, pinning her down and then thrusting deep again, deeper than before, his face a mirror of her own wild abandon, those blue eyes frenzied with the same desperate need. Mackenzie lost herself in them, lost herself in the slam of their bodies and the thick slide of him and the friction building, burning, raging deeper until she couldn't hold back, couldn't stop the supernova. He surged up inside her, stroking every last inch and *oh*, she shattered with a scream, ravished by the surge of pleasure, consumed by the sound of her name on his lips, a desperate, ragged prayer before his body tightened and she felt him come undone.

15

*M*ackenzie stretched, yawning. Jake was collapsed across her, pinning her to the rumpled sheets. It wasn't altogether a bad sensation, she decided, flexing her sore, tired muscles with a yawn.

"So, that's what a workout feels like."

Jake chuckled, his eyes still closed. "I wish. I'll take this over a five-mile run any day."

She nibbled on his bare shoulder, and Jake rolled them over, settling her in the crook of his shoulder as he let out an almighty yawn. "Down, woman."

Mackenzie cleared her throat.

"Babe?" he smiled, still sleepy. "Sweetheart? Darlin'?"

"Sure, snookums."

Jake's eyes shot open. "I'm going to pretend I didn't hear that." He smiled, pinning her down in an instant and kissing her deep enough to make every one of those tired nerve endings come screaming back to life.

Mmmm . . . Mackenzie luxuriated in the feel of him, the hard press of that magnificent body. Her hands couldn't keep from roaming, as if they had a life of their own, exploring up over his shoulders and down to the curve of his ass. "I've got to start dating more athletes," she murmured, teasing.

"You know what else we have?" Jake gave her a wicked grin. "Stamina."

Mackenzie laughed. "Well, in that case . . ." She bounced upright, looking around. "Where's the room service menu?"

Jake made a noise of appreciation. "See, I knew you were the perfect woman."

He got up and padded over to the bureau—giving Mackenzie an uninterrupted view. She flushed, realizing for the first time now that her afterglow was fading that this was happening.

She was naked, in a hotel room, with Jake Sullivan.

And it was about damn time.

"What?" Jake turned in time to see her victorious smile.

"Nothing." Mackenzie grinned. "Just admiring the view."

"Oh yeah?" Jake struck a muscle-man pose, showing off, until she tossed a pillow at him. "Hey!" he protested, throwing it right back. "Show a little appreciation. I'm out here hunting and gathering for you."

He grabbed the menu and collapsed back on the bed, making Mackenzie bounce. "I do appreciate you," she said, mock-serious. "Any man who can dish out orgasms like that *and* order ice cream wins my undying affection."

"Ice cream?" Jake reached for the in-room phone.

"Or fries." Mackenzie paused. "Or nachos. I can't decide."

Jake winked as he placed their order. "Hey, this is room 412. Can we please get an order of fries, nachos, and ice cream? Thanks." He hung up and kissed her. "Anything for my baby."

Mackenzie mock-swooned. "You're so good to me."

She fell back into the pillows, her heart singing. It was so simple with him: the laughter and easy jokes. She wasn't suddenly gripped with self-consciousness about her body, or awkwardly making small talk, the way it was with some guys. Instead, she felt perfectly at ease beside him, her head nestling against his chest, and his hand tracing idle circles on her bare shoulder like it was second nature to him.

"Excellent plan, by the way, staying in the city," she said, turning to smile up at him. "Who knows how dangerous the roads would have been."

Jake smiled back. "Sure. It's a blizzard out there."

Mackenzie laughed. The drapes were open, and she could see the gentle sprinkle of snowflakes spiraling down outside. "A real storm," she agreed, snuggling closer. "Who knows how long we might be trapped?"

"That's just fine with me," Jake said, his voice turning husky. "I've got everything I need right here."

He kissed her, a leisurely, morning-after kind of kiss that slipped through her veins, sweet as whiskey. Mackenzie sighed in pleasure, automatically pressing closer, and just like that, the kiss wasn't so leisurely anymore. Jake caught her lower lip between his teeth, nipping lightly, and Mackenzie teased her fingernails across his chest, loving how his breath hitched at her touch. He shifted, crushing her against him—

There was a knock at the door.

"To be continued," Jake promised, dragging himself away. He grabbed a robe from the wardrobe and tossed one to Mackenzie too, waiting until she was covered before opening the door. She slipped through to the bathroom while he chatted to the bellhop, and what seemed like a lifetime later, she finally heard the door close again.

"Sorry," Jake said when she stuck her head back out. "Turns out he was a fan."

"No rest for the famous," she said lightly, and danced over to explore the tray. There were crispy French fries with little individual bottles of mustard and ketchup, loaded nachos, smothered with cheese . . . Mackenzie sighed with satisfaction, sinking down on the couch and digging in.

When she looked up, Jake was watching her with a smile. "What?" she asked, wiping her face. "Do I have salsa all over me?"

He chuckled, strolling over to join her. "No, you're good. I was just making a mental note to get groceries in. At this rate, you'll eat me out of house and home."

"Your mom's pies won't stand a chance," she agreed.

"Actually, I moved in to Cooper's place," he said casually, reaching for a wedge of nachos.

Mackenzie stopped and turned. "What? When? Why didn't you say anything?"

He shrugged. " 'Cause I was being a jealous asshole. I saw you with Declan," he admitted.

She paused. Maybe it was petty, but she still felt pretty good knowing he'd been jealous. "Declan's just a buddy," she reassured him.

"So, you've never . . . ?" Jake was still studying the food like it was the most interesting thing in the room, but Mackenzie could see through his casual questioning.

"Nope. He's way too much of a playboy," she said. "We never clicked like that."

"OK." Jake seemed to relax. "And, yes, I know it's crazy of me to be jealous when we haven't even been talking for the past ten years, but . . ."

"I get it," Mackenzie agreed quickly. "I'm choosing not to think about you and any gorgeous groupies, either." She dunked a fry in the ice cream.

"There weren't any groupies."

Mackenzie looked up. Jake gave her a sheepish smile. "OK, maybe there were a few, but it wasn't like you think."

"Let's just not talk about them full-stop."

"Deal."

She munched on the food, her endorphins settling again. That first wild elation was melting, and now she just felt sleepy—sleepy, and safe, and wrapped in the delicious haze of the two of them, snuggled together companionably. It could have been any other of the hundred evenings they'd spent together.

Except for that whole "mind-blowing sex" part of the equation.

She glanced over, blushing, and as if reading her mind, Jake gave her a smoldering smile.

"Come here," he said, beckoning softly.

Mackenzie arched an eyebrow, but still, of course, she went: leaning over and slowly crawling up his body to drop a kiss on his perfect mouth.

He tasted like vanilla and chocolate sauce, sweet on her lips as she grazed over his cheek and then lower, to his collarbone, and the broad, tanned expanse of his chest. She felt him inhale as her hands slid lower, pushing his terry-cloth robe aside to explore her territory.

"Mac . . ." he whispered as she teased lower, licking a path along his hipbone, and down the cut lines of his abdomen. She heard him groan as she closed her hands around him, and then it was past the time for words. She had better things to do with her mouth.

16

*I*t was morning when Mackenzie woke again, and the gray, clear light was pouring through the window.

The bed beside her was empty.

She stretched, still sleepy, until she heard the sound of the shower from the bathroom, and suddenly, it all came rushing back.

The hotel. The snow.

Jake.

She sat bolt upright, her heart pounding. What happened now? Was this night the start of something more between them, or was it a fluke, one crazy, wild adventure that would never be repeated?

The shower shut off, and a moment later, Jake emerged—dripping wet, with a towel around his waist. He saw her sitting there, and smiled. "Good morning."

It was now.

"Hey." Mackenzie fought to keep her live-wire emotions in check. She bounced out of bed and quickly belted a robe around her. "What time is it? I feel like I've slept for hours."

"You did. It's past ten."

Mackenzie yelped.

"Don't worry," he chuckled. "I already called and got us late check-out."

"But the gallery," she said, already hunting in her purse for her cellphone. "And I was supposed to walk Debra's dogs again. What should I tell her?"

"That you got waylaid with a sex god?" Jake grinned with a cocky look on his face.

She laughed, tapping out a text. "I said I crashed in the city with a friend."

"A friend, hmmm?" Jake's hands slipped around her, inside her robe. "A good one, I hope."

Mackenzie's heart caught. She wasn't ready to have the talk about what they were to each other now—not when she didn't know for sure what his reply would be. So, she danced away with a kiss. "The best. I hope you left some hot water for me," she changed the subject lightly, heading for the bathroom. "Because the only thing I love more than hotel room service is hotel bathtubs."

"Is that an invitation?" Jake asked, already reaching for his towel.

"Definitely."

BY THE TIME they checked out and hit the road again, it was after noon. Mackenzie curled in the passenger seat, letting the sound of the radio wash over her, the snow-dusted scenes of the Cape speeding by as they headed back for home.

Jake was steady at the steering wheel, his profile framed against the pale sky. She watched him, marveling that such a familiar face could still be so new. Even after all this time, there was still so much to discover: the look in his eyes when he reached for her; the way his body felt as he came undone.

He glanced over. "All good?"

She nodded. "We'll be home soon," she said, pressing her fingertips to the cool glass. "It's weird. It feels like we've been away for weeks, not just one night."

"The best night of your life," Jake teased, and Mackenzie laughed.

"Sure thing, snookums."

But it was. And now that the glow was fading, Mackenzie was left with too many unanswered questions, so she pushed them all aside and turned the radio up: singing along and joking with Jake until they turned off the highway and passed the familiar sign welcoming them back to town. The streets were busy for the weekend, even with the snow, and she could already see the first tourists of the season snapping photos on the square. It was a good thing Phase One of the Starbright Festival was already underway, with decorations in every storefront and twinkling lights strung from every streetlamp across the square. "We should get everything stored over at the Town Hall," Mackenzie said, remembering the van-load of toys and decorations they were carrying in the back.

"It's OK, I can take care of it," Jake said.

"Are you sure?"

"What are errand boys for?" he asked.

"Well, I'm thinking of a few more things now," Mackenzie said flirtatiously, and was rewarded with a devious smile.

"Keep thinking, sweetheart. There'll be a quiz later."

He drew up outside the gallery and idled by the sidewalk. Mackenzie paused. "So . . ." she started, suddenly feeling awkward all over again. But Jake clearly didn't have the same concerns, because he just leaned over and dropped a casual kiss on her lips.

"I could come over tonight?" he suggested easily.

Relief flooded through her. "Sounds good," she said, matching his tone. "See you later."

She climbed out of the van and watched him drive away with a wave. As the van disappeared around the corner, she caught Hank, from the hardware store, on the corner. He raised his hand in a wave, then walked on.

She cringed. If he'd seen them kissing . . .

But no. Mackenzie straightened her shoulders, unlocking the gallery door. She was a grown woman now, an adult. If she wanted to make out with a man in broad daylight in the town square, then she would just go ahead and do it—to hell with the gossip.

And if she wanted to take the rest of the day off work, leave the gallery closed, and go straight to the bakery for a cup of tea, an afternoon pastry, and some much-needed girl talk? Well, she would do exactly that.

Mackenzie turned on her heel and set out along the winding roads that led just out of town. Summer's bakery was set back from the road, surrounded by a thicket of blackberry bushes, and when she stepped through the door, Mackenzie was hit with a rush of warm, cinnamon-scented air.

"Perfect timing!" Summer declared, looking up from behind the counter. "My afternoon shift just went home sick, and I have a whole batch of fruitcake that needs tasting."

"God, you're a difficult friend." Mackenzie grinned. "So demanding, you just take, and take, and take."

Summer laughed. She had her hair caught up in a messy braid, and an apron that declared *#bakerboss* over a bright red holiday sweater. She beckoned Mackenzie back towards the kitchen. "You say that now, but poor Grayson is sick of the stuff. I've been serving it to him for breakfast, lunch, and dinner."

Mackenzie followed her into the kitchen, then stopped. There was fruitcake on every surface. Round ones, square ones, cakes gleaming with fruit topping, and cakes drizzled with thick frosting. "Wow, OK, you really weren't kidding."

"I told you!" Summer exclaimed, with a note of despair in her voice. "I just can't get the recipe right. I had the most amazing slice once in France, it was like, life-changing cake, perfect for the holidays. But no matter what I try, I can't get mine to taste the same."

"Well, I better get started then," Mackenzie said, eyeing the nearest platter.

Summer cut her a slice from three different cakes and put the teakettle on to boil. "So, what's new with you?" she asked. "I'm sorry I haven't been around the past couple of weeks. Things have been crazy here, getting the new winter menu up and approving all the photos for the cookbook."

"How's that going?" Mackenzie asked, taking her first bite. "With your mom, I mean?"

Summer gave her a look. "It's . . . interesting. As always, when it comes to the great Eve Bloom. But she's making an effort, I guess. She only suggested I change my hair and drop five pounds twice during the whole shoot."

"That's progress for you," Mackenzie joked. She pointed to the cake she'd just sampled. "This one is amazing. It's got this spicy—"

"Ginger," Summer finished for her. "I used the sugared crystals, then grated some fresh for an extra kick."

"Well, whatever you did, it's amazing. Although . . ." She sampled the next cake. "Ooh, this one has chocolate."

"See my problem?" Summer cried.

"Yes, it's a terrible problem," Mackenzie agreed with a smile. "You're such a talented baker, you've created too many amazing cakes!"

Summer laughed. "OK, point taken." She poured them some tea, then joined Mackenzie at the counter, hopping up on a stool. "So, your turn. How was Thanksgiving? Did you do anything fun?"

Mackenzie stuck a forkful of cake in her mouth, and spoke

through the crumbs. "I stayed in town. Jake and I had dinner, it was pretty casual."

"Oh?" Summer paused, her tea cup halfway to her lips. She searched, and Mackenzie couldn't stop the smile creeping over her face. "*Oh!*" Summer's eyes widened. "Details. Spill. Now!"

Mackenzie flushed. But this is why she'd come looking for Summer, after all. She needed someone to talk to, to make her feel like it was really happening. "We, um, spent the night in the city," she said, and Summer's eyes got even wider.

"And?" she demanded.

"And . . ." Mackenzie gave a shrug. "A lady doesn't kiss and tell."

Summer clapped her hands together in glee. "Finally! We were wondering when you two would ever get it together."

"Who was?"

"Everyone!" Summer beamed. "This calls for celebration— wait, does it?" she checked, looking anxiously to Mackenzie.

She nodded. "I think so. I mean, yes. It does."

"Perfect. Call the rest of the girls, and tell Eliza to bring the wine. I just mixed up some mulling spices. Plus, you know, I'm going to need some help eating all this cake!"

THREE BOTTLES OF WINE, two hours, and more cake than Mackenzie could count later, she finally pushed her plate away. "No more!" she protested when Eliza offered her another slice. "You'll have to roll me home."

"Call it carb-loading," Eliza answered with a grin. "You're going to need your strength later."

Mackenzie flushed. "Don't!"

"Aww, come on!" Eliza protested. "Only one of us is banging a hot athlete. Let me live vicariously, at least."

"It's not like that," Mackenzie argued, still feeling her cheeks burn.

"Fine." Brooke smiled. "Making sweet, sweet love."

They all laughed. Summer had long since flipped the bakery sign to "closed," and now the five of them were in the apartment upstairs, poring over the details of Mackenzie's love life. A part of her felt guilty for gossiping, but the other part of her knew that without the bright laughter of her friends' teasing, those whispers of uncertainty would be back.

Besides, after years of bland dates not even worth a second thought, she finally had something worth talking about.

"So has he said anything?" Poppy asked. "You know, about . . ."

"The status of our relationship, and-or a declaration of his intentions and affection?" Mackenzie finished for her.

"I was going to say, your future plans, but sure, that works too." Poppy grinned.

Mackenzie shook her head. "It wasn't really the time for talking."

"I bet it wasn't." Eliza winked.

"He was driving!"

"Still possible." She smiled.

"Remind me to stay far away from you on the road," Mackenzie laughed. "But to answer your question . . . no. We haven't really talked at all about us. But that's OK," she added quickly, trying to reassure herself. "I mean, there's plenty of time. We don't have to rush anything."

"So he's decided he's staying in town? That's great!" Poppy exclaimed.

Mackenzie paused. "Well, no. We haven't talked about that either. But he did move into Cooper's rental. That has to be a good sign, right?" She looked around the table. They all nodded.

"Absolutely."

"Plus, there's nothing sexy about a man living in his parents' basement," Eliza added. "He's putting down roots."

But for how long?

Mackenzie knew deep down that he was only back in Sweetbriar because of his injury. He was already itching to join his teammates again, so there was no doubt he'd be on a plane back to Miami the first chance he got.

So where did that leave her?

Her expression must have shown her doubts, because Poppy quickly gave her hand a comforting squeeze. "You don't need to have the answers just yet. I mean, it's barely been twenty-four hours since you guys got it together. Have some fun!"

Mackenzie nodded. "You're right. It's way too early to be asking big questions."

Even if those big questions had been ten years in the making.

She pushed her fears aside. For now, she had her friends, wine, and a hot pro footballer waiting to rock her world all over again that night. She was going to enjoy this moment; the future could wait.

Her phone buzzed with a text and she fished it out of her bag to check.

Pick you up at the gallery at 7?

"Is it him?" Brooke asked. "I bet it's him."

"No sexting at the table," Summer warned her with a cheeky grin.

Mackenzie laughed. "You guys have dirty minds. It's nothing." She read the screen. "Just arranging to meet later."

"For all that sweet, sweet loving," Eliza finished her wine with a gulp. "It's a good thing I'm working on a kickass cover profile right now, otherwise I might—*might!*—just be jealous. What about you, Poppy? How's the new book coming?"

Poppy groaned. "Terrible! It turns out being in a happy relationship is the worst thing for my writing."

They all laughed. "Seriously?" Summer asked.

"I know, it's weird, but I can't bring myself to give my characters any emotional angst. It's all just, 'they met, they fell in love, they stayed happy with no major traumas or issues, the end.' My editor is at her wit's end."

"Aww, you'll find something," Brooke reassured her. "Tell Cooper to be a real jerk, just for this draft."

Poppy smiled. "He woke me up working with the power saw this morning. That helped. Until it turned out he was just building me a new desk."

"What an asshole," Mackenzie teased.

Summer let out a yawn. "OK, kids, I need to call it a night. I need to be up at four a.m. to start the bread."

"I'm so glad I never grew up wanting to be a baker," Eliza noted, getting to her feet.

"Much better to be the friend of the baker," Mackenzie agreed.

They helped clean and pack up the leftovers, then they all headed out. Mackenzie turned down offers of a ride and strolled the dark street back towards town, enjoying the brisk chill of the cold night air. Her stomach was already full of butterflies, just thinking about seeing Jake again.

And kissing him.

And . . . *more*.

She took a deep breath, the air fogging as she exhaled. This was all unknown to her, not just having someone in her life who could make her feel this way, but the whirlwind of emotions that came along with it, too. She knew her friends were right, they didn't need to rush anything, but still, Mackenzie couldn't help feeling like she'd been waiting on this moment since high school, and now that it was within her grasp, she wanted to hold on tight and know for certain exactly what it meant. What Jake meant by any of it.

Down, girl.

She took another breath. There was no point trying to fool herself that this was any other guy—a man to play it casual with, and not place any expectations on the relationship—but she could keep from diving in over her head right away. Enjoy it. Savor the moment. Like the fact she was practically power-walking across town, just to see him again.

Any man who could make her break a sweat was something special, for sure.

Mackenzie was smiling by the time she reached the gallery. Then she saw that the lights were on, and the door was unlocked.

"Hello?" Mackenzie paused on the threshold, feeling a flicker of fear. Had she left it open? "Is anyone there?"

She took a step inside. Everything looked fine in the main room, but she heard a noise in the back, and froze.

"Hello?"

She held her breath, looking around for a weapon. She grabbed an umbrella that was resting by the desk, and tiptoed closer. "You should come out now!" she called. "I'm armed!"

"Whoa, easy there." Jake stepped out of the back, his hands raised in surrender.

Mackenzie exhaled in a whoosh as she took in his broad frame. "What are you doing?" she exclaimed, tapping him with the umbrella. "You nearly scared me half to death!"

"Sorry. It was open when I got here, so I figured I'd wait inside." Jake came closer and pulled her into a hug. "What did you think, that I was some rogue thief out to steal all your sugar bowls?"

"It's not funny," Mackenzie said, even as she relaxed in his arms. "I could have hurt you."

"By protecting me from the rain?" he teased. She shoved him lightly, and he caught her closer, leaning in to capture her lips in a searing kiss.

All thoughts of danger left her mind. Mackenzie melted into him, loving the feel of his body so solid against her, and the taste of him, still so brand new.

Finally, he drew back. "Did you get much work done?" he asked.

"Not exactly . . ." She smiled. "Summer needed help with her tasting, so it turned into a girls' night."

"Any leftovers?" Jake looked hopeful, already eyeing her bag.

"Maybe," Mackenzie said. "Just let me close up here."

"I like the new stuff you're working on," Jake said, looking around. "Very festive."

"I know my market." Mackenzie smiled. The tables were full of pottery waiting for another coat of glaze: berry-red dishware and plates ringed with tiny green holly leaves. "There's a holiday craft fair up in Provincetown next weekend, I usually sell out."

"And those sculptures are cool," Jake continued. "Weird, but cool."

Mackenzie froze. "What sculptures?" she asked, with her heart in her throat.

"The ones in the studio," Jake continued, still browsing. "You know, the weird curvy ones."

"You looked in my studio?" Mackenzie's voice rose in panic. She pushed past him, rushing into the back. But it was too late. The drop cloths had been pulled down, revealing everything. The arc of the figures, the desperate yearning in their pose. Everything she'd been hiding, working on in secret all this time was suddenly standing right in front of them for him to see.

What did he think of her now?

She felt sick. "Jake!"

"What?" Jake appeared behind her, looking confused.

"I can't believe you!" She scrambled to cover them again, but she knocked the first sculpture off balance, and it was only Jake's quick hands that stopped it from tumbling to the ground.

"Whoa!" he exclaimed, pushing it upright again. "I've got it."

"Leave it!" she insisted, finally managing to get the figures hidden again. "Please, just stop!"

Jake stepped back, wary now. "What's wrong?"

"What's wrong?" Mackenzie echoed, feeling painfully exposed. "You came back here, into my private studio, and looked through all my work!"

"I'm sorry, I was just curious—"

"So? Did you even think if I would be OK with it?" she demanded. "You could have damaged something!"

"But I didn't," Jake said calmly.

"That's not the point!" She was horrified to feel tears stinging, hot in her throat. "This is my place, OK? You don't poke around an artist's work unless they invite you. The things here, there not finished, they're not ready. I might never show them to anyone, and that's *my* call."

"Hey, relax." Jake tried to draw her closer, but Mackenzie flinched away. "I really am sorry, I didn't know—about privacy, or the rules for someone's studio. In case you hadn't noticed, I'm pretty much a novice when it comes to art," he added, with a calming smile.

But Mackenzie was wound too tight to be soothed. She felt cut open, exposed, in the worst way possible. Her studio was her safe place, full of unfinished scraps and random musings, a controlled chaos from her mind onto the walls. Even then, she could have forgiven him for looking, if it wasn't for those damn sculptures. She'd known from the start they were too abstract, too personal to ever see that light of day. That's what Jake had said, wasn't it?

Weird.

She'd always been the weird one—as a kid, in her hand-knitted sweaters, eating smelly hummus and doodling in the back of classes. She'd told herself the teasing didn't bother her, but she'd always known exactly what they meant. She saw the world differently, in color and line and abstract form, and although she knew it was something to be proud of, not ashamed, it didn't stop the sting.

Now, she practically shoved Jake from the room, her cheeks burning. She would have preferred to march through the town square in her birthday suit rather than have him see those sculptures, but she didn't get the choice. She was naked, and he didn't understand.

"Please, just go," she said, swallowing back her tears.

Jake frowned. "You're really mad over this? I said I was sorry."

"And I said it was private." Mackenzie turned away, making sure everything was locked before she strode to the front door. "Look, it's been a long day. Let's take a raincheck on hanging out tonight. I need to get some sleep."

"Oh." She could hear the disappointment and confusion in his voice, but she didn't want to look. One glance at Jake's puppy-dog eyes, and she knew she'd crumble, and try to pretend that everything was OK.

"See you tomorrow," she said instead, and started walking away on the dark street.

17

*J*ake watched her leave, feeling totally bewildered. One minute they'd been talking—*kissing*—and the next, she was almost in tears. It wasn't as if he'd broken anything, he'd been extra-careful not to touch. And sure, maybe he shouldn't have gone poking around, but it was only because he was so curious to see what she was working on and get a glimpse of her creative life these days.

But clearly, he'd made a big mistake.

Mackenzie's red curls disappeared around the corner, leaving him alone on the dark street.

So much for the romantic night he'd planned.

Jake drove back to the barn and parked out front. He'd spent the afternoon moving the rest of his stuff over and stocking the fridge—in case of Mackenzie's late-night cravings. Now, he pulled out a beer and sat on the back porch, spinning his cellphone in his hand. He had a list of voicemails and unanswered messages from his agent racking up, but with an empty evening stretching ahead of him, he finally had no excuses for not returning the call.

Reluctantly, he dialed.

"Jake, my man." Trey sounded over the moon to hear from him, but his voice was muffled under loud music and a thudding bassline.

"Have I got you at a bad time?" Jake asked.

"There are no bad times when it comes to you, my friend." There was the sound of movement, and then the music receded, replaced by muffled street noise. Jake could just picture him, in LA maybe, ducked outside of the hottest new restaurant or bar. "OK, I'm all good now. What's new?"

"Not much, just checking in," Jake replied, and took a swig of beer. "How are things with you?"

"Can't complain. This new season is shaping up to be killer. A lot of hot picks out there with something to prove."

"What's the word on Sanchez?" he asked, naming the player who'd moved off the bench to fill his spot.

"Aww, you know these rookies. No finesse," Trey said.

"Liar. I've seen the buzz online." Sanchez was more than holding his own. And even though Jake was glad for his team, he had to admit it hurt too, knowing he could be so easily replaced.

"Don't believe everything you read," Trey insisted. "I guarantee the moment you step back on the field, they'll forget his name. How's rehab?"

"It's . . . coming along."

Jake felt guilty. With everything happening with Mackenzie, and the festival planning, he'd let his usual grueling routine slide.

Trey must have heard it in his voice, because he chuckled. "Hey, we've all been there. Thanksgiving, the holidays . . . it's hard to turn down another helping of turkey, am I right?"

"Something like that."

It wasn't the turkey putting a hiccup in his workout routine, it was the French fries dipped in ice cream.

And the red-head doing the dipping.

"Listen, you'll get back on track," Trey said confidently. "You've got more discipline than any other player I've worked with. If you want it, you'll make it happen."

"Thanks," Jake said, warmed by his faith.

"Hey, don't tell my other clients!" Trey laughed. "I tell them all that they're my favorites."

"Of course you do." Jake smiled. "Anyway, I've got another physio appointment in a week or so, we should get an update on how the knee is healing."

"Keep me in the loop," Trey said. "Remember, I don't get paid if you won't play!"

Jake laughed, hanging up. Trey liked to make out like he was a cut-throat hustler, but the guy had a softer side, too. His clients were like family to him—which is why he'd camped out in the hospital after the accident with Jake's parents, fetching coffee to help pitch in like he didn't have multi-million dollar deals waiting on the other line. His faith in Jake never seemed to waver, even when Jake's own confidence came up short.

Like now.

He stretched his knee in front of him, shifting the weight from one side to the other. He was pleased to note it had been feeling better the past few days, the constant hum of pain lessening to where he barely even noticed it. Still, that was no excuse for slacking off. If anything, it meant he should be pushing his body harder now, trying to get his fitness back on track.

He headed indoors and traded the beer for water, then changed into some loose-fitting sweatpants and a T-shirt so he could go through Dr. Lashai's movement routine. Carefully, he stretched and manipulated the joints, testing his muscles and ticking off the boxes for how long he could hold each pose. He was pleased to see improvement since his last set of numbers, and vowed to practice twice a day now, to really push his progress. He should be running now, too, he decided, jotting down his plans for a daily schedule, and working on his diet, hitting the weights.

His body may not look any different from six months ago, but he knew his stamina and strength had probably been cut in half with all this time out.

Luckily, his muscles would remember. And after hitting them with this new training regimen, they'd definitely get the message. He'd be game-ready by the spring, and then it would be like this terrible year had never happened at all.

Terrible, except for one thing.

Jake paused for breath, sweating at the exertion. He knew he was focusing on his workout plans so he wouldn't have to think about that fight earlier—or just how guilty he felt. He didn't understand what happened to make Mackenzie so upset, but he didn't like it either. The thought of her feeling hurt or angry with him made his chest clench hard in a way that had nothing to do with the exercise.

Had he just screwed the whole thing up without even realizing?

Jake gulped. Last night had been something else: something hotter, and wilder, and more vivid than he could imagine. Even now, the memory of her spread beneath him made his blood run hot. The tempting look in her eyes, the way her hair felt, brushing over his body as she moved lower . . .

He was going to need a damn cold shower.

He finally quit on the workout, but he was just heading upstairs when there was a knock at the door.

He went to open it, expecting Cooper, maybe, or a friendly neighbor with another welcome bushel of apples (he had received two already), but instead, he found Mackenzie on his front porch with her arms folded and a reluctant expression on her face.

And just like that, his night got a whole lot better.

~

"I'M SORRY," Mackenzie blurted, without any small talk. "I might have maybe freaked out on you, just a little."

Jake smiled back at her, annoyingly calm. "You think?"

Mackenzie glared. She'd been pacing up a storm back home, torn between her own humiliation and Jake's confusion over her meltdown. She'd thought the least she could do was come over here and explain herself, but it turned out he hadn't given her anguish a second thought. He'd been lounging around, looking gorgeous and sweaty . . .

She dragged her eyes back up to his face and took another breath. "I'm trying to apologize here."

He chuckled. "It could use a little work."

That was too much. She went up on her tiptoes and kissed him hard: hot, and sweet, and tasting like Christmas. "How about now?" she asked, her head spinning.

"Better," Jake said gruffly, and then his hands were around her waist, and he was practically dragging her inside.

Mackenzie went willingly, stealing another kiss right there against the slamming door. He peeled her coat off in record time, and then she was gasping as his mouth moved to the arch of her neck, nuzzling the sensitive spot right there beneath her ear. "So you don't think I'm a freak?" she managed to say, before her brain shut off completely.

Jake pulled away. "No. Why would you say that?" he asked, his gaze searching hers.

She cringed. She was overreacting all over again. "It's fine. Don't worry."

But Jake paused for breath, smoothing down her sweater. "Talk to me," he said gently, tugging her over to the couch. "What happened earlier?"

Mackenzie braced herself. "I just . . . don't show my work to people. Not the pottery, that's fine," she explained quickly. "But the sculptures. Nobody even knows I'm working on them.

They're too . . . personal. So when you just walked in . . ." She trailed off. "It felt like you forced it. That you saw something I wasn't ready to share."

Jake looked at her with a new understanding. "I'm sorry, baby," he said, squeezing her hand. "I didn't realize. You always seem so casual about your work, I didn't think you would mind."

"Normally, I wouldn't. But those pieces . . ." Mackenzie shrugged and looked away, feeling self-conscious all over again. "I wasn't planning on letting anyone see them. Ever."

"So you would just keep them covered up in your studio forever?" Jake frowned. "But that would be a waste."

"You said it yourself," Mackenzie reminded him. "They're weird."

"Weird-good!" he exclaimed. "I mean, I couldn't really tell what they were, but they were beautiful. You shouldn't let some dumbass who knows nothing about art make a difference," he added, his face open and sincere. "Seriously, Mac. You should be sharing your art. Don't just hide it all away."

She flushed. "Maybe . . ." she said evasively. "Anyway, I know you didn't mean any harm, and I'm sorry I blew up on you."

"That's OK." Jake gave a smile. "I can take it."

He pulled her against him, nestling her head against his chest. Mackenzie slowly exhaled, relaxing. It was a relief to know she hadn't just sent him running, but she still felt off balance knowing he'd seen her most personal pieces.

She looked around, wanting to change the subject. She knew Cooper's place well from their friendship, and had always liked the warm, rustic barn. "So, you're settled in now?" she asked.

"All one suitcase," Jake chuckled, his chest vibrating against her face. "But it definitely beats my old childhood room. I don't feel like my mom is going to come downstairs and tell me to keep my feet off the couch."

Mackenzie smiled. "And turn that music down," she mimicked.

Jake groaned. "Please, never imitate my mom again. That's just wrong." He looked around. "I don't suppose you brought those cake leftovers as part of your apology?"

Mackenzie made a face. "I may have eaten my feelings."

He laughed. "Then it's a good thing I stocked the pantry. I figured you might get hungry," he added with a wink.

"I don't think I'm going to eat for another week," she admitted.

"You might change your mind later." Jake shot her such a smoldering look that she flushed.

"Oh really?" She arched an eyebrow, trying to hide how her body was already hot with anticipation. "And why's that?"

"I can think of a few reasons," he said, stroking softly over the curve of her body. He dipped his head and kissed her cheek, her jaw, teasing her earlobe before he finally claimed her mouth. Mackenzie sank into the kiss, everything slipping away under his expert hands. He drew her into his lap, molding her body to his, as his mouth caressed hers with a sensual purpose.

God, she could kiss him forever, but already, the spark between them was burning hotter, and she craved the touch of him, skin to skin. From zero to sixty in a few seconds flat: Mackenzie would be embarrassed about how quickly she wanted him, if she couldn't feel the proof of his desire hard against her, just as insistent.

She drew back. "So, are you going to show me the bedroom?" she asked, nibbling lightly on his lower lip.

Jake scooped her up in an instant, carrying her up the stairs like it was effortless—and to him, it probably was. His bed was on a loft sleeping platform above the living area: simple, but everything they needed. Mackenzie braced herself to tumble back on the mattress, but instead, he placed her gently on the sheets, like she was made of glass. Her breath caught as he stripped his T-shirt over his head, and she devoured the sight of him, there in the dim light. The smooth planes of his muscles, all that coiled power bound up in a body that was a testament to his years of training.

Mackenzie bit her lip to keep from sighing, and Jake's mouth curled into a devastating smile, like he could read her mind. He leaned in and kissed her slowly, sweet and smoldering, setting her blood on fire as tension coiled tighter, deep between her thighs.

Slowly, he tugged her sweater over her head, and then her camisole too. Piece by piece, kiss by kiss, he stripped her bare until she was naked and gasping for him.

This time, he took her slowly.

Easing her open, he rocked her with a steady pace that was somehow hotter than any wild, frantic lust. She came apart. Not her body—that was still climbing, tighter, craving release—but something else, a part of her she'd never known existed. He knew her, all of her, and when he claimed her mouth, kissing hard and aching, she couldn't hold anything back.

This man, God, this gorgeous, reckless, sweet, infuriating man . . . He'd had her heart since she was sixteen years old, and now he had her body too, a pleasure like no other, so deep and swift it took her breath away. She felt cut open, every last nerve and hope and dream exposed. It was too much, too much to look at him and risk baring her heart like this, so she clenched her eyes closed and held on for dear life, telling him with her body the words she could never risk saying out loud. Over and over, he surged into her, and Mackenzie arched right back, giving and demanding until she was drawn taut, right there on the edge.

"Don't stop."

The words were crying out in her mind so loud she almost didn't realize they came from Jake this time: a fevered murmur, over and over. "Don't stop," he whispered in her ear, holding her tightly, his body braced and panting. "Please, don't ever stop."

So she didn't. Mackenzie loved him the only way she could: with her mouth, and her hands, and the slick arch of her body, until there was nothing more to give. She took them over the edge together, and in that sweet, exquisite rush, she knew there was no going back.

She was his.

She'd always belonged to him.

18

*T*he next morning, Mackenzie was woken by the sound of footsteps moving around the room, even though the light was still dim before sunrise. She squinted through the shadows and made out Jake's figure, already dressed in workout gear, lacing up his sneakers.

"What time is it?" she murmured, yawning.

"Shh, go back to sleep." Jake smoothed her hair from her forehead and leaned in for a kiss.

"You're . . . exercising?" She took in his outfit. "But it's dark out."

"Just a little," Jake replied, zipping up an all-weather vest. "But the roads are still good."

"You're crazy." Mackenzie could barely move for tiredness. They'd barely slept all night. There were too many other things to do.

"Just getting back into the routine. Don't move, I'll be back in an hour or two."

"Masochist." Mackenzie sat up. "I guess I better get up too."

Jake looked guilty. "I didn't mean to wake you."

"No, it's fine. I promised my mom I'd go hang out today, and we have the toy drive this afternoon at the library."

Jake blinked. "Since when?"

Mackenzie laughed. "Didn't you sign up for the Starbright email alerts?"

"The what now?"

"ADD IT TO YOUR LIST," she said, yawning again. "Once you're done chiseling yourself into peak physical form."

"Why stop there?" Jake teased. "I'm aiming for perfection."

"Don't expect to brainwash me with all these fitness shenanigans," Mackenzie warned.

"I'd never dream of it."

Jake headed downstairs, and Mackenzie lay there a moment longer, cocooned in the warmth of the covers and the flush that still lingered from his touch. She almost wished it was a blizzard outside, instead of the light dusting; then, perhaps, they could hole up here for days. But she had a busy schedule ahead—one that she couldn't exactly deal with while wearing last night's clothes.

Their lazy weekend would just have to wait.

AFTER STOPPING BACK HOME to shower and change, Mackenzie made the drive down the Cape, across the bridge to the overgrown farm where her parents lived now—alongside twenty chickens, six goats, and a dozen alpacas. Thankfully, they'd waited until she left for art school before going full hippie and buying up their ramshackle plot. Her childhood had been zany enough without livestock wandering through the front room.

Now, she turned down the winding dirt road that led off the highway and bumped along towards the house. The snow was melting, and she could see her mom's figure in the distance, wearing a bright red parka as she scattered feed for the livestock. Mackenzie rolled down the window and slowed as she approached.

"Hi, love," her mom greeted her breathlessly. Linda's gray hair was peeking out from under her no-doubt-hand-knitted cap, the same spiral curls that Mackenzie had inherited.

"Hi, Mom. Want a ride back to the house?"

"I've got the chickens still to feed. You go ahead and put the kettle on. And tell your father to stop fussing with that circuit board of his," she added. "He's been tinkering with the thing for days. I swear, he thinks he's going to program the vacuum to take orders or something!"

"OK." Mackenzie smiled. "See you there."

She drove on another half mile and pulled in by the main farmhouse. Sure enough, she found her father inside, with the kitchen table covered in screws, wires, and tools.

"Hey, Dad." She kissed the top of his head as she passed. "Mom says to put that stuff away."

"Hey, pumpkin." Phillip Lane looked up, every inch the mad professor in his cable-knit sweater and spectacles. He paused. "Did you do something with your hair?"

"Six months ago," Mackenzie replied, filling the kettle at the sink. "You ask that every time I see you."

"Oh. Well, it looks lovely." He gave a sigh, then began to clear his things with obvious reluctance.

"How was the retreat?" she asked, remembering their Thanksgiving plans.

"You know." Her dad gave Mackenzie a smile. "A little bit woo-woo for my liking, but your mother enjoyed herself. A nice group of people, too," he added. "We had some nice conversations, and on the last night, there was a naked moon-dance ceremony—"

"I don't need to know!" Mackenzie cut him off quickly. "In

fact, take it as a rule that I don't need to know anything involving you and Mom and the word 'naked.'"

Her father chuckled. "I won't tell you about the Eighties, then."

"Please don't."

Mackenzie shook her head, smiling. They'd always been like this. Linda and Philip Lane marched to the beat of a different drummer—or, more often than not, a different drum circle. They'd met at a reiki retreat in the Catskills thirty years ago and bonded over transcendental meditation and their love of beat poetry before taking off in an RV together across the country for a few years. By the time Mackenzie was born, they'd settled down a little, at least—to a home on solid ground. But still, Mackenzie had to live with being uprooted and moved around every few years, starting over in another town with a new school before she'd ever gotten comfortable with the last. It was how she'd found herself the new girl in Sweetbriar at sixteen, the odd one out in a small class where everyone had known each other since birth. At least, until Jake had struck up conversation that day, and she didn't feel so odd anymore.

Linda came in the back door, stamping her muddy boots on the matt. "We're going to need more of that feed," she said, her cheeks red from the cold. "Stevie's looking pregnant again. I wouldn't be surprised if she was eating for two."

Stevie Nicks, one of the alpacas. Not to be confused with Joni Mitchell, the queen-bee goat, or Carly Simon, their grumpy tabby cat.

"Maybe give Julie a call at the vet's office," her dad suggested.

"Julie's on sabbatical, remember?" Linda replied. "It's that new kid they've got in to cover, he doesn't know a llama from an emu."

Mackenzie watched her mom strip off her coat and scarf and bustle around the kitchen—moving more of her father's bits and bobs aside, keeping up a running monologue about the leaky roof on the henhouse and their plans for the wool yield that spring.

Phillip got cups down and made the tea, the pair of them moving around each other in the cluttered space in a perfect, unconscious ballet.

Thirty years . . . Mackenzie knew it was a rarity, but it had never registered before just how special that kind of partnership was. She always took the fact of them for granted: partners in whatever harebrained new hobby they thought up next. But building a marriage that strong must have taken work: thousands of days that they chose to be together, facing the world as a team instead of alone, with kind words and support and a friendly smile at the end of the day.

She wanted a partner like that.

Mackenzie felt a wave of longing so swift and powerful it took her by surprise.

Where did that come from? She'd never been the one pining over love or relationships. Sure, her parade of bad dates over the years had been disheartening, but she hadn't been searching for some vision of happily-ever-after, not when she had so much going on in her life right now.

But if this was that happy ending—two people in a drafty kitchen who knew each other by heart, a refrigerator door covered with snapshots of their life together, and his-and-hers mugs sitting on the countertop—then Mackenzie wanted it all.

And she wanted it with Jake.

"Mac, honey?"

Mackenzie snapped back. Her mom was holding up the tea box. "Assam or Oolong? Or you could try my new rose-hip blend," she suggested eagerly. "I've added dandelion this time."

Behind her, Phillip shook his head frantically.

"Oolong is fine, thanks, Mom." Mackenzie smiled. Her mom was certain that her hand-blended herbal teas were the source of all her energy, but Mackenzie only knew them as a source of a bitter aftertaste. "Here, you sit down. I've got this."

She took over tea duty, and soon her dad was heading out to the garage—"Just for a moment"—and Mackenzie and her mother were left alone.

"So were you planning on telling us about your new boyfriend, or was I just supposed to wait for the engagement?" her mom asked, only half-teasing.

Mackenzie should have guessed news would travel this far, this soon. The Sweetbriar gossip tree could rival any command center.

"I heard it from three different people this morning," Linda added, looking put out. "You were the talk of the farmers' market. 'What's the news?' they all asked me, and I had to admit I didn't know a thing. Your own mother." She sniffed dramatically.

"Cut it out," Mackenzie said lightly. "You don't ask about my love life, remember? It's called having healthy boundaries."

"They said this one was serious." Linda searched her face. "But I would have thought you'd be happier if it was."

"It's . . . complicated." Mackenzie looked away. She took a sip of tea and promptly scalded her tongue. "It's Jake Sullivan."

"I heard that part," her mom said brightly. "You guys used to be friends, didn't you? I remember him clearing out the fridge every time he came around."

Mackenzie nodded. "He's back in town with an injury, but I don't know for how long."

"Oh." Her mom nodded. "Long distance can be tough."

"It's not like that. We're not even . . . We haven't said . . ." Mackenzie paused. "I don't know what we are. Maybe that's the problem."

"It isn't necessarily a bad thing," Linda pointed out, getting up to rummage in a cabinet. "I refused to marry your father for years. I didn't see why a piece of paper would change what we were to each other."

"That's different," Mackenzie said. "You always told me you

both said the first night you met that you were going to be together forever."

"Because we were eighteen and high as a kite on mushroom tea!" her mother laughed. "We still had plenty to work out. Like your father's girlfriend, for one."

"Mom!"

Linda smiled. "Oh, hush, honey. There's never a straight line through these things, and don't believe anyone who tells you otherwise. The only thing you need to ask yourself is, are you willing to make that journey?"

Mackenzie paused. Sure, it was dressed up in her mother's usual hippie language, but she had a point. Despite the history echoing in Mackenzie's chest when they were together, she and Jake had barely begun.

"Thanks," she said, "I think you're right."

Her mother looked startled. "Really? Phillip, get in here!" she called. "Mac just said I was right about something. I need witnesses!"

Mackenzie laughed. "Stop it!"

Her father appeared in the doorway, brandishing an old-fashioned tape recorder. "Say it again, sweetheart," he urged. "We should capture this one for the records."

"Both of you are ridiculous," Mackenzie informed them, still giggling.

"Unlucky for you, it's in your genes!"

MACKENZIE DROVE BACK to Sweetbriar and arrived at the library to find Eliza waiting on the steps, bundled up in a big parka jacket and scarf.

"The interview!" Mackenzie exclaimed, leaping out of the car. "Oh my God, I'm so sorry. It completely slipped my mind!"

"That's OK." Eliza greeted her with a hug. "I know you have

other things on your plate." Her eyebrows waggled suggestively. "So, what's the latest with Jake?"

Mackenzie laughed. "I saw you yesterday!"

"A lot can happen!" Eliza protested. "Whole lives can change in an instant. Twenty-four hours is tons of time."

Mackenzie smiled, leading her inside. Eliza was right. Her life had spun on a dime with just one kiss—that Halloween night in the gazebo upending Mackenzie's dangerously content world. "Well, there's nothing to report," she said lightly, glossing over that whole "artistic meltdown" part of the proceedings. "We hung out last night, that's all."

"I highly doubt that's all," Eliza teased, "but my editor says I need to work on not badgering people to death, so I'm going to let that one slide. For now, at least, until Jake gets back."

"He was here?" Mackenzie asked, surprised.

"Sure. He was hauling boxes all morning. I think he left to go get lunch," Eliza added. "He said something about finding a salad, but I figured he was just dizzy with dehydration."

Mackenzie was touched. "I didn't even ask him to help."

She pushed open the door and found the rec room was already stacked with boxes and trestle tables, set up into wrapping stations and gift selections, too.

"Wow," Eliza looked around at the stacks of toys. "Did you empty Santa's grotto or something? I thought the point of a toy drive was to get people to come donate."

"Jake and I went a little crazy buying up supplies," Mackenzie admitted with a smile. "Well, Jake did the buying—not that he'll take the credit."

"It's not his thing," Eliza agreed. "It's like all his charity work in Miami."

Mackenzie raised an eyebrow.

"You know, the Big Brother program, the team summer camps," Eliza explained. She must have seen Mackenzie's surprise because she laughed. "Try googling sometime. In fact, how are you not looking up your dates? It's literally the first thing I do. To check they don't have a criminal record, or post on Nickelback fan sites," she added. "You know, due dating diligence."

"OK, *that* we're definitely talking about later," Mackenzie warned her. "And no, I didn't know about his charity. He doesn't really talk much about the team, or anything from back in Miami." She paused. "I know the injury is tough on him," she said quietly. "So I'm trying not to push. I don't want to be the buzzkill always asking how he's doing."

Eliza gave her a sympathetic smile. "I'm sure he'll talk when he's ready. Or even if he has anything to say about it. From what I was reading, recovering from those kinds of injuries is pretty boring: just a long slog of training and rehab."

Mackenzie made a mental note to do her own research. Just because Jake wasn't opening up about it, it didn't mean she couldn't find out what he was dealing with and be supportive in whatever ways she could.

Eliza got out her cellphone and tapped a few buttons. "So, come on, O great organizer of all things Starbright, tell this intrepid reporter what you're doing here today."

Mackenzie began explaining about the toys they collected every year to donate to shelters and churches on the Cape. "Of course, everything in Sweetbriar has to be a party," she said, "so one year, I guess Debra decided to make the toy drive a big group effort. Now everyone comes to wrap gifts and write cards—and gossip, of course."

"Naturally." Eliza grinned.

The doors swung open and Jake came in, almost hidden behind a stack of pizza boxes.

"So much for the salad," Eliza joked as he deposited them on the snack table and unloaded a grocery bag of chips, too.

"This isn't for me. And hey, you." Jake turned to Mackenzie and kissed her lightly on the lips. "How are your parents?"

"A trip, as ever. They say hi," she added. They also said to invite Jake out to the farm for dinner soon, but since that would involve her mother's nut loaf casserole and the Spanish Inquisition, she was keeping that part to herself. "I can't believe you set up everything already. Thank you so much."

"It's no problem. According to my email account, it's the least I can do."

"Yeah, sorry about that." Mackenzie winced. "The town appreciation committee likes their news bulletins."

"Are you kidding me?" Jake asked, a teasing smile on his face. "Who wouldn't want to know the sleigh-ride schedule—and the amended schedule, and the debate over whether the amended schedule clashes with the town history tour? You should sign up," he said to Eliza. "You'll never have a quiet inbox again."

Eliza laughed. "Actually, that's tempting. My email is nothing but weight loss spam and takeout coupons right now. Because I'm such a loyal customer. I've started inventing company when the delivery guys arrive. You know, yelling 'food's here' into my empty apartment so they don't think all three boxes of pad thai are mine."

"Hey, if you ever need help getting through those orders, this is your girl." Jake pointed at Mackenzie.

"You can talk!" she protested. "Or are those double pepperonis going to eat themselves?"

"Those are for the party." Jake gave her a virtuous look. "I'm back on my training diet again. Power smoothies and lean protein, baby. All the way."

"Great." She made a show of sighing. "I guess I'll be the one eating ice cream at midnight alone."

"I guess I could make a few exceptions," Jake said, drawing her closer. He kissed her again, and Mackenzie let herself fall into the simple pleasure of it, until the sound of Eliza clearing her throat made her turn.

"Don't mind me."

"Whoops. Sorry." Mackenzie winced. Eliza waved it away.

"Please. If I had one of those, I'd never come up for air. No offense."

"None taken," Jake said cheerily. The doors swung open again, and people started arriving, toting bags full of toys and books, and reams of wrapping paper. "I guess the show's starting. Where do you want me?" he asked Mackenzie.

"Right here is fine."

Just a heartbeat away.

19

*W*ithin an hour, it seemed to Jake like half the town had descended on the toy drive, and soon the whole building was packed with noise and laughter. Someone brought a well-worn collection of swingin' holiday classics, someone else pitched in a CD player, and more volunteers showed up with snacks and drinks, until he couldn't move for festive cheer. Franny was testing out her eggnog recipe, and even Debra held court from a chair in the corner, her ankle propped up on a cushion with the cast covered in bright signatures.

"Not bad," Debra said, looking around approvingly. "I was worried you'd drop the ball on the planning, what with all your other distractions."

Jake didn't have to ask which particular distraction she meant; Mackenzie was over manning one of the wrapping stations, swathing toy baseball kits in sparkly wrapping paper, with tabs of tape stuck to the side of her face.

"Just trying to live up to your good example," Jake replied instead.

Debra snorted. "Would you believe I actually miss it?" she

asked. "I'm going stir-crazy waiting to get this damn cast off. I can't imagine how you must be feeling with your knee."

"I'm getting by," he said noncommittally. He was frustrated with his slow progress, too, but any progress at all was welcome after such a long time out of shape.

"So you'll be wanting to get back to the team, I expect?"

That was Debra for you, she didn't even try to disguise her loaded questions. Jake glanced over at Mackenzie again. "That's the plan."

"Still?"

Jake shot her a look. "As far as I know."

"Hmm." Debra didn't seem satisfied with that response, but it was the only one she was getting. For now, Jake was going to focus on what was right in front of him. Like four dozen gifts that were awaiting gift wrap, and a woman in need of kissing.

He joined Mackenzie at the table just as Riley and Brooke arrived with their own bags of toys, and a steaming jug of mulled wine.

"Look at you!" Brooke admired Mackenzie's handiwork. "Any time you want to come wrap wedding favors at the hotel, just give me a call."

Mackenzie shook her head. "Oh no, I know your Bridezillas. They'd set their bridesmaids after me if I folded the party favors wrong."

"I wish you were exaggerating." Brooke winced. "But we just had a wedding this weekend, and I swear, the bride had the whole day timed down to the minute. She cut off her father's toast with an alarm!"

Riley gave Jake an amused look over the women's heads. "So, how about them Yankees?"

Jake sucked in a breath. "You don't say that name in this town. We're all born dyed-in-the-wool Red Sox fans."

"My bad." Riley grinned. "And the Patriots? Or are you still loyal to the home team?"

"I haven't been watching recently," Jake admitted. "I tape every game, but I can't bring myself to turn it on. I second-guess everything. You know, the plays I'd make, the interceptions . . ."

"That's got to be rough," Riley agreed. "But it looks like you're on the mend. I saw you out running this morning. Looking good."

"We'll see." Jake found himself answering vaguely again. He understood why they were all asking, it was only out of friendly concern, but still, something in him bridled from the questions, a reflex from all the months he'd spent wondering if his reply would ever be good.

He was more optimistic now. Hell, the way his rehab was coming along, he was pretty damn hopeful. But that didn't mean he wanted to jinx it, not until the day he was back in uniform, throwing that perfect pass.

"What are you guys doing?" Mackenzie slipped under his arm and smiled up at them. "Don't tell me you're still scoring manly points talking about sports?"

"You can score a ribbon or two instead, you know," Brooke agreed. "We won't think any less of you."

"Scoring what now?" Riley looked confused.

The women laughed. "Maybe not."

They kept talking, about the hotel and the gallery and their big holiday plans. Jake took a mug of mulled wine and looked around the room. Mackenzie, his old friends, the town . . . He was hit with a sudden sense of belonging that took him by surprise.

This had always been his home, right here, and all the years away hadn't changed a thing.

Except Mackenzie.

She was laughing along to something Riley said, her expression bright. She saw him watching her, and gave him a cheeky smile.

He could see it in an instant, a lifetime spent just like this. Waking up to that smile and falling asleep to the steady sound of her heartbeat, with long days of laughter and easy conversation in between.

Jake looked away, shaken. What the hell was he thinking? He'd always known exactly what the future held: a full recovery and then a trip back south to take his rightful position on the team.

But where did Mackenzie fit into that plan?

"Yo, man, how's it going?"

Jake stumbled forwards as an unexpected slap came down hard on his shoulder. It was Moose, with a grin on his face and a slice of pizza in his other hand. "Don't worry, I'm not here to fight you."

Jake was still off balance from his thoughts, and he looked at Moose blankly.

"Over our girl, Mac." Moose winked. "No hard feelings, bro. All's fair in love and war."

"Uh, sure," Jake said. "Thanks."

"Anyway, I figured you two would get it together eventually," Moose continued, leaning past him to grab another slice of pizza from the table. He sandwiched the two slices together and took a bite. "I mean, everyone knew she was in love with you back then."

Jake shook his head. "No, we were just friends."

Moose snorted with laughter. "Sure, *you* were. But Mac was panting after you like a dog in heat. Isn't that right, babe?"

Jake turned. Mackenzie was standing right behind them, with the strangest expression on her face. "Hey," he said, relieved. "You're just in time, tell Moose he's full of crap. He's got some crazy idea you had a crush on me in high school."

Mackenzie blinked. For a split second, her face changed, then she laughed. "That is crazy," she said loudly. "Please. I had better taste—no offense."

Moose chortled along, but something made Jake keep

watching her. Her cheeks flushed, and she met his eye for a moment before quickly glancing away.

And just like that, he knew.

It was true.

Despite her laughter and deflection, Moose had somehow stumbled onto the truth that Jake had somehow been too blind to see.

She'd been in love with him?

All this time?

"So, what did you bring for the toy drive?" Mackenzie was asking Moose brightly, as Jake tried to reassess everything he thought he remembered about their friendship.

"We were supposed to bring something? Aww, sorry. I just thought it was a party."

Jake spoke up. "Why don't you pick something out from the pile and get it wrapped." He gave Moose a look, and for the first time in his life, the other man took a hint.

"Cool, see you guys." Moose strolled away, and they were left alone.

Jake drew Mackenzie aside, into a quiet corner. "It's true, isn't it?"

"What? No," she protested. "That's just Moose. The guy spent most of high school drunk or high. Or both."

"Mac . . ." Jake searched her face again, and Mackenzie's pretense finally slipped.

"Fine. It's true."

"But, you had that secret boyfriend." Jake thought back, reeling. "You were hooking up with him. Someone saw you guys on prom night."

"They saw *me*." Mackenzie exhaled, looking reluctant. "There was no other guy. I was going to tell you how I felt. Only, I heard you talking to your friends, about how you would never touch me. I had to climb out your bedroom window, and my dress got caught, and . . ." She gave a self-conscious shrug. "It was easier just to let everyone think the other story."

Jake tried to process the revelation. "So all that time, hanging out . . . I don't understand," he said, feeling like he just got hit by a truck. "You never said a thing."

Mackenzie looked away. "There was no point. I knew you didn't feel the same way."

Jake blinked. He'd always thought back to their friendship as some rock-solid thing, but now it was shifting, and he didn't even know how to begin to feel about it.

"It's not a big deal," Mackenzie said quickly. "Really. It was just a crush. You went off to college, and I moved on, too. I didn't even think twice about it until I saw you on Halloween, and then, well . . . Like I said, it's ancient history."

But this wasn't. Whatever was happening between them now was more real than ever, and somehow, knowing that Mackenzie's feelings had run so deep sent Jake's head spinning.

"Jake?" Mackenzie looked at him anxiously. "I'm sorry I didn't tell you before, but I didn't want to make it into some big thing." She paused. "Are we OK?"

"Sure, we're fine." Jake leaned in and dropped a kiss on her lips. But he wasn't. He felt a strange burn: tension, coiled in his muscles, needing to get out. "Are you OK finishing up here?" he asked Mackenzie.

"Why?" She blinked, looking uneasy. "Are you leaving? I told you, Moose is making this a much bigger deal than it really was."

"No, it's not that. I forgot to do my rehab exercises today," he lied, hating himself even as the excuse slipped effortlessly from his lips. "My physio said I shouldn't miss a day."

"Of course." Mackenzie reached up and kissed his cheek. "You go, take whatever time you need. There are plenty of people here to give me a hand."

"Thanks."

Jake felt like a traitor, slipping out early with the sound of the party still going strong behind him. He headed home to change into his workout gear, and then hit the road, jogging a steady loop out through the woods and along the outskirts of town.

He'd already run a couple of miles this morning at a punishing pace, and the doctor had warned him to take it slow, but Jake couldn't just sit around for the rest of the night, not with all these new questions spinning in his mind. Mackenzie, their history, and where the hell he was going to go from here.

It used to be so simple.

Train. Play. Let off some steam after the game, sure, but then start the whole cycle again come five a.m. Monday morning. The past ten years of his life were devoted to the same thing. Be better. Stronger. Faster. And damn, if he hadn't smashed those goals every time.

But what else did he have to show for it?

Jake picked up the pace, his footsteps slapping on the frozen sidewalks. It was easy to feel like a success down in Miami, where he and his teammates were treated like royalty at every bar and club in town. But here, where his sporting achievements were far away? It was harder to ignore the fact he'd built his entire life around the game—leaving barely any room for anything else.

Family. Community.

Love.

Looking back now, Jake felt like a fool not to have noticed Mackenzie's feelings. Sure, they were just kids, but there must have been signs.

But even if he had known, what difference would it have made?

None—then. But now?

Would he have been more careful with her feelings? Would he have stayed away, knowing the stakes were something real?

Maybe he should have, but if he was honest with himself, Jake knew, nothing could have kept him away. The connection between them had been undeniable, from that very first night. Everything they'd shared as teenagers only made that stronger: the trust and ease between them was the reason why the rest of it was so damn good.

He hadn't known it could be like this.

Jake stopped, breathing hard. He tried to block the thoughts whirling in his mind, and all these new questions that he was nowhere near ready to answer.

On a whim, he detoured via the old high school. It was closed, of course, after-hours, but he could see the lights of the football field still lit, and when he came closer, he saw Coach Wilson out beneath the goalposts, watching the gangly team throw drills. He was always a taskmaster, making them practice long hours after school.

Jake strolled over. "Hey."

Wilson turned and took in Jake's workout gear. "Docs gave you the all-clear, huh?"

"Just some gentle training," Jake said evasively. "So, this is your current crop?"

"For my sins." Coach looked back at the field, then let out a yell. "Pick those feet up, Kyle! Come on, keep the pace."

Jake cast an assessing eye over the kids on the field. There were some steady arms out there, a couple of solidly built guys too, who he knew would make the difference when it came to blocking interceptions. Then one of the guys fell back, further than the rest of them, all the way to the SOMETHING YARD LINE. He gestured for his partner to go long, then arched back his arm and threw a spiraling pass so far and swift that Jake whistled in admiration.

"Yeah, that's the kid I was telling you about," Coach said, following his gaze. "Billy Taylor. He's always been fast, but he got a growth spurt this year, shot up. Six-two now and counting."

"That's good." Jake nodded. Build mattered for the pros, and while you could bulk up in the gym, there was no creating those extra inches of height out of thin air. "How are his reflexes?"

"Could be better." Coach watched the field with eagle eyes. "But the kid's got no discipline. Some days, he brings it; others, he doesn't even try. Remind you of anyone?" he added.

Jake chuckled. "Give the kid a break. When you're seventeen, it all seems like a game."

"Well, this game could get him a free ride to college—if he buckles down and works for it. His family could use the break, too," Coach added. "A scholarship might be his only shot."

Jake watched the lanky teenager as Coach blew his whistle, breaking up the practice. The rest of the team jogged for the sidelines to retrieve their things and leave, but Billy stayed out there, collecting footballs and practicing his throw. One of the footballs came bouncing nearby, and Jake scooped it up, strolling out to meet him.

"Nice arm," he said by way of greeting. Billy was even skinnier up close, with a shock of blonde hair and a wary, cocky look.

"You're Jake Sullivan," he said, looking Jake up and down.

"That's right."

"My mom says you fumble too many interceptions."

Jake laughed. "Does she now? I'd like to see her hold on tight with five two-hundred-pound linebackers racing straight for her."

Billy grinned. "She supports the Packers, so what does she know?"

Jake rocked the ball from side to side. "Want to show me your moves?" he said, suddenly tossing it straight to Billy's face.

The kid's hands came up fast, stopping it a split second before it broke his nose. "Hey!" he protested, but Jake was already walking away.

"Try the YARD LINE," he called. "And get your elbow up, it'll help with the height."

Billy jogged down the field, into position. He wound up and threw long, the ball arcing in an elegant snap that made it easy for Jake to catch.

Jake was impressed. He returned the ball, and Billy sent it back again. Jake mixed up the next passes, making Billy run for it, testing his reflexes and hands.

The kid had talent. Raw, for sure, but his instincts were there.

He spiraled it hard and wide, and Billy missed the catch. He went to retrieve the ball, and when he sent it back, it was mimicking Jake's throw: mean, and wide. Jake broke into a sprint, closing the distance and plucking the ball out of the air, the way he had a thousand times before. He landed hard, weight on his right foot, and suddenly, pain jarred through his knee.

Jake gasped, bent double, and almost collapsed to the ground. It was white hot and shattering, and for a moment, the pain consumed him so much he could barely breathe.

Goddamnit.

"Hey, man." Billy jogged over. "Are you OK?"

Jake nodded, fighting to catch his breath. "I'm fine," he lied, even as the pain throbbed—that familiar agony he'd thought was behind him for good.

This wasn't happening. It couldn't, not after all his months of recovery.

Fear gripped him, and it took everything he had to force himself up. He took a cautious step.

The pain shattered him all over again.

"Let me go longer next time." Billy was still chatting eagerly. "I think I've got it down now."

"Next time," Jake said, gritting his teeth to keep from cursing out loud. "I need to call it a night. But good work."

"Thanks." Billy smiled at him. "I can really feel the difference, with my elbow."

Jake nodded wordlessly, limping for the sidelines. Every step was agony, but he didn't have a choice. What else was he going to do: fall to the ground in the middle of the frozen field and lay there for the rest of the night?

Next time, you won't be so lucky.

His doctor's words echoed in his mind. God, what had he just done?

"You want a ride?" Billy was eyeing him warily. "I've got my truck out front."

"Thanks," Jake ground out, and gave him the address. It wasn't until he was sitting in the cab with the weight off his knee that he could finally exhale. The memories came flooding back, all those agonizing hours recovering from surgery, the weeks he'd spent doing battle with the walker and cane.

Had he just pushed himself all the way back to square one again?

The fear turned thick and ice-cold, and he didn't even notice the drive until they pulled up outside the barn.

"When can we practice again?" Billy asked eagerly.

"I'll see." Jake tried not to be angry at him. It wasn't the kid's fault, after all. He was the one who'd had to catch that pass, to prove himself. For what? "Just focus on regular practice for now. Coach knows what he's talking about. You'd do worse than listen to him."

"Fine," Billy sighed, every inch the sullen teenager. "I guess I could give the old man a shot."

Jake carefully eased down out of the truck and was relieved to find he could manage a slow limp. The screaming pain had dimmed to a throb, and he found his footing again, slowly climbing the front porch to the door. Inside, he grabbed a couple of ice packs and slid to the floor, trying to keep panic at bay.

This was just a hiccup, he told himself. It had to be. Pain was the body's way of getting stronger, wasn't that what they always said?

Still, he couldn't keep his doubts from flooding his mind. Like, if he wasn't even ready to toss a ball around with an amateur, then how was he supposed to take on a pro game filled with brutal hits and guys who wouldn't think twice about taking him to the ground?

For the first time, it dawned that it wasn't just about him and getting his own game back in shape. There was a team out there: a board of moving pieces that could all work in perfect harmony—or send him crashing out on the wrong pass because someone sent him reaching too far, stopping too short, or landing on just the wrong angle.

He'd always been a fearless player, that was part of his strength. But trying to imagine himself out there, in the middle of a game, it made his chest clench with fear instead of hope.

One bad tackle. One wrong landing. That's all it would take to bring him down again. And if that happened . . . would he ever get up again?

Jake took a deep breath, trying to stay calm. For months now, his biggest fear had been that he might never make it onto the field again. But now, for the first time, another question loomed larger, just as terrifying.

What would happen *after* he got back out there?

20

*M*ackenzie didn't hear from Jake the next morning. She tried her best not to read anything into it. She'd been reliving Moose's unwelcome revelations all night, and still didn't feel any better about Jake's assurances everything was OK.

She deliberated texting, but forced herself to play it cool. He was probably out training, and besides, after playing hooky all weekend, she couldn't ignore the gallery—and all her customers—any more. December was always her busiest time of year, and from the moment she unlocked the door, she was flooded with a busy stream of browsers, all looking for that perfect holiday gift.

"I can't decide between the blue swirly ones or this snowflake pattern . . ." An exhausted-looking woman already laden down with bags held up the two dishes and frowned. "They're all so beautiful, and I still have so many other gifts to find!"

"Who are you shopping for?" Mackenzie asked.

"My mother." The woman sighed. "She hates everything I pick out for her. But not as much as my mother-in-law."

Mackenzie smiled. "How about you get the sugar bowl and

creamer sets for both of them?" she suggested, nimbly steering her over to the display in the corner. "I can wrap them up in a box with a teacup, too. Moms love it."

"You haven't met mine." The woman deliberated a moment longer. "What the hell. I'll take four sets. Aunt Carol and my nana can get one too."

"That's the spirit!"

Mackenzie ducked in back to find the pre-packed boxes. She was down to her last few already, and quickly scribbled a note to fire another two dozen this week. She was going to be working late nights at this rate, but she wasn't complaining. Bless the difficult mothers of the world and their love of simple tea sets!

"Here you go," she said, once everything was wrapped up safely and adorned with tasteful blue bows. "Happy holidays!"

"You too." The woman bustled out and was immediately replaced by three more, and she caught sight of a familiar face. "Ellie, hi." The younger woman was bundled up with her brunette hair tucked under a woolly beret. Her family ran the inn on the outskirts of town, and Ellie helped local businesses with their bookkeeping—Mackenzie included. She smiled at Ellie as she finished ringing up a sale. "I like the hat. Very French."

Ellie gave a wistful sigh. "It's about as close to Paris as I'm getting for a while. Anyway, things look good here?"

"Fingers crossed." Mackenzie smiled. "What can I help you with?"

"Aunt Maggie." Ellie glanced around. "I was thinking a salad bowl? Everyone loves a salad bowl."

"They love it even more when you call it an ice-cream bowl." Mackenzie plucked one down from the shelf in a shimmering blue.

"Love it. Love the fact I don't have to spend more than five minutes shopping even more. Things are crazy at the inn," Ellie added. "And I'm the only one holding down the fort."

"Ouch." Mackenzie gave her a sympathetic smile. "Good luck." She quickly wrapped the bowl and rang it up—with a friends and family discount. Then she spotted a new customer. "Ooh," she whispered. "I spy a lost-looking husband who had absolutely no idea what to buy. My favorite!"

Ellie laughed. "I won't stand in your way. See you soon!"

Mackenzie sidled over with a smile, and sure enough, by the time she was done, he was walking out with a full set of dinnerware, with extra salt-and-pepper shakers, and even some matching plant pots to boot.

"God, I love the holidays," she said, shutting the register with a *ding!* of satisfaction.

"I don't know whether to be proud or scared."

She looked up to find Jake in the doorway. "Hey!" Mackenzie couldn't deny the way her heart leapt, just a little, to see him standing there.

OK, a lot.

She leaned up for a quick kiss. "You're really slammed today, huh?" he said, looking around.

"It's not just me," she said, nodding to the busy town square outside. "The tour busses started running this week, 'Quintessential Cape,' and all the rest. They like to bring people down from the city for a day of shopping and local charm."

"Well, there's plenty of that here," he grinned, and Mackenzie laughed with pure relief.

They were OK.

"I can give charm for days, as long as they're buying," she quipped.

"That's my vicious saleswoman," Jake said affectionately. "I won't keep you. I just wanted to drop by and see how you were doing. Want to grab dinner later?"

"I'd love to, but it better be a late one. Eight-ish?"

"Works for me," Jake agreed with a smile.

"Everything's OK with you?" she checked, just to be sure.

"Sure," Jake said. "Fine."

She thought she saw a flicker of something on his face, but there wasn't time to ask about it, not with a busy line forming at the register. "See you at the pub?"

"Perfect." She quickly went back to work, and when she looked up again, Jake was already gone.

AFTER THAT, the flood of customers turned to a tidal wave, and by the time she closed the door that evening on the very last one and flipped her sign to "closed," Mackenzie was worn out.

Tired, and also elated at the empty spaces on all her shelves. She wanted nothing more than to go consume her body weight in fries and roll into bed—preferably with someone warm to snuggle up to —but there was work to be done. She closed out the register, then headed into the back to check her stock levels. Luckily, she'd been throwing extra pots and bowls all fall, and her shelves were full of the plain fired pots just waiting for a layer of glaze and their final turn in the kiln. She picked down a dozen pieces, and quickly set out her paints. The snowflake and blue styles had been selling best, so she mixed up the colors, and then efficiently smothered the pottery in their first layer. It would take a couple more to get the depth of color she really loved, but that could wait until morning.

Fries waited for no (wo)man.

She was just washing her hands when there was a tap on the door. Mackenzie went over, expecting to see Jake there, maybe with a hot cup of coffee if she was lucky, but instead, it was a slim, dark-haired woman dressed in a chic red coat.

Mackenzie opened the door. "I'm sorry, I'm closed," she said.

The woman's face fell. "No, really? I'm only in town tonight, and I so wanted to see your work."

She was English, with such a stylish air, it looked like she'd stepped off the cover of a magazine.

"I went to dinner at a friend's a few months ago," the woman added. "And fell completely in love with this darling fruit bowl of hers. It was nautical, with little sea monsters and drowning sailors all around the rim."

"Oh, that one." Mackenzie laughed, remembering the series. She'd been so sick of turning out Fourth-of-July-themed things for the tourists, she'd gone a little crazy. "There was a matching serving platter too, with ships getting wrecked on the rocks while the octopuses had their fun."

"I don't suppose you have anything like that in stock?" The woman peered past her hopefully.

"Not right now, no." Mackenzie took pity on her. "But come on in, and I'll take your details, if you want. I work on private commissions sometimes, and have a mailing list for my new collections."

She stood aside, and the woman followed her in. "Thank you so much," she said. "I'm Vivian, by the way."

"Mackenzie." She went to the desk and found a spare scrap of paper and a pen. "Here, just write it all down, and I'll put you in the system."

Vivian pulled a heavy silver pen from her purse and started writing in elegant cursive. "Let me know if you do anything like it again. I loved the dark whimsy, so charming."

Suddenly, Mackenzie remembered something. "You know, I might have something for you. I started doing a series like the sailors, but inspired by Greek myths. You know, Icarus burning to death and all that."

Vivian lit up. "That sounds darling."

Mackenzie would have said "disturbing," but she wasn't about to stand in the way of a potential sale. "I have a couple of the pieces in the back," she said. "If you wanted to make an order, I could finish the set for you."

She showed Vivian into the studio, and searched on her cluttered shelves. "Hmm . . . Oh, there they are." She went up on her tiptoes, fetching down the plates. They were dusty from sitting in the corner too long, and she gave them a surreptitious blow to clean them off. "Is this the kind of thing you were talking about?" She turned, the plates in her hands.

Vivian was looking at her sculptures.

Mackenzie took a deep breath and tried not to freak out. Jake hadn't run screaming from them, and she was an artist, remember? Artists should be able to stomach people looking at their work without wanting the earth to open and swallow them whole. "That's just something I'm working on for fun," she said, blushing. "I'm not . . . I mean, I'm not trying to sell them or anything."

"No?" Vivian arched an eyebrow. "They're very interesting pieces. Yes," she said, narrowing her eyes thoughtfully. "Very interesting."

"Oh."

Mackenzie blinked. Interesting-good, or interesting-waste-of-space?

Vivian seemed to come to a decision, because she reached into her designer clutch purse and pulled out a card. "I have a gallery in New York," she said. "There's a show coming up in the spring, a small collection of exciting new voices. I could use some sculptural impact."

Mackenzie took the card slowly. Was Vivian saying what she thought she was?

"When they're finished, send me the pictures," Vivian added. "I think they would work in the show."

"I . . . Umm, I mean, sure!" Mackenzie blurted in shock. For probably the first time in her life, she was speechless.

Exhibit her sculptures in a gallery? As in, a real art show?

She was still silent in stunned disbelief as she followed Vivian back out to the front of the store. "Let me know about the dinnerware," Vivian said, "and the show, of course. Lovely to meet you."

She disappeared back onto the street, leaving the doorbell tinkering behind her.

Mackenzie stared at the card in her hand.

Vivian Blythe, The 8th St Gallery.

Did that really just happen?

Mackenzie locked up and practically sprinted across the square. She found Jake by the bar at the pub and threw her arms around his neck. "You won't believe what just happened!" she exclaimed, and quickly filled him in with Vivian's unexpected offer.

"That's amazing!" Jake grinned, hugging her tightly. "And totally well deserved."

"I don't know," Mackenzie said, coming back down to earth. "She only got a glimpse of them, and the pieces aren't even finished. The final series might not be what she's looking for, and—"

"Stop." Jake silenced her with a kiss. "Don't talk yourself out of this. Just enjoy it."

Mackenzie exhaled. "OK." She smiled. "I will. What about you?" She perched up on a stool and smiled at him, at eye level this time. "How has your day been? Let me guess, training hard?"

"Sure. You know, the usual . . ." Jake looked around and gestured Riley over. "How about some celebration fries?" he suggested.

"And burgers," Mackenzie agreed. "Oh, wait, I'm supposed to be supportive of your new fitness routine, aren't I?" She looked at the menu for the first time. "I mean, I guess we could get salads?"

Riley whistled. "I never thought I'd hear the words."

"Don't bother," Jake said. His voice had an edge, and

Mackenzie turned. "I mean, get whatever you want," he added. "We're celebrating, remember?"

Mackenzie beamed. "Thank God. I was worried I'd have to chew through a bowl of rabbit food. No offense," she said to Riley. "I'm sure your salads are delicious."

He grinned. "None taken. Extra cheese?"

"Always."

THEY TOOK a table by the fireplace to eat, and Mackenzie chattered happily about her day, and the long, long lines at the gallery. "It's only going to get busier this month," she said with satisfaction. "Especially now there are only a few days to go."

"Until what?" Jake asked.

"The festival!"

"Oh. Right. That." Jake picked at his food, and Mackenzie paused. He'd barely touched his burger, and had been quieter than usual all night. He'd even lost a game of pool without comment, which for Jake, was unheard of.

"Is everything OK?" she asked quietly.

"Of course." He gave her a smile. "Why wouldn't it be?"

"No reason. You just seem, distracted, that's all."

"I'm just a little tired, that's all," Jake said, then tugged her closer, so he could murmur in her ear. "Plus, I'm thinking about all the things we can do when I take you home."

Mackenzie's breath caught. "Oh really?" she said softly. "Well, you better get started showing me." She got to her feet and reached for her coat.

"You haven't finished your fries," Jake said with a lazy grin.

"I know. Priorities," she winked, and Jake chuckled out loud.

"If that isn't the greatest compliment you could give a man, I don't know what is."

He followed her to the door and outside to where he'd parked on the street. There was something different, though, and it took Mackenzie a moment to realize he was moving slower than usual, cautious on the sidewalk. She opened her mouth to ask if his knee was OK, then stopped. Jake was probably sick of people asking about it, and if he wanted to talk to her, he would. So, she bit back her concern and talked about the festival plans instead, and the thousand candles she'd ordered for the closing carol concert.

They arrived at her place, and she unlocked the door. "So, about those things you were planning . . ." she said, drawing him inside with a kiss. Jake's mouth was hot on hers, and she shivered with anticipation, letting her coat slip to the floor as they stumbled backwards, hands cool and searching.

Jake wrapped his arms around her, kissing with a hunger that thrilled her. She responded instantly, leaning into him, locking her arms around his neck and shifting her weight—

Jake winced, and immediately, Mackenzie stepped back. "What is it?"

"Nothing."

He reached for her again, but she could see it on his face, and when he leaned in, she could tell he was keeping his weight shifted to one side.

"Jake," she finally said, unable to keep it bottled up any longer. "You don't have to lie to me. It's your knee, isn't it? You've been trying to protect it all night."

Jake clenched his jaw. "Great. So it's obvious."

"No," she said gently, "I just know you, that's all."

Jake turned away, and for a moment, she was worried he was leaving. Instead, he stripped off his coat and then cautiously walked over to the couch. He sank down with a sigh.

"I messed it up again."

Mackenzie's heart ached to see the pain on his face. "Oh no, how?" She went to him and curled up beside him on the couch. "What happened?"

"It doesn't matter," Jake said angrily. He sat forward, fists clenched with frustration. "None of it matters now. If I can't even do the most basic things without setting it off, how the hell am I supposed to play again?"

"Don't say that," Mackenzie urged him. "With time, and healing—"

"Stop." Jake cut her off harshly. Then he exhaled. "Look, I know you're just trying to be supportive, but I can't deal with anymore platitudes, OK?" His expression was desperate. "I've heard it all before, how these things take time, and how the body has its own pace, but none of that means a damn thing if I can't play again."

Mackenzie took a breath. She couldn't imagine what he was going through. Because it wasn't just about the pain in his knee right now, it was the end of his career: all those dreams he'd spent his life working for. All that training, day in and day out. It was all slipping away from him, and the only thing she could do was watch.

"So what would help?" Mackenzie asked simply. "What do you need from me?"

Jake shook his head. "I don't know," he said. "I don't know if anything's going to help me now." His voice caught, raw with emotion, and his face crumpled, like he couldn't keep it together a single moment more.

"Shhh . . ." Mackenzie drew him to her. She rested his head against her chest, and just held him, feeling the tension and terrible fear in his body, and wishing like nothing else that she could take it all away. "It's going to be OK," she whispered, stroking his hair. "We'll figure it out. I promise, we'll find a way."

Jake held her tightly, taking ragged, gasping breaths as he fought the tears. Mackenzie didn't move, she just held him in the quiet of the dim room until finally, Jake's body seemed to relax.

He slowly sat up. "I'm sorry," he said, looking away, clearly embarrassed.

"Don't be. I'm here." Mackenzie took his hand. "Is there anything you can do, for your knee, I mean?"

He shrugged. "I made an appointment with my doctor for tomorrow. She'll take some more scans, and see if I completely fucked it up."

Mackenzie squeezed his hand. "What time should we leave?"

He looked surprised. "You don't have to come."

"I know. I want to," Mackenzie said firmly.

"But the gallery . . ." Jake frowned. "You said it yourself, this is your busiest time of year."

"The gallery will survive," she reassured him. "I'll get someone to cover for me. You don't have to do this alone."

He looked like he wanted to argue again, but then slowly, he gave a nod.

"Thank you."

It was almost a whisper, but she knew, it couldn't have been easy for him—acknowledging that something was wrong enough to need the support.

"We'll figure this out," she said again, praying that the answers from the doctor would be good ones. "Whatever happens, I'm here."

---

21

*J*ake tapped his good foot impatiently, staring at the pale Boston skyline just outside the windows. They were back in the city, and it was snowing again, but romance was the last thing on his mind. He'd spent the morning getting fresh scans on his knee, and now they were just waiting on the results: sitting out in the quiet waiting room, ignoring the magazines on the table as every hour stretched into an eternity.

The wait was killing him. He'd been here before, too many times. Waiting on tests, and news, and the latest doctor's report. He'd thought he was finally past it, but here he was, all over again.

Mackenzie's hand came down gently on his thigh. "It won't be much longer," she said, giving him an encouraging smile.

Jake didn't reply. He'd been so wrapped up in his own thoughts, he'd almost forgotten she was there. He gave her a guilty nod instead. "You want a coffee or something?" he asked, getting up. "They have a cafeteria downstairs—"

"I can go." Mackenzie bobbed up. "You stay here. Sit."

"I can walk, you know," Jake told her, trying not to get

annoyed. He could catch her anxious glances out of the corner of his eye, checking if he needed help.

That wasn't how he wanted her to look at him.

"I know." Mackenzie's reply was steady. "But I don't want you to miss the doctor when they're ready with your scans."

"Oh. OK." Jake sat again and watched Mackenzie head down the hallway. She exchanged a few words and smiles with a nurse by the elevator, then disappeared out of sight.

He was being an ass. He knew that, but somehow, he couldn't stop his fears and insecurities boiling over in her direction, which only made him feel guilty, as well as scared. He'd thought it would be easier with Mackenzie there by his side, but now, he just wondered what she was thinking, having to spend her day playing babysitter to an ungrateful ass like him. He hated that she'd seen him fall apart like that last night, and although he'd found something close to solace in her arms, now he was staring down his future again, and he knew the outlook wasn't good.

"Jake, there you are." Padma joined him with a file under her arm, just as Mackenzie reappeared. He introduced them, and then Padma said, "Why don't you come into my office?"

Jake started to follow her before he realized Mackenzie was waiting behind. He stopped, and held out his hand to her.

Are you sure? her expression seemed to ask.

He nodded, and Mackenzie quickly fell into step beside him, her hand tucked snugly in his own. Jake couldn't explain it, but he still felt that pull to have her near, even in the worst of times.

Inside Padma's office, they sat, and Jake braced himself.

"I've taken a look at the scans," she began. "You took a nasty shock to the tendons. What were you doing?"

Jake guiltily cleared his throat. "Just tossing the ball around," he said, and Padma fixed him with a look.

"Well, I'm afraid there'll be no more of that. Not unless you want to do more permanent damage."

He felt Mackenzie gasp at the words, but he couldn't feel a thing. He watched, as if from far away, as Padma kept talking them through the end of his career.

"We were able to visualize the injury clearly, here and here." She pointed to the scans. "The tendons were torn away from the cartilage again. You were very lucky not to sever them completely. You won't need surgery, but I'm afraid it's put the recovery back another five, ten months maybe. I'd imagine you're in a fair amount of pain just walking, so it's going to be a long road back. You know the drill," she added. "Rehab, healing, and no stress on that knee of any kind."

Mackenzie leaned forward, looking stricken. "So he can't play?"

"No," Padma said firmly. "No more high-stress activity of any kind. You were lucky this time, but that's all it was: sheer luck. The connective tissue hardly ever survives a tear the first time around, let alone second. There won't be a third. Next time you push it, the reconstructive surgery might not even work again." She took a breath and softened. "I know this must be difficult, Jake, but it's like I've been telling you: your body can only take so much. If this had happened on the field, during a real game . . . you wouldn't have been walking into my office today, I can tell you that."

"So I should be grateful?" Jake's reply came, angry, before he could check himself.

Padma didn't flinch. "Yes. You should be." She stared back, empathetic but firm. "Grateful that you even have an option for recovery. I've seen guys in your place just starting out, twenty-two, twenty-three, they'll never step foot on a football field again in their lives. You at least had a long career behind you."

"And that's supposed to be a consolation?" He couldn't believe this.

"I'm not going to sugarcoat it for you, Jake, because I know this is the last thing you want to hear. But you *need* to hear it." Padma's voice remained steady, even as she spoke his death sentence. "This is the only strike you get. Next time you ignore your doctors, it won't be such an optimistic result."

Optimistic.

Jake stared at her numbly. This was the end of his whole career, and she was talking like he should be relieved.

His blood roared in his ears, and he had to grip the arms of his chair to keep steady.

"What about if I follow your rehab instructions to the letter this time?" he started, feeling a desperate panic in his chest. "I go slow and take things step by step, the way you want. Maybe in six months, or a year, I could try playing—"

"I'm sorry, Jake." Padma cut him off. She shook her head sadly, and to his horror, he saw pity in her eyes. "This shows us exactly what will happen if you try again. Your football career is over now, and your focus needs to be on a steady recovery now. Slow and managed. With time, and work, you'll be able to get a full range of motion, and live your regular life. But there's no chance of playing at a professional level. I'm afraid that's out of the question now."

He sank back in the chair, the words swimming in his mind. He barely noticed as Padma wrapped things up and gave him his new rehab schedule. She chatted with Mackenzie, showing them to the door, and then he was back in the hallway again, except this time, everything was different.

It was over now.

No distant chances, no planning, no determination to prove them all wrong and heal better than ever. The doctor had been clear, there was no way back this time.

No hope left for him at all.

They were out on the street again before Mackenzie finally spoke. "I'm so sorry, Jake. I can't imagine what you must be feeling right now."

Traffic hurtled past, the street wet with melting snow, but Jake didn't register a thing.

Your football career is over now.

"What do you want to do now?" Mackenzie continued. "We could drive straight back, or go somewhere . . . Talk . . . Whatever you need."

What he needed was to turn the clock back a year and sidestep that Falcons linebacker. Skip the play, or make the pass a fraction of a second sooner. What-ifs spun suddenly in his mind, and he felt every last one like a punch to the gut. But there was no going back now. No changing one damn thing. That chapter of his life was over, maybe it had been all along, and he was only just realizing it now: the last fool in the room.

"Jake?" Mackenzie's voice came again. She was still standing there on the sidewalk, looking at him with the same expression Padma had inside.

Pity.

He recoiled from it, hating the worry in her eyes. "I need to take a walk," he said abruptly. "I need . . . to think."

"Of course," Mackenzie said quickly. "We can meet back later, just call me when you're ready to go home."

Home.

The word echoed with him as he turned down the street alone. Sweetbriar hadn't been his home in a decade. He still had an apartment in Miami, filled with all his stuff. A doorman holding packages, a phone full of buddies and dates.

Buddies he hadn't heard from in months now.

Dates who wanted the thrill of walking in on the arm of a pro player, not some washed up invalid who'd never score another touchdown again.

198

He tried his best not to give in to the bitterness. Maybe the doctor was right, and he was lucky, but it didn't feel like good fortune to be limping down the street with the dull echo of pain jolting every step. But it wasn't the pain that mattered, he'd endured worse. No, the part that cut him open was knowing his days on the field were over for good.

Jake walked in a numb daze. It didn't feel real. He'd been in denial for so long, ignoring all the words of caution, but now it was hitting him all at once. He was done. Game over. This past year had been bad enough, feeling sidelined and far away from his team, but now he would never get to go back.

Where did he belong now?

The dull pain rang out sharper, and he looked around for a bench. He would have appreciated the irony if it didn't cut him so damn deep. He'd pushed his body to the limit for too long, and now it was pushing back.

He looked around. He'd been here before, after his last appointment. Jake looked around, recognizing the curve of the bridge and the icy river-walk. It felt so long ago, but it had only been a month or so—before his own foolish mistakes had wrecked any chance at recovery for good.

Before Mackenzie.

Jake shook away the memory of her concern, the care in those wide eyes. He couldn't think about her now, not with anger and frustration boiling harshly and the sick lurch of defeat like an iron in his chest.

God, he'd been so naïve, planning his return to form, like all it would take was a few extra miles on his run and some time to knit those tendons back together again. He wanted to run, hard, pounding the asphalt along the icy river until his lungs screamed for air, but he knew he would fall down in agony before he'd even taken ten steps.

What was left now?

Jake had been avoiding the question ever since that first, brutal hit. But there was no avoiding it anymore. The future lay in front of him, as cold as the icy river, and for the first time in his life, he didn't know where to turn. He missed his friends, his teammates, and that sense of belonging that came every practice and game day, no matter what. When he stepped out on that field, he'd always felt like he was exactly where he was supposed to be. He'd never felt anything even close to that, nothing except . . .

Her.

Jake remembered Mackenzie's embrace last night, holding him so tightly and promising that everything would be OK. For a few hours, at least, he'd believed her.

But how long would that patience last? How long until she realized he had nothing to offer her now, not even the promise of a future back on top?

He couldn't let that pity linger in her eyes; it would kill him, if the failure didn't first. She deserved so much more from him. He needed a game plan, and he needed one fast.

Jake got out his phone and dialed.

~

MACKENZIE TRIED NOT to watch her phone, but she couldn't focus on anything else. She browsed some stores downtown, trying to distract herself, but in the end, she gave up on trying to wait Jake out. She needed help, and when she found herself a couple of blocks from Eliza's newspaper office, she took it as a sign. She bought coffees from the cart in the lobby and then called up.

"I'm downstairs," she said, paying the vendor. "And I have caffeine."

"Come on up!"

She took the elevator up to Eliza's floor, and then navigated her way through a rabbit warren of cubicles to a dim spot in the corner, where her friend was squinting at a computer screen. "Sorry to just show up like this," she said, setting the coffees down. Eliza leaned up from her computer and gave her a quick hug.

"Are you kidding? You're always a welcome distraction. Just let me finish this email . . ."

Mackenzie looked around as Eliza typed. She'd always thought newsrooms were bustling, busy places, but this one was half-empty, with a grim, quiet air.

"OK, done!" Eliza spun her chair to face her and grabbed one of the coffees. She gulped happily. "God, I needed this. I have five million more things to do before lunch."

"What's with all the sad faces?" Mackenzie asked. "Did someone die?"

"Just the independent press," Eliza sighed. "They announced a takeover yesterday. We got bought out by some trust fund kid who wants to play media mogul. Now everyone's braced for layoffs."

"Ouch, I'm sorry."

Eliza shrugged. "What are you going to do? I've been polishing my resume, and sending 'remember me?' emails to every editor around. Finger's crossed I don't wind up unemployed and living back at my mother's. Again."

"Hey, if the worst happens, you can always come crash on my couch."

"Don't tease," Eliza warned with a grin. "I might very well have to take you up on that. Except, three's a crowd. I wouldn't want to get in the way of your 24/7 sexy party."

Mackenzie sighed.

"Uh oh." Eliza's eyes widened. "That can't be good."

Mackenzie bit her lip. "I just came from the hospital, with Jake.

He injured his knee again, it's bad. The doctor says he won't play again."

"Oh no," Eliza said, sympathetic. "How's he taking it?"

"How do you think?" Mackenzie gave her a rueful look. "I just feel so useless. I know this is a lot for him to handle, and there's nothing I can say."

"Just be there for him, I'm sure that's all he wants."

"I don't know if he even wants me around for that," Mackenzie said, remembering how fast Jake had bolted after the hospital. "Maybe he just needs some time . . . but I can already feel like he's pulling away from me."

"Men." Eliza tsked. "Nothing like a little emotion to make them shut down completely."

"Hey, Jake isn't like that," Mackenzie protested.

"No, you're right." Eliza smiled. "That's just the Neanderthals I've been dating. I'm sure Jake will figure it out."

Mackenzie nodded, hoping she was right. "He's probably just in shock right now. With a little time, he'll figure it out."

"Sure he will," Eliza said brightly. "And anyways, it's the holidays soon. That will help distract him, all the fun Starbright events."

"Maybe." Mackenzie perked up a little. "And if all else fails, we can just get him drunk on Franny's spiced apple cider."

"Is it lethal?" Eliza asked.

"That's right," Mackenzie realized. "This is going to be your first Sweetbriar Christmas. How is that possible?"

"We only ever spent the summers there," Eliza shrugged. "And you know I run away from town spirit."

"You say that now, but we'll get you in the end," Mackenzie teased. "There's a spot on the town beautification committee with your name on it."

"Never!" Eliza joked, but her smile wavered. "To tell the truth,

I'm kind of dreading it. The holidays," she explained. "It's the first one since my dad passed."

Mackenzie inhaled. "I'm so sorry, I didn't think." Eliza's father had passed away back in spring, before they'd even met. She didn't talk about it much, but of course, with the holiday coming, it would bring her loss into focus again.

Eliza gave her a rueful look. "It's OK. Maybe it's a good thing, having all this Starbright stuff to distract me. I'll see if my mom and Paige want to come, too. Start a new tradition." She shook her head, as if putting the thought aside. "Anyway, this is about you and Jake. How long has he been off wandering?"

Mackenzie couldn't help checking her phone again. "A couple of hours now," she answered. "I should call him," she said, feeling uneasy. "I know he wanted space, but I should at least check in and see what his plans are."

"Good luck." Eliza gave her a sympathetic smile. "I should get back to work—while I still have a job."

Mackenzie gave her a hug goodbye and headed back to the lobby. She dialed Jake with trepidation, and was relieved when he answered on the second ring. "Hi," she said cautiously, "how are you doing?"

"Great!" Jake's answer was muffled by a sudden burst of music and conversation. "You should . . . Downtown . . . For six."

"Sorry, I can't hear you." Mackenzie covered her ear to try and make out what he was saying.

"I'll text you," Jake said, still hard to hear. "Come over and meet everyone!"

He hung up, and Mackenzie slowly lowered the phone. He sounded upbeat, which was something, at least. Her phone vibrated, and then there was a text with a single word.

Deluxe.

Mackenzie quickly searched for it online. It was a restaurant over near Boylston, too far to walk, so she hailed a cab outside and drove over. It was a trendy spot on a street full of expensive boutiques, and as soon as she stepped inside, a hostess moved to block her path

"Yes?" The woman looked her up and down. "Do you have a reservation?"

"I'm meeting someone." Mackenzie tried not to feel out of place. She'd dressed for comfort that day, in jeans and a sweater, but every other diner looked like they were out for a fancy meal. "Jake Sullivan? He should be . . ." She caught sight of him across the room, in a booth with a group of people. "Oh, he's right there." She pointed, and the hostess gave her a skeptical look.

"I'll go check."

Her voice was dripping with skepticism. Mackenzie blinked. "Really, I'm not some stalker fan."

"Wait here."

Mackenzie sighed, impatiently watching as the woman crossed the room and leaned in to speak to Jake. He looked around, and saw her, then leapt up, waving her over.

Mackenzie gave the hostess a triumphant smile and went to meet him. "Hey! What is this place? I thought they were going to frisk me at the door."

"Isn't it great?" Jake replied with a wide grin, before turning to the booth. "Mackenzie, this is JD, and Mickey and Bob and Rich."

"Umm, hi." Mackenzie gave an awkward wave. Two of the guys were built like Jake—broad-shouldered and clearly athletes— while the other two were dressed in casual designer suits, with expensive haircuts and watches to match. They were spilling out of the booth, the table covered in plates of food.

"Great to meet you." One of the men—Bob, maybe?—enthusi- astically shook her hand. "Here, you can squeeze in next to me."

Mackenzie looked to Jake, confused by this 180-degree change in mood, but he was ordering champagne from the server. "Are we celebrating?" she asked. She wasn't sure what to make of his broad smiles and laughter, not after the bad news this morning.

"We sure are," Bob grinned. "Our boy Jake here has finally decided to come on board and join us on the sidelines. You're looking at the newest member of the ESPN sportscasting team."

"Straight to the West Coast, baby!" one of the other athletes whooped. "All the way to the top."

22

*M*ackenzie looked around the table, wondering if she'd heard them wrong, but the men kept talking, happily congratulating Jake on his new job.

His new job in Los Angeles.

Her heart clenched.

"I didn't know you were thinking about broadcasting," she said quietly, meeting Jake's eyes across the table.

He glanced away. "Well, you know, it's always an option for retired players."

"A great option," Bob butted in. "Let me tell you, Jake here drives a hard bargain."

"But he's worth every penny," Rich agreed, smiling widely.

The champagne arrived, and Bob uncorked it with a cheer. Jake smiled and toasted, laughing along with all their big plans, and all the while, Mackenzie sat there, her heart sinking lower by the second.

Los Angeles. Two and a half thousand miles away, give or take a few. She knew they hadn't talked about their future, there hadn't been the right moment, but Mackenzie had thought he would be in the same time zone, at least.

Instead, he was heading right back across the country again—back to his old life, the game, as if the past few months had never even happened.

Like she didn't matter at all.

She was horrified to feel tears stinging, bitter in the back of her throat. "Excuse me," she said, struggling to slip out of the booth again. "I'll be right back."

Jake didn't seem to notice as she fled for the bathroom, finding a cool expanse of mirror and tile. Mackenzie ran the cold water over her wrists and then sank against the countertop, her head still spinning.

He was leaving.

Of course, he was leaving all over again.

What had made her think it was any different this time?

Except, it *was* different. Back then, they'd been kids. As much as she'd pined for him, it wasn't anything real. He'd had no idea how she felt, and even if he did, she would never in a million years have expected to change their future plans for each other.

But now?

Now, she knew the taste of his kisses, and the way his face changed when she took him over the edge. Now, they'd whispered through the night and woken curled in each other's arms when morning came.

Now she loved him, with all her heart.

And he was leaving her.

Mackenzie gasped for air, trying so hard to hold back the tears, but she couldn't stop them from silently running down her cheeks.

She'd through this was real, that he felt something for her, more than just a passing distraction. From the moment he'd kissed her that night in the gazebo, she'd tried so hard to play it safe, but she couldn't help it. Then, and now, Jake Sullivan was the only one she'd ever wanted.

The only man to see her, really see her for everything that she was. Encourage her, and laugh with her, good days and bad.

And love her, the way she always dreamed.

Except, he hadn't. Not really. Mackenzie thought back over the past months with a sickening sense of dread. What had he said, really? No promises, that was for sure; no sweet talk of the future, or plans for them to keep in mind. He'd taken her to bed in a whirl of passion and pleasure, but he'd never sworn to be there in the morning, now, or in the days to come.

She'd fallen for him so fast, she hadn't stopped to realize that he was standing still in place, as far out of reach as he'd ever been.

The door swung open, and a couple of women entered in a clatter of high heels and chatter. Mackenzie turned away, hiding her face until they'd touched up their lipstick and gossiped about their lunch dates, and strutted back out into the restaurant.

She sucked in a desperate breath, and then another. She had to pull it together, until she was back in Sweetbriar Cove, at least. Then, maybe, she could collapse into the aching tears that gripped her chest, but for now, she still had to make it through the rest of lunch.

She could do this. It was just Jake.

Her Jake.

Mackenzie took a quick look in the mirror, swiping away the smear of mascara under her eyes. She fixed a smile on her face and forced herself back out of the door and over to their table. The group had swelled now: two more athletes, and a couple of shiny-haired girlfriends, spilling out of the booth and onto an adjoining table. Jake was the center of attention, and it was clear how much he was enjoying it: leaning back with a broad smile on his face, laughing right along with everyone.

He looked like his old self again, and despite everything,

Mackenzie was glad. He deserved this, another chance to be happy again in his old world, and even though it cut straight through her to see she wasn't a part of the equation, she knew anything was better than seeing him in pain.

"Hey babe," Jake beckoned to her, making space beside him. "Do you want something to eat? We've got everything here. Or I can order for you?"

"No, it's fine." Mackenzie tried to smile. "I'm not hungry."

"Then have a drink." He thrust a champagne flute at her, as everyone at the table raised their glasses in another toast.

"To Jake!" Bob declared.

"LA, all the way!"

LUNCH LASTED HALF THE AFTERNOON, and somehow, Mackenzie managed to keep smiling the whole time, even as her heart was slowly breaking. At last, Bob and Rich called for the check, and they all clustered out on the street, flagging down cabs and saying their goodbyes.

"See you soon, man." The guys slapped Jake's back, and he grinned.

"Can't wait."

Mackenzie slid into the back of a cab and directed him to the hospital, where they'd left Jake's car. It felt like a lifetime ago, but it was only a few hours. Was it really just this morning she'd woken in his arms and felt like they could face anything —together?

Jake climbed in beside her. "Great guys, huh?" he said, already scrolling through his phone. "Apparently, I'm going to need all kinds of social media accounts, they like their on-air talent to have a profile, you know? And I talked to my agent, he says I might not even lose my endorsements, not if I get enough screen time."

"Is that what you want?" Mackenzie asked, as the city streets blurred outside the windows. "To be on TV?"

"I mean, it wasn't the plan, but you heard what they said, I can be right there for all the big games, doing locker-room interviews. It'll be like I never left."

Jake was amped up, his excitement clear. Her heart beat a slow, broken beat.

"So when do you leave?"

He didn't notice the ache in her voice. "Soon. The network wants me out there next week for screen tests and contracts, you know. If things go well, I could even be doing the Super Bowl coverage. Giving DeJay a run for his money," he grinned, and Mackenzie swallowed back her pain.

"That's great."

Jake's expression wavered, as if he knew something was wrong. But he didn't ask, he just looked back at his phone again, and the rest of their short ride passed in silence. They drew up beside his car.

"Thanks." Jake paid the driver and climbed out. He had his keys in his hand, but Mackenzie headed for the driver's side all the same. "You were celebrating," she said. "I can drive."

"It's OK, I'm good."

She shook her head. She needed the distraction, something to focus on, because she knew two hours in the passenger seat would be unbearable. "You shouldn't stress your knee, remember?"

Jake tossed the keys over. "Good point. Commentating isn't the same as playing, but I'm still going to have to be careful, all that standing around in the studio."

She got behind the wheel and turned the radio on, just loud enough to make talking hard. The miles blurred past, the city streets unfurling to the cool gray tones of the waterfront heading up the Cape, and all the while, she waited for Jake to say something. Anything. About their future, maybe, or why he'd spun his life on a dime and signed up to a whole new career, in less time than it had taken for her coffee to get cold. What it meant for the two of them—or if there was even a two of them in his mind.

But Jake just kept playing with his phone, until finally, they drew up outside her place. Mackenzie turned off the engine.

"Well, this is goodnight, I guess," she said quietly.

Jake stopped, his hand already on the door handle to get out. "You don't want me to stay?"

He looked surprised, and she fought to corral her whirlwind emotions. "I don't think that's a good idea," Mackenzie said slowly. "Do you?"

Jake's expression settled in a stubborn frown. "Is there something you want to say? You've been in a mood all afternoon, so clearly something is on your mind."

Mackenzie felt a pang. She'd seen that expression a dozen times before, and she knew exactly what it meant.

She shook her head. "I'm not going to do this, Jake."

"Do what?" he asked. "I don't know what's going on."

"Yes, you do," Mackenzie said gently. "I know you, remember? I know that you're feeling guilty right now, only you don't want to, so you're getting resentful instead. If you come inside, you're just going to pick a fight," she continued, "so you can tell yourself I'm acting crazy and unreasonable, and then you won't have to feel guilty anymore. You did the exact same thing junior year, remember? We agreed to go to the winter formal together, and then you found out Sophie McAllister wanted you to ask her, so you picked that stupid fight so you could cancel on me and take her instead."

"You're mad about some high-school dance?" Jake asked, raising his eyebrows. "That's ridiculous."

"No, I'm not. But you already know that." Mackenzie grabbed her purse and got out of the car. She was halfway to her door when Jake's voice came from behind her.

"I thought you'd be happy for me."

She turned. He was standing there on the sidewalk, his arms folded, with that familiar stubborn expression on his face.

"I am happy for you," Mackenzie replied sadly. It would be a lot easier if she could just feel betrayed, or mad, but she wanted this for him. He deserved it.

"So why are you being like this?"

Her patience finally ran thin. "Why do you think, Jake? I find out that you're moving all the way across the country, and all you do is pour champagne."

His jaw clenched. "It's a great opportunity."

"I know."

"And in case you hadn't noticed, my options are kind of limited these days!" he exclaimed. "What am I supposed to do, now that I can't play anymore? At least this way I get to still be part of the game, part of a team."

"In California," she said quietly.

"Sweetbriar Cove isn't exactly bursting with professional football teams!" Jake shot back. "I can't play, I can't do anything. There's nothing for me here!"

Mackenzie felt the words like a blow. She reeled back.

"There is something," she said, aching. He looked away.

"I didn't mean it like that."

"No, you did." Mackenzie was blinking back tears now, all her worst fears confirmed. "This was just a temporary thing for you, wasn't it? A distraction, while you waited to get back to your real life in the spotlight."

"Mackenzie—"

"No, don't apologize! I get it." She wiped her cheeks furiously, hating herself for letting him see her cry. "I should have known from the start, from the way you kept pushing me away. But I wanted you too much, I didn't stop to think about . . ." Her voice cracked, but she forced herself to keep going.

"...About what would happen when you were done."

"It doesn't have to be like this," Jake said, moving closer. "We can do long-distance. You can visit, all the time. And I'll be traveling, for the games—"

"No." Mackenzie shook her head so hard her hair rustled around her face. "I'm not going to sit around waiting for you. Wondering where you are, and who you're with. And then what? Where could it possibly go?"

Jake looked uneasy. "Maybe you could move out there. LA's a great city. You'd love it: the weather, the bars..."

Mackenzie gave a hollow laugh. "This is my home," she said. "I've built a life here, one that I love. My family, and my job, my friends... Am I really supposed to give all this up for a man who can't even look me in the eye and tell me how he feels about me?"

Jake stared at the ground. "I don't know what to say to you. I mean, we've just been dating a few weeks."

"No, we haven't," Mackenzie said, feeling a calm wave of clarity that almost numbed the bitter ache. "This hasn't been some casual thing, and you know it. I'm in love with you," she said simply. "I've been in love with you since I was sixteen."

Jake's head snapped up at her words, his eyes filling with emotion, and for a moment, Mackenzie almost thought he was in reach.

Then he took a step back. "I'm sorry," he muttered, and Mackenzie's last hope scattered on the cold December wind.

"Sorry," she repeated numbly. That was all he had to offer her, after she'd laid her heart out for him to take.

"You deserve better than me," he said, his voice twisting. "See, I'm fucking things up without even trying. I just... I have to do this. I'm nothing without football, OK? It's been my whole life, and now... now I can't just sit around and talk about the glory days, like some washed-up hack."

"So don't," Mackenzie urged him desperately. "You can build a new life, you have brains, and determination, you can figure it out. We could," she added, "together."

But Jake shook his head. "I don't want your pity."

"This isn't pity!" Mackenzie exclaimed, "I'm telling you that I want this. We could be something real, something incredible. But it's no use," she added, deflating as reality slipped back in. "This never meant anything real to you, did it?"

His silence told her everything he needed to know. The truth right there in the empty space between them.

"God, how stupid do I have to be, falling for you all over again?" She shook her head bitterly. "I would do anything for you, but you don't want me enough to even try."

"Mac—" Jake's voice was twisted and raw, but she didn't want to see the guilt on his face.

"No, don't." She forced herself to draw up to her full height and look him straight in the eyes, for what would be the last time. "You go to California. Go where you think you belong."

She unlocked her door with shaking hands and then slammed it shut behind her. She sank back, sobbing against the wall and slid to the ground. Her heart still ached, hoping against the odds that she'd hear his footsteps coming closer, and his fist pounding on the door. She'd open up, and he'd tell her that he loved her, and they would hold each other tightly and never let go.

But the footsteps never came. His headlights flared, bright through the window, and then she had to sit there on the floor, listening to him drive away.

23

*J*ake almost went back.

Driving away that night with Mackenzie's cottage getting farther in the rearview mirror. Packing up his stuff at Cooper's place. Getting on a flight to California, and watching the snowy curve of the Cape drop out of view. He almost did it, a hundred times.

But what could he say? That he was sorry for hurting her, but he didn't see another way to make himself worth something again? That he hadn't realized what guilt truly looked like until he felt the crushing shame of putting that heartache in her eyes?

That he'd loved her all along.

It was too late for that now. He saw it on her face, he'd failed her. She'd given him her heart, and he'd been so caught up in his own stupid pride that he didn't see what was right in front of him.

She was best thing that had ever happened to him, and he hadn't even realized it until she was gone.

24

The worst part about living in such a small town was that word of her breakup traveled fast. All Mackenzie had to do was send a heartbroken text to her friends, and by Monday morning, she was getting sympathetic looks from passers-by on the street as she walked to go get breakfast. Was it really so obvious? She'd washed her hair and even put on a clean pair of jeans, after spending the weekend in sweatpants, wrapped up in a numb, heartbroken haze. But clearly, Mackenzie's half-hearted attempts to hide her pain weren't working, because the moment she stepped through the door of the bakery, Summer was at her side.

"Hey," Summer said, her voice warm. "Come sit down. I just baked a fresh batch of cinnamon rolls, and there are two with your name on them."

"And have a cup of tea," Franny pitched in from the next table. "Nothing's so bad with a nice cup of Earl Grey."

Her phone buzzed with a text. It was her mom. *I'm here if you want to talk.*

Mackenzie sighed and looked around. "Is there anyone on the Cape who doesn't know I've been dumped?"

Summer winced. "Sorry."

"Maybe Hank at the market?" Franny suggested. "You know his hearing isn't what it used to be."

"Nope," said Ellie Lucas, who was just leaving with a paper bag of pastries. "I was just in there getting detergent, and they were talking about it. He offered to go whoop Jake's ass, if that helps."

Mackenzie sighed. "He'd have to go all the way to California."

She didn't want to sit out in the café, with all the tongues wagging, so she followed Summer into the kitchen in back. Every surface was covered in holiday treats, and for good reason: the Starbright Festival officially kicked off that night, and the whole town had gone celebration-crazy.

Mackenzie leaned against the counter and snaffled a broken piece of gingerbread. She knew it must be delicious, but she couldn't taste a thing. Maybe she was still in shock: after Jake had left, she'd dragged herself to her potter's wheel and spent the weekend turning out new stock for the gallery, losing herself in the steady spinning of the clay until she could barely feel anything at all.

"So, how are you feeling?" Summer asked, piping some frosting on a line of star-shaped cookies. "Or is that a dumb question?"

Mackenzie gave a helpless shrug.

"What happened?" Summer shot her an anxious look. "I mean, you don't have to talk about it if you don't want to. All I heard was that he went to take that job in LA."

Mackenzie took a deep breath. "That's pretty much the whole story. I told him I loved him, and he left." Her voice twisted on the words, and Summer dropped the frosting tub to sweep her into a hug.

"I'm so sorry, babe."

"Me too." Mackenzie gulped back the tears. "I hate it. I hate feeling like this. I can't even hate him, because he didn't do anything wrong. I was the one diving in the deep end, not waiting a second to see if he felt the same."

"If he didn't, then he's crazy," Summer said firmly. "Who wouldn't love you?"

Mackenzie gave a wistful smile. "Pretty much every guy I've ever dated."

Summer didn't have a reply for that. She held out a cookie. "Well, we love you. And I'm proud of you, you know."

"For what?" Mackenzie asked, surprised.

"For knowing what you're worth." Summer gave her a rueful look. "I've been in your shoes, and I know how tempting it is to just take whatever he's willing to give you—even if that's not enough."

"But Grayson realized he couldn't live without you," Mackenzie said sadly. "He didn't get on a plane and fly thousands of miles in the other direction."

"True," Summer agreed. "But planes go both ways. It doesn't mean he can't fly back."

Mackenzie shook her head. "I've been over it in my mind a hundred times. He just doesn't feel the same way about me. Whatever we had—the chemistry, the spark—it wasn't real, not in the end. It was just some casual thing to him."

"But I saw the way he looked at you," Summer argued. "That wasn't casual."

Mackenzie's heart ached. "It doesn't make a difference either way, not anymore. He made his choice, and it wasn't me."

Summer looked stricken. "I didn't mean to upset you more."

"You haven't," Mackenzie reassured her. "It's just going to take me some time. I would still be hiding out in sweatpants if I didn't have to go open the gallery."

"And the Starbright kick-off is tonight, too."

She nodded. "I don't know if I'll make it. Debra's almost back on her feet, so she's going to oversee the candle-lighting ceremony."

"But you have to come!" Summer exclaimed. "Everyone will be there. Even Grayson, and you know how he feels about town events."

"I want to, I just don't know if I want to face all the gossip." Mackenzie sighed. "What am I supposed to tell people when they ask about Jake?"

"Whatever you like." Summer gave a wicked smile. "Maybe he ran off to join a Buddhist meditation group, or eloped with a Real Housewife."

Mackenzie laughed. "I couldn't."

"I know. But I could." Summer winked. "We'll come pick you up at seven, and I won't take no for an answer."

TRUE TO HER WORD, Summer was on Mackenzie's doorstep at seven. Mackenzie, however, was already in her pajamas. She'd managed to keep it together all day at the gallery, but the moment she'd arrived back home, all her determination melted away.

She missed him.

She wanted him.

He was gone.

"Oh no," Summer said, looking her up and down. "Unless you want to give the town a glimpse of Snoopy, you need to go change."

"You go ahead without me," Mackenzie said listlessly. "I don't feel so good."

"A broken heart isn't like the flu," a voice came from further down the path, and then Brooke pushed inside. "It won't go away with chicken soup and Netflix."

"It might," Mackenzie argued, feeling pathetic. "It's Aunt June's chicken soup. That stuff is magic."

"Oh, you're right." Summer's face changed. "But that's still no excuse. Come on, chop chop." She pushed Mackenzie down the hall and into her bedroom. "Unless you pick out something in the next ten seconds, I'm choosing you the most hideous holiday sweater I can find."

"Since when did you become so mean?" Mackenzie protested.

"Tough love, baby."

"I could just throw on a coat?" she suggested. "I'd be so bundled up, nobody would even know."

Brooke shook her head. "Just listen to yourself. Friends don't let friends go out in their pajamas."

"They should," Mackenzie grumbled. "We'd all be much more comfortable."

She reluctantly gave up her cozy flannel and dressed in a sweater and jeans. Soon, she was cocooned in her winter gear and shuffling down the street towards the town square. "Everyone knows he dumped me," she said, checking around to see if the gossips were still out in force. "I may as well have 'spinster' written on my forehead."

She'd always joked about her title before—the Spinster of Sweetbriar Cove—but that was when a future going solo (with a dozen cats) seemed like a happy fate. Now that she knew what happiness she could have had with Jake, it cut deep to think of being alone.

"You're allowed to wallow in self-pity for exactly one more hour," Brooke declared, linking arms. "Then I'm cutting you off."

"Here." Summer sandwiched her from the other side. "This will help."

She passed a hip flask, and Mackenzie took a swig. Hot milk and spices burned the back of her throat—and a healthy dose of bourbon. She whistled. "Is this your entry in the nog-off? You'll give Franny a run for her money."

"Damn straight." Summer grinned. "I've got my eye on the big prize."

"There's actually no prize," Mackenzie confided. "Just an old trophy, and the glory, of course."

"I'll settle for that!"

They turned the corner and reached the town square, and despite the ache in her chest, Mackenzie couldn't help but smile. One tree, of course, wasn't festive enough for the Starbright Festival, so instead, they had half a dozen ringing the town square, each of them decorated by a different class from the grade school —which meant dazzling pink lights in one corner, and another adorned with superhero ornaments. And in the center of the square was the crowning glory, a majestic fir tree towering thirty feet in the air. It was still cast in darkness, but hundreds of people were gathering all around, bearing candles and torches that lit up the night.

"It's so pretty," Brooke cooed. "You did a great job."

"It was nothing." Mackenzie dismissed the praise. "Everyone in town pitched in. I just made a few calls to keep everything on track."

"We both know that's a lie."

Mackenzie turned. Debra was there in a brightly-knitted poncho, leaning heavily on a cane. "Lovely work," she said, giving Mackenzie a rare smile of approval. "I knew I could leave the planning in your capable hands."

"Jake helped too," she felt obliged to say. "I couldn't have done it without him."

"Yes. Well. He's not here, is he?" Debra's lips tightened with disapproval. "Are you sure you don't want to flip the switch? It's a perk of the position."

"No thanks, you do it," Mackenzie said. "I like the view from here."

Debra nodded, and made to head through the crowd. But she paused before she went, and touched Mackenzie's arm. "I'm sorry," she said softly. "I shouldn't have meddled, pairing the two of you up. I never dreamed it would turn out like this. I just wanted the best for you . . ." Her voice faltered, her pale eyes getting watery. "You deserve someone special."

Mackenzie covered her hand with her own. "It's OK," she said, feeling choked up herself. "I know you only meant well. I'm fine," she insisted. "I'll be fine."

"Of course you will." Debra nodded firmly. "And when you feel up to dating again, my niece just broke up with a lovely man—"

"I'll let you know." Mackenzie cut her off. "Thank you."

Debra headed off, slowly through the crowd. Mackenzie watched her go, touched by her concern. She realized suddenly that all the gossip she'd felt so self-conscious about was really just people wanting the best for her. They were her friends and neighbors, and they cared.

Just maybe they could care more discreetly next time.

She looked around the square, feeling a sense of belonging, which dulled the pain. Grayson had come to meet Summer, and Riley was snuggled up with Brooke, too, blowing on a steaming Thermos. Poppy and Cooper were over with her Aunt June, and even Ellie was on the outskirts of the crowd with a dark-haired man Mackenzie didn't recognize. Eliza hadn't been able to make it, but she would be back for the caroling on Christmas Eve.

And Mackenzie was there in the middle of it all, alone.

Not alone, she corrected herself. She was surrounded by people who cared about her.

She watched as the crowd fell silent, and Debra announced the official start of the Starbright Festival. She ceremoniously flipped a switch on the electric board, and the main tree suddenly flared to life: a thousand tiny white lights blazing all the way to the top, stars bright in the crisp, clear night.

It was magical.

Mackenzie's heart lifted for the first time since Jake had walked away. She decided she wouldn't spend another moment pining after him; she'd spent too much of her life doing that already.

She didn't know where he was, or what he was doing, but she could bet he wasn't giving her a second thought.

25

*J*ake was two thousand miles away, but he couldn't get Mackenzie off his mind. He should be having the time of his life. The network was wining and dining him, his agency had rolled out the red carpet again now that there was a deal on the horizon, and he was back on the town with his old teammates and friends again.

It was everything he'd wanted, the whole damn reason he'd taken the job. But even as the party whirled around him, he didn't feel a damn thing.

"Not too shabby, huh Jake?" One of his old buddies, Reggie, raised a glass from across the table. They were hanging at some VIP-only rooftop bar in Hollywood, the kind of place crammed with booze, and music, and beautiful women, with the city lights laid out below. "I told you, this is the way to go. If you can't be on the field, get the sideline pass instead."

"Right." Jake tilted his glass, but his heart wasn't in it. He was just thinking about calling it an early night and heading back to his apartment when Trey appeared, followed by a server with a fresh round of drinks.

"How are my favorite former players doing?" Trey beamed at them. He was dressed to kill, California-casual in dark jeans and a white button-down, with designer shades tucked in his open collar.

"Seriously?" Jake asked, smirking. "Shades. At night?"

"Oh, these things?" Trey acted like he'd forgotten they were even there. "I've got to wear them when I drive, man. Sensitive eyes."

Reggie whooped with laughter. "Dude. You Uber everywhere."

Trey laughed it off. "You like them? I know the designer, I can hook you up."

"No man, I've got a deal coming with All-Star," Reggie said. "I can't be promoting the competition."

"Good point. We need to get you one of those deals," Trey said to Jake. He pulled out his phone and tapped a note. "And sneakers, too. Maybe an energy drink, or something. Water's getting big, I hear."

"Right," Jake said slowly, trying to take it all in. "Water. Because it's always been so underrated."

"Hey, the opportunities are out there, it's what you pay me my percentage for," Trey grinned. "I know you never chased this stuff while you were playing, but now you're a civilian, we've got way more options on the table."

"I know it seems weird," Reggie spoke up. "But he's right. You don't have any conflicts with team sponsors now. You can rack them up, anyway you like. I'm doing a duster commercial next month."

Trey's head shot up. "No way. Domestic products," he translated to Jake. "Big market. Huge."

"They sent a truckload over to the house," Reggie laughed. "Now we've got dry mops for days. The wife says I better do diamonds next time, and get some better freebies."

"Cleaning products," Trey repeated, still tapping his phone.

Jake nudged him. "Cut that out. I'm not going to go hawking dish soap."

"If they offer the right price, you will." Trey caught himself. "Hey, I get it, we only want top-draw deals. Leave it with me, you'll be protected."

Jake stifled a sigh. Ever since he'd stepped off the plane, it had been like this. Business lunches and sponsor drinks. Everyone was talking big money and lining up the next deal, and nobody had uttered a damn word about football. But that was his job, they told him. Look great for the camera and talk good game, and he'd be cashing those checks all day long.

It was what he'd wanted, wasn't it? A slice of his old life again, to prove he still mattered. As if the size of his bank account would give him purpose, or fill the empty space that playing the game had left behind.

"You're quiet tonight," Trey said, looking concerned. "You know I'm just kidding you about the sponsorship deals. We won't do anything you don't want to do."

"I know." Jake sighed. "I guess I'm just not feeling it tonight."

"I know one sure-fire way of turning that around." Trey winked, and then waved across the rooftop.

Jake followed his gaze straight to a trio of women, out on the town in LA-cool jeans and plunging tops. One waved back at Trey and then leaned in to murmur to her friends. "No man," he protested quickly, but it was too late, they were already making their way over, sashaying on stiletto heels.

"Paulina, look at you, and Krista." Trey got up to greet them all by name. He never forgot a face—or a single detail of their bio. "How was the Barcelona shoot? I bet you crushed it."

One of the women, with striking dark hair, gave a casual shrug. "I think it's the cover next month."

"I'll have to check it out. Ladies, this is my good friend Jake, he's the newest on-screen talent for ESPN." Trey looked so proud, it was like he was the one with the shiny new title. "He's just recovering from a broken heart, so be gentle with him."

"Trey!" Jake glared, but Trey just winked and leaned in. "Trust me, women love to help you heal."

He was right. The dark-haired Paulina immediately moved in close beside him on the couch and murmured her sympathies. "I just got out of a long-term relationship, too," she said, gazing up at him with wide eyes. "We were together three months."

Jake couldn't judge. He'd spent, what, a few weeks with Mackenzie, and it had been more than enough to fall for her. "I'm sorry," he said.

She put her hand on his thigh. "Time heals," she said, still looking so sincere. "Time, and *support*."

The hand moved higher.

Jake slid away and got to his feet. "I really need to call it a night," he told Trey, who already had his arm draped around Paulina's friend.

"Sure man, whatever you need. Remember, you've got the eleven a.m. with our publicity team, and then I've lined up a stylist at two."

Jake frowned. "A stylist?"

"You're not going to go shopping for all your new clothes, are you?" Trey countered. "This girl's great, she does all the pro names."

"It's Christmas Eve."

"No rest for the wicked!"

Paulina was still making eyes at him, so Jake wasn't going to hang around to disagree. "Fine. I'll see you then."

He made his way out through the rowdy crowd and down to street level, where his car arrived almost immediately.

"Hey, I know you," his driver said, glancing in the rearview mirror. "Miami, right?"

"Not anymore," Jake said.

"Oh yeah, that hit. Heard it was a rough one. Glad to see you're on your feet again."

"Thanks."

The city slipped past his windows.

It didn't hurt like it used to.

The compliments and sympathies used to cut deep, but now they rolled off him with barely a flinch. It was bound to happen, he guessed—or maybe it was because that old wound had been replaced by something fresh and bloodied.

After all, his pride didn't hurt nearly as much as a broken heart.

BACK AT HIS RENTAL, Jake let himself in and tossed his keys to the empty countertop with a clatter. He looked around at the polished floors and sleek, modern furniture, and remembered the cozy chaos of Mackenzie's tiny cottage. Her whole house could have fit in his master suite, but he'd never felt more at home than when he was curled on that overstuffed velvet couch in front of the roaring fire, her legs draped across his lap, and the red in her hair blazing in the dim light.

He fought the urge to call her. It was late on the East Coast, and she was probably fast asleep. Not that she would even pick up the phone. No, Mackenzie had always been the stubborn one, with a pride to match even his own. There were no second chances with her, not once you crossed her. And now he was on the outside, and he had nobody to blame but himself.

Was this really what he'd turned his world upside down for?

Jake slid open the terrace door and stepped out into the balmy night air. He had a million-dollar view, surrounded by the lights of downtown, but he hadn't slept in days from all the hum of traffic and the echoes of street noise downstairs. It had never bothered him before, just the white noise of city life, but coming from the thick, dark midnight back in Sweetbriar Cove, he just couldn't find his old rhythms again.

He leaned against the balcony railing and took it all in. The city lights, the buzz—everything he thought he'd wanted. He'd traveled before, all over, sometimes for months at a time, but he'd always been able to slip effortlessly back into his routine.

It didn't feel like home, and he didn't even need to wonder why.

She wasn't there. And he wasn't with her.

Why?

Because he'd needed to prove himself and feel like a man: with status, and a paycheck he didn't need, and all the trappings of his old life, like they could ever turn the clock back. It was bullshit, all of it, and she'd known that from the start. He flinched to remember that last fight, how she'd seen right through him.

You're feeling guilty right now, only you don't want to, so you're getting resentful instead.

Yeah, that was about right. It still blew him away how she knew him so well, better than he knew himself sometimes. She'd seen he was pulling away, trying to blow the whole thing up, but still, she'd put her heart on the line and told him everything. How she felt.

I'm in love with you. I've been in love with you since I was sixteen.

How could he have missed it, the first time around? She was his friend, his best friend, the one he could always count on, but he'd never even noticed that she'd wanted more. And then when they'd met again after all these years, he still hadn't realized. He'd been so caught up in his own drama, pushing her away, he'd ignored how special what they shared could really be.

The passion. The white-hot chemistry. And more than that, the feeling of total ease and safety when she was in his arms—where she belonged. A man could go his whole life never feeling that bond, and what did he do when he was finally blessed enough to have it right there for the taking?

He shut down. Turned on her. Ran scared, because the thought of facing the unknown there in Sweetbriar with her was more terrifying to him than taking the easy way out here. Without her.

Damn, he'd been a fool.

Was it really too late for them?

Jake paused, a small flash of hope cutting through the darkness.

He wasn't a quitter. That was what had made him a relentless player: whatever it took to make it happen, no matter how long he had to train, no matter how punishing the process. He fought, and he won, every time.

So why wasn't he fighting for her?

He turned on his heel and stepped back inside, already pulling out his phone to call a car. It was forty minutes to the airport, six hours on a plane, another two on the road to make it to the Cape, but that was nothing compared to a lifetime without her.

He was late already, and there was no time to spare.

26

*C*hristmas Eve dawned bright, with an icy-blue cloudless sky and the perfect thick layer of snow on the ground. Mackenzie leapt out of bed, determined not to let her heartache ruin her favorite time of year. She was going to take her traditional stroll around town to see everyone's festive displays, and then the whole town closed early for the final day of the festival. Sleigh rides and carol-singing, and the famous Sweetbriar nog-off tasting contest.

She was going to find her holiday cheer if it killed her.

"Look at you, Ms. Klaus!"

When she stepped out of her door, she was surprised to find Eliza just approaching, bundled up in a massive parka with two steaming cups of coffee in her hands. "Love the outfit," she grinned, and Mackenzie did a little spin. She was wearing a red knit dress with thick tights, winter boots, and a white faux stole, with a Russian-style fur trapper hat to finish the ensemble.

"Is that coffee?" she asked eagerly.

"Yours is vanilla with whipped cream," Eliza announced, thrusting one at Mackenzie. "Mine is black, like my heart."

She took it. "What are you doing here? I thought you were on deadline, trying to keep your job."

Eliza waved her concern away. "They sent us all home early for the holidays, which I'm sure is a great sign for my continued employment. Besides, I need to make sure you don't disappear in a pile of takeout boxes and despair. Wait, that's my way of handling a breakup. You seem remarkably healthy," Eliza frowned.

"I'm past shock, and into denial," Mackenzie said cheerfully.

"Sounds good to me." Eliza laughed, and the two of them began strolling towards town. "Now, I'd tell you to be gentle with me with all this holiday stuff, but I'm guessing that's not an option."

"It depends," Mackenzie grinned. "Does 'gentle' include a sleigh ride and making our own gingerbread houses?"

"Uh oh." Eliza began to look worried. "I don't think there's enough coffee in the world for that."

But despite her anti-holiday stance, Eliza didn't protest as Mackenzie dragged her around town, sampling everything the Starbright Festival had to offer. From photos in Santa's grotto, to a bracing sleigh ride through the snow, they tried it all. Mackenzie was glad for the whirl of distraction, and it was fun to share her beloved traditions with a newcomer. By the time the sun was setting, even Eliza was humming along with Bing Crosby in the pub—in her new holly-trimmed holiday hat.

"Not you too!" Riley exclaimed, pouring them both a mug of mulled wine. "I thought if anyone could stand strong against the tide of festivities, it was you, Eliza."

"Sorry, not sorry!" Eliza grinned.

"I took her to the dark side," Mackenzie gloated. "Or rather, the red-and-white side."

Brooke joined them, leaning up to give Riley a kiss. "Aww, are you playing Scrooge again? He won't tell you, but he watched *Love Actually* last night," she added with a wink.

"For you!" Riley protested. "Because a good boyfriend makes sacrifices."

"Sure," Brooke teased. "That's why you had me pause it while you got up for snacks."

They all laughed, just as Summer and Grayson entered, bearing a shiny trophy. "I did it!" Summer announced, striking a pose. "You are now looking at the official title-holder of the best eggnog on the Cape."

Mackenzie led the applause. "Congratulations!"

"Does this mean you're getting a liquor license for the bakery?" Riley asked, looking worried. "Because let's be honest, I can't compete with those pastries."

"No, your business is safe. For now!" Summer beamed. Then the door swung open again, and Poppy and Cooper arrived, looking so happy and in love that Mackenzie let out a little gasp.

"Is it official?" she asked, looking back and forth between them.

Cooper cracked a smile, and then Poppy thrust out her hand, showing off a gorgeous engagement ring.

The shrieks were deafening.

"Oh my God, when did you do it?" Mackenzie demanded, smothering Cooper in a hug.

"This morning." He looked bashful. "I was planning on waiting until New Year's, but, well . . ."

"That's not the only thing," Poppy added, practically glowing. "I'm pregnant. Officially," she added with a grin.

This time, the wave of congratulations included almost everyone in the pub. Mackenzie hugged her tightly, overwhelmed with excitement for them. She'd known Cooper for years, and for a while, it had seemed like he would grow old and bitter, alone.

But his good heart had just needed the right partner, and Poppy was the perfect fit.

"I've finally got an excuse to take up knitting," Eliza exclaimed. "This baby's going to have onesies for days."

Poppy laughed, and then her expression grew teary. "I can't believe it," she said, looking around. "This time last year, I had a whole different life. And now here I am, and it feels like I've been home forever."

"This place has a way of changing everything," Mackenzie agreed. She suddenly felt choked up, and had to step away to get a glass of water from behind the bar.

Jake should be here.

It was silly to think. After all, he hadn't spent long in town, not this time around, and he'd only just met her friends. But somehow, Mackenzie felt the space where he should be: shaking Cooper's hand and congratulating Poppy. Part of her world, here.

Part of her future.

She swallowed back the pain. It wasn't the day for it, not with so much good news to share in. So, she put it away, safe in a box in her heart for later, and went to celebrate with her friends, linking arms as they all bundled out into the cold again and followed the stream of people towards the town square. The trees were all lit up, blazing in the night, and the local choirs were starting to sing, the clean, crisp notes of the carols soaring through the dark sky.

Mackenzie noticed that Eliza was tapping on her phone. "Put that away!" she scolded her. "Unless you're looking up the lyrics to join in, no phones allowed."

"You're right." Eliza tucked it away and turned to Mackenzie with an innocent smile. "It's so busy out, let's go find a spot to sit and enjoy the singing."

"OK," Mackenzie agreed. The crowd was getting massive now, and she could use a little room to breathe, so she followed Eliza to the edge of the green and along the path to the gazebo. The structure was lit up, strung with a hundred tiny lights, all illuminating the—

"Snowflakes," Mackenzie breathed, recognizing the gleam of the ornaments, dangling from the roof in a shimmer of stars. She didn't understand. She'd searched that basement high and low, and they were nowhere to be found.

"Look—" she started, turning to Eliza, but her friend had vanished into thin air, and Mackenzie was alone. She climbed the steps, and looked around in delight. It was just the way she remembered, a frozen corner of the world, full of magic.

"But how . . . ?" she wondered aloud.

"I called every gift shop and décor place in Massachusetts."

Her heart stopped.

She almost didn't want to look, in case she was imagining things, but when she finally forced herself to turn, there he was, standing with his hands bunched nervously in the pockets of his coat, with snowflakes melting in his ruffled hair, and his eyes— those eyes that always took her breath away—looking at her with such a naked hope that Mackenzie forgot how to breathe.

Jake was here.

He'd come back. For her?

"I found them in a little store in Boston," he continued. "Luckily, the owner was a football fan, so she opened especially for me, on my drive down."

"They're beautiful," Mackenzie whispered, unable to drag her eyes away from him. "But . . . why?"

Jake gave her a bashful smile. "You said it wasn't Christmas without them."

She took a shallow breath, and then another, forcing herself not to leap into his arms. She couldn't do it again, not until she knew what he was doing back here, looking at her that way.

She loved him too much to settle for anything less.

"I'm sorry." Jake's voice was raw, and he took a half-step closer. "I messed this up, I know I did, I just . . . I couldn't deal with failing again. I spent so long with football at the center of my world, and then, after the injury, the only thing I knew for sure was that I had to get it all back. Until you." Jake paused, his gaze searching hers. "I've never known anyone the way I know you, Mackenzie. And I've never loved anyone like this either."

The world stopped spinning. Her heart was pounding so loudly, she almost didn't believe she'd heard him right. But then Jake moved closer and caught her hands in his.

"I love you," he said again, smiling this time. "And I know I don't deserve a second chance after the way I hurt you, but I swear, I'm not going anywhere this time. I don't care how long it takes, if you tell me there's even half a chance of making this right with you . . ." His voice caught with the urgency of his emotions, but she saw it written on his face.

Awestruck and reverent—the way she felt whenever she looked at him.

Her heart caught fire, blazing so hard she could have sworn it lit up the night sky. "But what happens now?" she whispered, still not quite believing it. "I told you, I'm not moving to LA, and long-distance—"

Jake shook his head. "I don't want you to," he vowed. "You were right, you belong here. Sweetbriar is your home, and . . . And, I want it to be mine, too. If you'll let me. I love you." He said it again, fiercely, moving to cradle her cheeks in his hands. "I love you, and I'll do whatever it takes to be with you. And if our future is here, then . . . well, you couldn't drag me away," he said, his breath whispering her skin with the promise she'd spent half her life waiting to hear.

"I'm here, Mackenzie. I'm yours."

It was simple, in the end. It had always been simple with him.

She knew his heart—every brave, strong, gentle, passionate beat—and Mackenzie knew she would gladly spend a lifetime loving him with every part of hers.

She pulled him closer and kissed him, holding tightly as the carols soared around them into the night.

"I love you," she whispered, coming up for air. "I think a part of me has always loved you."

Jake held her tenderly. "Then I guess I've got some catching up to do," he said, and she laughed, feeling gleeful and bold. She had everything in the world, right there in her arms.

"We're back where we started," she suddenly realized, looking around. The gazebo was a winter wonderland, twinkling with a hundred fragile snowflakes, but she could remember the pumpkin patch and the scent of hay bales that first night they'd kissed. "Do you remember?"

"How could I forget?" Jake smiled. "That was the night a mysterious assassin stole my heart."

Mackenzie laughed, but his eyes were true.

"I mean it," he said, dipping to kiss her cheek again, her forehead, her nose, and even her eyelashes, lavishing her with tenderness. "It's yours, sweetheart. It'll always be yours."

She felt choked up, overwhelmed by how precious the moment felt, like snowfall in her palms. But instead of melting away, she knew this was just the beginning: the first of a thousand nights in his arms, the first of a lifetime.

"Come on," he said softly, taking her hand. "Let's go see the rest of the show."

She shook her head. "Next year," she said, knowing in her heart there would be a next year for them, and a next after that. The years stretching out like the jewels of streetlights strung through the square, full of possibility. She drew him back to her again. "This one's just ours."

So he wrapped her in his embrace, and they held each other there as the snow fell softly, and the candlelight shone, and all was calm and bright.

27

*T*his year, New Year's Eve was different.

Usually, Mackenzie closed the store early and spent the afternoon busy in her studio with music playing and a cup of hot cocoa at her side. It was a tradition of sorts, throwing the first pots of the year and planning her collections to come, before she wrapped up, stopped by a local party, and shared a celebration with her neighbors and headed home, greeting the new year in front of the fire with a solitary glass of wine.

This year, she was anything but alone.

"Touch gently . . ."

"Like this?"

"Yes, feel your way along. Softer, softer . . . Yes, Jake, that's right."

"I told you, I've got magic hands."

Mackenzie laughed, and gently guided his touch on the clay. She was sitting behind him at the potter's wheel, showing him firsthand how to throw his very first bowl.

Jake half-turned to drop a kiss on her cheek. "I can see why you like this," he said. "I'm feeling all *Ghost* here."

"That would make me Patrick Swayze," Mackenzie giggled, her hands intertwined with his as the clay spun and shaped on the wheel. "And you're Demi."

She felt the rumble of Jake's laughter against her chest, and then he was kissing his way up her arm with hot, molten kisses that made it hard for her to concentrate on shaping the clay. "It'll fall," she warned him breathlessly, as his lips reached her shoulder.

"There's no danger of that," Jake teased, pressing closer. She laughed, and then willingly surrendered, shutting off the wheel as Jake lifted her around to straddle his lap. He brushed hair back from her face, and she didn't even care about the smears of clay from his dirty hands, not when his body was flush against her and he was smiling at her with those laughing blue eyes.

"You've got a little something . . ." he murmured, leaning in to kiss her shoulder. She shivered as his lips trailed over her skin.

"So do you," she whispered, tracing the trail of clay down over his biceps. She closed her eyes happily as his lips found hers for a slow, hot kiss. She was learning the shape of him by heart, the way she knew the curves of her clay, every ridge and hollow of his torso, every smooth expanse of muscle and knot of sinew. Still, she never tired of exploring, savoring the rise of his body and the tantalizing slide of his tongue against hers.

Her phone buzzed in her bag, and then again.

"That'll be Eliza," Mackenzie said, dragging her lips away.

"So?" Jake kept kissing her. She giggled.

"So, we're late for the party. We've been hermits all week . . ."

He stole her words with another kiss, and Mackenzie sank into him, reminded of the reason why. They'd barely come up for air since Christmas, wrapped in their cocoon at her cottage, eating and sleeping and laughing and making up for that lost time. It was thrilling and delicious, but it still almost felt like a dream to Mackenzie to have everything she wanted right there in her arms.

Finally, Jake drew back. "One hour at the party, then I get you home," he bargained, his hands still sliding over her body with a possessiveness that made her pulse skip.

"Done." She detangled herself from him, and went to the sink in the corner to hastily wash away the scandalous fingerprints he'd left behind. When she was done, she turned to find him examining the sculptures in the corner.

"You changed this one," he said, tracing the third one. She was surprised—and touched—that he'd noticed.

"I wanted to give the series a happy ending," she said, assessing the way the figures bent towards each other now, love joined, instead of denied. "I sent some photos to Vivian in New York, and she really likes them. So, I guess the exhibition is going ahead."

"You guess?" Jake echoed. He shook his head, clearly amused. "We're going to have to work on your confidence."

"I'm plenty confident!" she protested, laughing as he picked her up. "I'm the town charades champion. I make a killer spaghetti—"

"And you're an amazing artist."

"If you say so." Mackenzie flushed. She knew she would have to get used to sharing her work eventually, but it still meant a lot that Jake was behind her 100%. He set her down again, and she reached to pass him his coat. There was a crinkle of papers in his pocket, and she paused.

"What's this?"

Jake looked bashful. "Just some things from the realtor."

Mackenzie paused. "The realtor . . . here?"

"Where else?" Jake looked blissfully confused. "I told you, I'm staying."

She exhaled, that warmth spreading from her chest to every part of her. "I know. But I like to hear you say it."

Jake smiled and tugged her closer. "I thought in the new year we could start looking for a place. For us. I know you love your cottage," he added, looking apologetic, "but—"

"But it's not big enough for the two of us," Mackenzie finished for him. Jake had bashed his head on the low-slung doorways at least four times already, and her cluttered bathroom had barely enough space for his toothbrush, let alone any of his things.

"Cooper's place is larger," she suggested.

"I know. But, I like the idea of getting something that's just ours," Jake said. "Somewhere to put down roots. I mean, if that's OK with you," he added, shooting her a cautious glance. "I don't want to rush you."

Mackenzie felt like her smile would light the room on fire. "That's more than OK with me," she said, leaning up to kiss him. "I can't wait."

SHE LOCKED UP, and they headed across the square to the pub, where the party was already in full swing, spilling laughter and music out into the night. Inside, she found all her friends and neighbors dancing and celebrating as the clock ticked closer to midnight.

"You're just in time!" Eliza greeted them, her cheeks flushed, with a glass of champagne in her hand. "I would ask what kept you, but it's written all over your face," she added, reaching over to clean a stray smear of clay from Mackenzie's nose.

Mackenzie laughed. "You're just jealous," she winked.

"Of your hot boyfriend? Yes, yes I am." Eliza grinned. "At this rate, I'll be making out with old Hank on the stroke of midnight."

"I don't know," Mackenzie teased, "I think you could land Larry, if you tried." She sent a wave to the sixty-year-old harbormaster across the room, who was wearing his trademark peaked cap and cable-knit sweater. He waved back at them, looking confused, and Eliza snatched her hand down.

"Shush!" she hushed, laughing. "Don't even joke!" She pulled Mackenzie over to the bar, where Jake was already drinking with Riley, Grayson, and Cooper. Mackenzie sidled in next to him and claimed a glass drink—and a kiss.

"They live!" Poppy exclaimed, coming downstairs with Summer and Brooke. "I haven't seen you two in forever."

"We were talking about sending a search party," Brooke agreed. "But nobody wanted to volunteer to interrupt you."

"Probably for the best." Jake draped an arm around Mackenzie's shoulders. She flushed.

"Aww, leave them alone," Riley spoke up. "Everyone gets a pass when it's cold as balls outside."

"Enough talk of balls," Poppy said, laughing. "Does everyone have a drink? Good." They all raised their glasses. "Here's a toast, to the year ahead."

"Full of new arrivals," Cooper said, sharing a smile with her.

"And new adventures," Riley agreed.

"And new beginnings," Mackenzie echoed, squeezing Jake closer. The call went up, and then they hustled outside, everyone was counting down the final moments of the year.

"Seven! Six! Five!"

Jake drew her a little way from the crowd and tipped her face up to his. "Are you ready?" he asked, gently tracing her cheek.

"Four.. three... two..."

Mackenzie knew he was talking about the new year and the fireworks to come, but to her, it meant so much more. The start of their life together, and the love she'd hoped would be hers for so long.

"I'm ready," she vowed, and then he was kissing her: slow, and deep, and full of forever as the countdown blurred into the background and the stars burst overhead, and the year ticked over into something glorious.

THE END

Thank you for reading. It's not the end for Jake and Mackenzie—or any of their Sweetbriar Cove friends. See how their stories continue (and how Eliza meets her match) in NO ORDINARY LOVE.

Welcome to Sweetbriar Cove, where true love is guaranteed!

Book Five: No Ordinary Love

For journalist Eliza Bennett, summers in Sweetbriar Cove were her happiest childhood memories. Now that she's been unceremoniously fired, evicted, and dumped (all in the same week), she hopes the small town will work its magic again and help get her life back on track. She definitely isn't looking for a distraction like the handsome stranger she meets on her way into town... especially when she discovers he might be the man behind her recent misfortunes.

Cal Prescott is in Sweetbriar Cove adjusting to (or escaping from) his new role as head of the family company. He's always prided himself on his cool logic, but reckoning with the outspoken spitfire, Eliza, is making him forget his responsibilities - and why falling in love would be such a bad idea.

The sparks between them are red-hot, and soon, their passion is heating up the summer nights. But can Eliza and Cal find a way through their differences - or will this opposites-attract romance burn out before it even begins?

Find out in the latest swoon-worthy Sweetbriar Cove romance from New York Times bestselling author, Melody Grace!

---

*E*ver since she was a kid, summers for Eliza began with the drive out to Cape Cod.

The moment school was over, they loaded up the car: her and her older sister, Paige, crammed in the back of their faded Honda, squeezed between beach toys and books, and a cooler full of tuna-fish sandwiches. Their mom would complain about the traffic, and their dad would commandeer the radio with his old country mixtapes, but as the clogged freeway made way for the sandy two-lane highway, and that first glint of ocean glittered on the horizon, all the stress and arguments faded away.

Summer had arrived.

Even now, at twenty-seven, driving the familiar road alone with the brisk chill of Spring still in the air, Eliza could taste it. Melting ice cream, and saltwater taffy, evenings by the firepit, and mornings combing the rock-pools for new adventures. She crossed the Sagamore Bridge, the unofficial gateway to the Cape, and suddenly felt a well of sadness in her chest so sharp, she had to call Paige.

"Tell me you're nearly here." Her sister sounded harried.

"Another hour away."

Paige groaned. "Mom's driving me crazy. I swear, she's drawn up a list of every single man on the entire Cape, ranked by eligibility. Anyone would think we're in a Jane Austen novel!"

Eliza laughed.

"She's got one for you, too," Paige warned.

"What?"

"I took a peek. How do you feel about Tommy McAllister?"

"Tommy? I used to babysit for him!" Eliza exclaimed. "He would run around with no pants on, mooning everyone on the beach."

"And now he's legal." Paige giggled. "Hey, just be glad you get the toy-boys. I've got a couple of widowed bachelors on mine."

Eliza sighed. "That woman is impossible. Someone needs to stage an intervention."

"She's just looking out for us." Paige's voice softened. "She's probably just trying to distract herself. It can't be easy, coming back here."

"I know."

Eliza's heart ached again. It was just over a year since their father had passed away, a year of painful firsts that made the loss feel fresh, every time. She'd thrown herself into work and making new friends out in Sweetbriar Cove, moving on as best she could, but this was the first time the family was venturing back to the beach house—without him.

"Do you know why she asked us both to be out there?" Eliza asked, focusing on the road.

"You mean besides securing us good marriages?" Paige teased. "No, she hasn't said what the big deal is. She probably wants us both there for moral support. You know she hasn't even packed away his things yet."

"How long can you stay?"

"Just a week." Paige sounded reluctant. "Things are crazy at work right now, we have a big order due." Paige was a designer for a kids' clothing line. "But I figure we can both pop back on weekends if she needs. Will the newspaper give you any more time off?"

"About that . . ." Eliza eyed the backseat in her rearview mirror, currently piled with boxes containing all her worldly possessions. "It turns out, they're giving me all the time I need." She sighed. "They fired me."

"Eliza! What did you do?"

"Nothing!" Eliza protested. "It's this new boss. He laid off half the staff, he's turning the paper into some crappy website." A *revolutionary, forward-facing news vertical*, the memo had said, whatever that meant. "He put us all on probation, to prove we could 'evolve' with the company. And, well . . ." Eliza trailed off.

"I knew you did something."

Eliza exhaled. "It doesn't matter. I've got plenty of time to help Mom with whatever project she's got going now."

"I'm sorry," Paige said, comforting. "Who knows? Maybe Tommy will sweep you off your feet."

Eliza managed a smile. "I won't hold my breath. Listen, my cellphone's about to cut out. See you soon."

She hung up and took a deep breath, trying to inhale that summertime feeling again. But thanks to a passing truck, all she got was a lungful of exhaust fumes.

This year wasn't exactly going according to plan.

It was all Cal Prescott's fault. Or rather, Callahan Archibald Prescott IV, heir to the Prescott media empire, and her new boss. Not that Eliza had ever met the man. All his new rules had been handed down by memo—dozens of them, addressed to the staff in crisp, impersonal business-talk as he set about dismantling the most prestigious newspaper left in Boston. Probation was bad enough—they'd all been walking on eggshells since news of the takeover hit—but then the not-so-helpful suggestions started arriving too. More fluffy human-interest stories, more celebrity coverage. More advertisements, less investigative journalism. Eliza should have been pleased. Features was her beat, she loved profiling oddball people and writing up local events, but even she chafed at her list of assignments, nothing but ritzy society parties and puff pieces . . . until one of those puff pieces landed her in hot water—and out of a job.

It wasn't fair. How was she supposed to know that the mayor's wife was a Prescott cousin, and the paragraph about her screaming at the kids' nanny wasn't what Cal had in mind for a "behind the scenes" look at her new charity launch?

OK, Eliza had known. And maybe she'd written the story as a way to thumb her nose at the Prescotts. But wasn't journalism supposed to be about the facts—speaking truth to power? It was what her father had always said. He'd been her biggest supporter, from the time she'd decided, aged eight, she was going to be an intrepid reporter, all the way through school newspaper assignments and those nerve-wracking years out of college, pitching freelance articles and interviewing all over town. The day the Boston Herald had published her first byline, her father had gone out and had it framed. He kept it hanging in his office at the college where he taught, proudly telling anyone who'd listen about his daughter, the journalist.

It was a good thing he wasn't around to see her now.

Eliza swallowed back the pain and focused on the road ahead. She wasn't far now, just another few miles of highway before the turn-off to the house. Already, the light seemed brighter, the midday sun glinting off the ocean through the dense, green trees. Eliza felt her tension ease. Maybe some time on the Cape was what she needed right now. She could regroup, catch up with her friends, and try to figure out what she could do next to get her career back on track.

If Cal Prescott hadn't blacklisted her for good.

The radio switched to an upbeat song, and she was just reaching to turn the volume up and sing away her stress, when she saw a car pulled over on the side of the road. The trunk was open, and a man was waving a cellphone in the air, looking frustrated. Eliza was so close to the beach, she could almost taste the soft-serve ice cream, but her father had always taught her to help out where she could. *You never know when you'll be the one needing a hand.*

Eliza pulled over. "Having problems?" she called, getting out of the car.

"I can't get a cell signal." The man turned. He was dressed immaculately in navy pinstripe pants and a crisp white shirt, a jacket slung on the roof of his car. As Eliza came closer, she could see it was an expensive sedan, gleaming and spotless despite the sand on the road.

Rich people problems.

"This is a dead spot," she explained. "There's no signal for a couple more miles. Let me take a look." She bent over and examined the wheel. It was totally deflated, with . . . Ah. A rusty nail was embedded near the rim. "Here's your problem," she said, working the nail out of the rubber and holding it up.

She found herself looking straight into the man's eyes. His piercing, midnight-blue eyes.

Eliza blinked. He had a chiseled jaw, and tanned skin, and dark hair that fell in a perfect rumpled wave over his forehead like something out of a fashion shoot. It was movie-star hair, McDreamy hair, the kind of hair that came from $200 salons that valeted your car and gave you a special scalp massage.

The man took the nail from her and sighed. "Just perfect. Sorry," he added, with a rueful look. "It's been one of those days. Make it, one of those months. So, what now?"

"Now?" Eliza arched an eyebrow. "Don't tell me you don't know how to change a flat?"

"Sure I can," the man replied, looking amused. "But it's a little hard without a jack. It looks like my guy forgot to put it back after the detailing."

Make that, *really* rich people problems.

"No worries, I've got one," she said reluctantly. "Your spare should be enough to get you to the nearest garage. Save waiting on triple-A all afternoon, at least."

"Thank you." The man's face finally relaxed into a smile that lit up his handsome face and left Eliza breathless.

Hello.

She quickly turned on her heel, and went to fetch the jack from her trunk—and quickly smooth down her hair. She was wearing jeans and a sweater, picked for comfort on the drive down, but this guy made her feel like she was roaming around in her slouchiest pajamas.

You're doing *him* the favor, she reminded herself.

"And thank you for stopping," the man added, when she returned. "I swear, half a dozen cars sped right by. So much for small-town hospitality."

"Don't take it personally," Eliza told him, bending over to fit the jack in place. "It's just the summer people thing."

The man looked confused.

"You know, rich city people buying up houses and stopping by for Fourth of July," Eliza explained, starting to crack the handle. "You jack up the property prices, leave them empty, then come swanning around once a year demanding non-fat almond milk and gluten-free fries."

"Tell me how you really feel, why don't you?" The man grinned, looking amused.

Eliza smiled back. "You're a grown man, I figure you can take it."

He laughed. "You've got me. Well, almost. I haven't bought my place yet, I'm visiting a friend here, taking a look around. And I had almond milk by accident once, in my coffee. It was sacrilege."

"Amen," Eliza agreed.

"Here, let me." The man suddenly seemed to realize what she was doing. He rolled up his shirt-sleeves—revealing tanned, elegant forearms—and took over, expertly jacking the car up and then loosening the wheel nuts with a few turns of the spanner.

Eliza admired the line of his muscles rippling under his shirt. For a preppy summer guy, he was *toned*.

"So, you live around here?" he asked, pausing to wipe his brow.

"No. But my family has been coming here for years," she added quickly. Still, the man gave her a teasing look.

"Hmm. Every summer? Like . . . a summer person?"

She laughed. "It's not like that. My grandpa built our place himself, back in the Fifties. He and my grandma retired out here, so we've been coming my whole life."

"An honorary local."

"Pretty much. You should watch out," she added lightly. "You think you'll just stay a week or two, but the place has a way of growing on you."

"It's off to a good start."

The man held her gaze for a long moment, and Eliza's pulse skipped. She flushed and looked away, but the man didn't seem ruffled at all.

"So, do you have any tips for me, to blend in around here?" he asked, effortlessly moving the spare wheel into place.

"You could lose the suit, for starters."

He glanced up, looking amused.

She flushed. Why did that come out sounding so dirty? "I just meant, people dress pretty casually around here. It's a good place to switch off and leave your stress behind."

"Hence the lack of cellphone signal."

"That's just along this stretch of highway," she reassured him. "It's just Cape Cod, not the back of beyond."

"I don't know, maybe a forced detox would be a good thing," he said, with that rueful, tired look again, and out of nowhere, Eliza was struck with the sudden urge to push that stray dark lock off of his forehead . . . and run her fingers through that perfect hair.

Down, girl.

This was what happened when she spent her whole life working; she had inappropriate thoughts about the first vaguely attractive man to cross her path. OK, *very* attractive. But still, that was no excuse. He wasn't her type at all, with that knowing smirk, and clean-shaven jaw, driving a car that was probably worth more than her student loan.

And that was really saying something.

Still, that didn't mean she couldn't be friendly. "You should check out Sweetbriar Cove while you're here," she found herself suggesting. "It's a cute town, just a few miles farther. There's a great pub, and the bakery is world-class. The sticky buns aren't to be missed."

"Really?" He gave her that wicked smirk. "What man could resist an invitation like that?"

Eliza blinked. "I didn't mean . . ." She trailed off, flushing again, but luckily, she was saved by the buzz of his cellphone.

He snatched it up, and pressed it to his ear. "Philip, can you hear me? How about now?" He moved away, trying to get a clear connection.

Eliza finished up with the wheel, and went to stow his tools in the trunk of his car, still feeling flustered. She looked around for a rag to wipe her dirty hands on, but of course, the car was empty and spotless, save a leather overnight bag on the backseat, beside a stack of papers.

Eliza couldn't help but lean in to sneak a look, curious about the man who could rattle her so effortlessly—and look good while doing so.

Expansion proposal . . . Revenue projections . . . Prescott Foundation Agenda . . .

Wait, *Prescott?*

Eliza reached in the open window and moved his briefcase aside to get a clearer look at the papers below.

The envelopes were all addressed to Callahan Prescott IV.

She paused in disbelief. Seriously?

The handsome stranger was her boss.

Correction: her *ex*-boss. The reason she'd been fired from her dream job, perp-marched out of the building, and was currently broke, homeless, and unemployed.

Bastard!

Eliza quickly stepped away from the car, checking Cal hadn't noticed her snooping. He was still pacing by the roadside, bellowing into his phone to be heard.

Typical. She should have known it the minute she clocked his fancy suit and expensive watch. Men like him thought they could just bulldoze their way through life, never mind who got crushed underfoot. And to think she'd actually helped him!

Well, maybe it was time karma paid a little visit.

Eliza glanced around again, and then paused by the spare wheel. She reached down and felt her way to the tire valve, then quickly unscrewed the cap and slipped it in her pocket. She could hear the faint hiss of air escaping as she stepped away. It would take a little while to deflate completely, so he had a chance of making it to the next town. Or maybe not, and he'd have a chance to break in those leather shoes of his.

Either way, it would give him plenty of time to take stock of his life.

"I'm heading out," she called over to Cal.

He paused and lowered his phone. "Oh. Well, thanks . . . ?" He waited for her to fill in her name, but Eliza just gave him an innocent smile and got back behind the wheel of her car.

"Welcome to the Cape," she called. "I hope you have an . . . interesting trip!"

TO BE CONTINUED...
Eliza and Cal's story is just getting started. Fall in love in NO ORDINARY LOVE, available to order now!

The Promise

ABOUT THE AUTHOR

Melody Grace grew up in a small town in the English country-side, and after spending her life reading, she decided it was time to write one for herself. She published her first book at twenty-two, and is now the New York Times bestselling author of the Beachwood Bay series, which has over three million downloads to date.

She lives in Los Angeles, writing books and screenplays full-time with the help of her two cats.

Connect with me online:
www.melodygracebooks.com
melody@melodygracebooks.com

Made in the USA
Columbia, SC
29 December 2021